D0457086

MELCHIOR'S FIRE

BAEN BOOKS by JACK L. CHALKER

Tales of the Three Kings:
Balshazzar's Serpent
Melchior's Fire

The Changewinds
The Demons at Rainbow Bridge
The Run to Chaos Keep
Ninety Trillion Fausts
The Identity Matrix
Downtiming the Nightside

MELCHIOR'S FIRE

JACK L. CHALKER

This is a work of fiction. All the characters and events portrayed in this book are fictional, and any resemblance to real people or incidents is purely coincidental.

Copyright © 2001 by Jack L. Chalker

All rights reserved, including the right to reproduce this book or portions thereof in any form.

A Baen Books Original

Baen Publishing Enterprises
P.O. Box 1403
Riverdale, NY 10471
www.baen.com

ISBN: 0-671-31991-4

Cover art by Bob Eggleton

First printing, June 2001

Library of Congress Cataloging-in-Publication Data

Chalker, Jack L.
  Melchior's fire / by Jack L. Chalker.
      p.   cm.
  "A Baen Books original"—T.p. verso.
  ISBN 0-671-31991-4 (hc)
    1. Life on other planets—Fiction. 2. Treasure-trove—Fiction. I. Title.

  PS3553.H247   M39   2001
  813'.54—dc21   2001025184

Distributed by Simon & Schuster
1230 Avenue of the Americas
New York, NY 10020

Production by Windhaven Press, Auburn, NH
Printed in the United States of America

10   9   8   7   6   5   4   3   2   1

For L. Sprague de Camp
for old time's sake

MELCHIOR'S FIRE

Prologue:

THE LEGEND OF THE THREE KINGS

Rationalists predicted that religion would be the first thing to fall when humanity finally went to the stars and found no gods, no heaven or hell, that could not be explained by physics and the other sciences. Scientists never had been all that good at predicting or understanding human culture and sociology; they never even noticed that, when they finally went out there, every deity and supernatural belief system known at the time went right with them.

Humanity was late to the stars, considering how young in its life it had begun the quest, but, like all things it had done, once it decided to go and had the means, it went like wildfire.

The discovery of the wormgate system and the way it could stabilize and link wormholes, which folded space and took you many times faster than light by the simple

method of stepping around it, made space travel efficient and affordable.

First out were the unmanned, super-hardened ships
that could withstand the forces within a naturally
occurring wormhole and exploit it, go through, and estab-
lish a temporary stabilizing gate on the other side. Then
came the follow-ups, mostly robotics with some human
supervision, who would convert that makeshift gate into
a permanent and optimized one. Then a small maintenance station both for the gate and for ships that might
come after was built and stocked, so that parts and labor
were available as needed.

Natural wormholes created weaknesses within several
parsecs, allowing other holes to form. Most were quite
small and many were highly unstable, but the little probes
punched through and were successful, at least most of
the time.

Next came the government types, of course, in quasi-
military-equipped highly reinforced ships, looking for alien
lifeforms and new worlds to exploit.

And they found them! Not exactly alien civilizations,
but certainly alien lifeforms in incredible abundance in
a universe that seemed filled with potentially human-
habitable planets. Much of the alien life was basic and
primitive, the equivalent of Earth's insects and animal
and plant life, strange as it might be to the humans who
went out there. Still, while nothing was a precise match
to Earth forms, and much was surprising and even
revolutionary to science, nothing really broke the rules.

Nothing also seemed to have evolved intelligence, let
alone civilization, beyond the most rudimentary; evolution
was borne out, but the requirement for a fast-thinking
brain seemed to be a low priority in nature's schemes.
Humanity's fickle interest in the exploration program
waned, as it always tended to do in anything that went
along without real surprises, and the scientists and
corporations who depended upon it sought new methods

of funding. Ultimately, they came up with the idea of selling off some of the best planets to interest groups back on Earth and on the few planets that had been developed to bleed off excess Earth population. It seemed an outrageous and unworkable idea. How many groups would even *want* their own planet, anyway? After all, even if they were livable, the only reason to sell the planets at all would be because science and government had decided that the worlds had nothing profitable to offer. And who could afford it? Certainly all of the worlds in question could be used in a self-supporting mode, assuming settlers could import or develop Earth plants and animals that could thrive there and use the world's mineral resources for building. But all such a program would offer would be a return to a more primitive life with little to bargain with.

The answer was, just about *every* group and leader with a dream or a vision or a political theory wanted a world. Every established religious group, and every dissident religious group, and every cult open and secret that had survived history or had emerged from it wanted their own world. And they all seemed to have amazing abilities to raise sufficient funds to get one, too.

Soon there were hundreds of settled worlds, spread all over the near galaxy, connected by a network of self-powered and self-maintained wormgates that, mapped, looked like some drunken spider's webbing. But the one thing they weren't, not really, was independent.

The Earth System Combine wanted a single level of control, a single military force, and control of the economy of the entire expanding system, if only to pay for its expenses and expansion. But over such a vast distance and with so many quasi-independent "colonies," direct political and military control would be expensive and impractical. Instead, the economic system was divided so that none of the worlds established out there were in more than the most basic sense self-sufficient. Oh, most could certainly maintain a subsistence living, some much better than that, but for the latest technology, the cutting edge of what was possible, they were made cleverly interdependent, with no single world having more than a tiny part of the whole. Any worlds that matured and chafed at interstellar rules and regulations, or balked at their share of the "user and facilitation fees" paid to the Combine, were welcome to drop out. It was then that they discovered how dependent they really were, and what it was like to be on your own in a cleverly constructed system that even controlled access to its own parts. If you weren't a member, the costs and fees were huge, and prohibitive to a degree.

Some tried it anyway, but no terraforming was *that* far along or *that* absolute, and none of the worlds were true Earthly paradises. The ones who stayed out and cut all ties were often revisited out of curiosity decades later by Combine ships only to be found with no human survivors.

The skills that had originally made humans dominate their home planet were now dead; nobody knew them anymore. The machines did it, but who programmed and maintained the machines? And what happened if no more came?

And each rebel thus became an example, all without firing a shot. The Combine grew fat, and lazy, and rich, and complacent.

Nobody knew what had caused it, nor who. The best guess was one more grab for power by yet another faction back home who ran into a ruling clique who decided that if they couldn't have the power and control nobody else would. A miscalculation, a failure of intelligence or perhaps a misjudgment of will. Perhaps it was an unforeseen enemy in their midst or from somewhere else in the vast starfields. It didn't matter.

Whatever it was, what happened was that, one day, with no notice and no particular alarms, almost a third of the wormgate system, the part that led back toward the Earth System and the headquarters of the Combine, simply stopped. Nothing more emerged from the gates, even though ordinarily traffic was brisk; and, perhaps as ominously, nothing that went into the gates after that one point ever was seen or heard from again.

Messenger probes went in and never came out. There was some indication that they might not have arrived *anywhere.*

It was the Great Silence.

Two thirds of the wormhole system, and part of the military and commercial fleets, remained working and intact, but it was the part that ran from the developing to the least developed points. There was no longer any direction, and the finely tuned interdependency that included the third now gone could not exist any longer. Worlds did not fall into savagery, at least not most of them, but they were far more on their own than before, and the ones who now ran what was left of the show were the ones with operating spaceships.

The trouble was, spaceships were a commodity that had originated strictly from the Combine and near Earth systems; there weren't any spaceship factories in the remaining two thirds, nor the automated systems to create and power them safely. There was maintenance, yes, but that was it, and going through artificially enlarged and artificially maintained wormholes left little tolerance for error.

The military tended to become a force unto itself, claiming all jurisdiction over interstellar space and the gates, financing itself by taxing the commercial ships that still ran. The commercial ships became the prizes, trying to continue their runs, keep themselves safe and maintained, and avoid the military, potential pirates, and privateers at the same time.

Things were breaking down and fast. Only the most profitable worlds and markets were of interest; most of the other worlds were forgotten, neglected, or just ignored.

It was another century before the Supreme Cardinal of Vaticanus, a world maintained and developed as a religious retreat by the Roman Catholic Church before the Great Silence, became one of the first to try and put some order back into the system. Without contact with the Pope or even knowing for certain if there still *was* one, but maintaining out of faith that there *had* to be, the board of cardinals who'd run the retreat and seminary world had run things as they hoped God wished, awaiting a relinking with Earth. It hadn't come, and now they were finally using some of their wealth, some of their connections on the more developed colonies, and their backup of the vast Vatican library system to send out a few dedicated priests to try and find the lost worlds.

It was probably because his name really *was* Ishmael.

The small probe ship came out of the void with the keys to Heaven, Hell, and perhaps someplace in between; it brought with it evidence of fabulous riches and more, but what it didn't bring back was a road map to the stars.

Along with the spiritual part of humanity, the legends, both good and bad, had also survived, particularly among the few who still knew of or could follow the patterns of the scouts to the stars. Fear, doubt, and death were out there, it was true, but perhaps not only that. Somewhere out there, in stories and songs and legends from forgotten origins, were the Three Kings.

Every civilization had at least one such legend; every faith as well. It might be the kingdom of Prester John, or the fabled El Dorado, or, on a more ethereal plain, it might be called Paradise, Heaven, or a state of Nirvana. On a more secular level, it was the big one, the find of a lifetime, the jackpot, the ultimate strike. Nobody really knew what it looked like, but everyone had their own vision, their own dream, and their own deep-down conviction that, sooner or later, they would find it.

The major difference between all of those and the Three Kings was that almost everyone was convinced that the Three Kings existed, and there was in fact physical evidence of it. The trouble was, its location was as mysterious and mystical as any of the others.

Ishmael Hand was one of the breed of loners the church called Prophets and everybody else called scouts. Half human, half machine, merged into cybernetic ships that were almost organisms in and of themselves, able to build—or perhaps *grow* would be a better word—the probes and contact devices they required, these volunteers sent into the eternal void in search of the unknown had a million motives. Hand was a mystic, and not the only one in that category of scout; he had turned himself into the ultimate pilgrim, searching among the stars, praying, meditating when in between, looking for something that might be out there, might actually be within his own mind, or might not exist at all. To those who sent the volunteers out, the motive didn't matter, so long as the supply of them continued.

It was initially done entirely by machines; smart machines, machines that were every bit the observer and evaluator—but those machines proved lacking in several ways. They had never been living beings, born and raised in organic environments, feeling what organic sentient beings feel, understanding in non-academic ways what organic sentient beings really wanted or needed. They could only send back samples and reports; they could never send back impressions that others might understand and interpret. They could quantify, but they could not dream.

Sentient beings like the human Ishmael Hand, however, also had their limits, not just physical but mental and emotional as well, and they didn't live long enough to cover vast distances; nor did they have the precision and detail that cybernetic equipment could bring to a job. The marriage of creature and machine was, after much trial and error, found to be the perfect vehicle.

Within, of course, limits.

For if they were not a little bit mad when they left, they certainly were after centuries of roaming the vastness of the universe; yet their machine sides stayed precise and detailed. As time went on, it often became difficult to interpret all the data properly. . . .

Once an uncharted system was sighted, scouted, and thoroughly investigated, the procedure was simple. The ships themselves were almost organic; they could take in debris, dust, rock, whatever was out there and convert it to what was needed, just as their external scoops could turn some of it into interstellar fuels. From this material they grew small probes according to designs within their complex memory banks, and sent them everywhere in system. Every type of analysis was performed, every part of everything evaluated. The most dead of worlds could contain something of great or unique value.

Premiums, of course, were first and foremost lost colonies; then solid planets within the life zone that could be the source of new life or, if there was anything particularly interesting, could be turned with minimal cost or effort into new colonies. Beyond that, the ships looked for things they had never seen before, beautiful and unique creations, *knowledge*.

There was a lot of life in the galaxy; that was well known. The trouble was, only a minuscule portion of it had any brains at all; and of the handful of races bumped into by expanding humanity, none had been anything but primitive.

Ishmael Hand had recognized what he'd stumbled on almost immediately. Long before the Great Silence there were half-whispered tales of them, but never, until now, solid physical evidence of their existence. Three planets in the life zone that had not gone bad over the eons was just about unheard of; even two was almost never seen. That was why, Hand speculated, nobody had really found the Three Kings since early and messed-up machine-only scouts had first reported them.

Because the Three Kings weren't three planets, not exactly. There was one *enormous* planet, a world at the outer limits of even gas giants, and three moons, very different, yet each with thick, oxygen-rich atmospheres and water.

The largest one, bigger than the Earth, wasn't the sort of place you wanted to visit. As big as it was, it contained vast, active volcanic fields, and in some places the land was forever changing, floating and twisting where lava fractured it.

And yet there was water, even two vast oceans, making almost a dance of solidity and water, and then fire and flux, then water and solid land again, and then another fiery area. Much of the surface was concealed in clouds, but now and then there were breaks—and those breaks showed the bizarre and fractured landscape below. It was hot on its surface, even in the "cool" solid regions, but perhaps not *too* hot. There was vegetation, in a riot of colors, wherever it could cling and not be burned off or knocked off by internal forces. It wasn't a nice place to live and work, but it was fascinating if only because nobody, not Ishmael Hand nor the vastly larger and more complex thinking machines of the home empire he'd abandoned, could figure out how the heck a planet that dynamic and contradictory could possibly exist. Although the Three Kings name was ancient, it remained for the scout to make sense of it, and he called this huge planet Melchior.

And then there were the other large moons, among countless rather ordinary small ones. One of the larger ones was warm but not a raging madhouse like the huge planet below that held it captive; almost 25,000 kilometers at its equator, a small planet in captivity. It was a wonderland of islands large and small in a continuous sea, more than forty percent land yet with no major gaps, so that any part of the water could be called an ocean, nor land masses so huge that they might be considered continents. It was a world of lakes and islands, teeming with plants and perhaps small animals, wild, primitive, and beautiful. This moon Hand called Balshazzar.

The third moon also had an atmosphere, but it was farther out, cold, full of bizarre and twisted rocks and spires, great desertlike regions of red and gold and purple sand. Yet somehow, without large bodies of surface water, nor the thick vegetation that would normally go with such an atmosphere, it retained in the air a significant amount of water vapor that rose in the night from the ground in thick mists and vanished in the light, and oxygen, nitrogen, and many other elements needed for life. The atmosphere was thinner than humans liked it, but they could exist there, as they'd learned to exist atop three- and four-kilometer mountain ranges on their mother Earth and elsewhere. This third moon Hand christened Kaspar.

"None of the figures make a lot of sense, I admit," the scout's report said, "but it will make some careers to determine how these ecosystems work. God is having fun with us here, challenging us. I do not have the means to start solving these riddles, but I feel certain that you have ones who have more than that."

The worlds, in their own ways, also lived up to their ancient reputation, judging from the samples sent back.

Here was a small sack of apparently natural gems, gems as large as hens' eggs and colored in translucent emerald or ruby or sapphire, with centers of some different substance that, when viewed from different angles, seemed to form almost pictures or shapes—familiar ones, unique to each viewer, subjective and ever-changing devices of fascination. Machines could make synthetic copies that were almost but not quite like the real thing, of course—but the real thing was unique in nature and thus precious.

There was sand in exotic colors, mixed within containers but nonetheless unmixed, as if the colors refused to blend with each other and the individual grains appeared to prefer only their own company. The properties were electromagnetic in nature but would take a long time to yield up their secrets, particularly how such things could have come about in nature.

Plant samples at once familiar and yet so alien that they appeared to be able to convert virtually any kind of energy into food, including, if one was not careful, any living things that touched them. Rooted plants that nonetheless responded to sounds and actions and would attempt to bend away from probes or shears and whose own energy fields could distort instruments and short out standard analyzers.

But most fascinating of all were the Artifacts.

They were always afterwards called the Artifacts, with a capital "A," because there was nothing like them and no way to explain them. Ishmael Hand found no signs of any sentient lifeforms on any of the three worlds, nor ruins, nor any signs that anyone had ever been there before, but he, too, understood what was implied by the Artifacts.

They were not spectacular, yet they were the greatest of all finds. One was a simple cylinder, perfectly machined, with tolerances so small, with dimensions so perfect, that one had to go down almost to the atomic level to find a flaw. And it was machined out of an absolutely one hundred percent pure block of titanium.

It also looked very much as if it had been manufactured in a lab within the past few hours, yet the tag with it indicated that it was lying half buried in the surface. But the entire thing was coated, to the thickness of only a dozen atoms, in a hard coating that was close enough to one used in human manufacturing that it was inconceivable to think of it as natural.

The second was a gear, perhaps a half a meter around, with one hundred and eighty-two fine and perfect teeth. It, too, was machined just like the cylinder, to absolute perfection, and it, too, had the synthetic protective coating.

The third and final Artifact was a one-meter coil, made out of a totally synthetic and absolutely clear polymerlike substance and created to the same perfect tolerances as the other two. The coil had nineteen turns and its ends were smooth, not broken. The substance was unlike any that had ever been seen before, yet made of stuff that contemporary labs would have no trouble duplicating. In fact, it was easily as good as what was being used but cheaper and easier to make.

"There must be a lot of this junk around," Ishmael Hand's report noted. "Consider that my probes were able to discover these three pieces with ease, although none are all that large. Don't try and put them together, though. I doubt if they're from the same device. In fact, I'm nearly *positive* that they aren't. You see, the coil came from Balshazzar, the gear from Melchior, and the cylinder was sticking out of the purple desert sands on Kaspar."

After all this time, Ishmael Hand could only have faith that anyone was even listening. He had been sent out from a holy world, a retreat and monastic place designed to help you to find what God had in mind for you. One of its orders had trained many of the scouts like Ishmael Hand in the mental disciplines required for such a life, and had carefully prepared them for the long, lonely Communion. Once the Great Silence came about, they had but a few dozen scout ships fully outfitted and not many more candidates than that. They sent half back in the direction of the Arm and Old Earth in hopes of reestablishing contact; the others, like Hand, were sent forward to find the colonies and remap what might be out there. Thus it was that Hand had discovered what had already *been* discovered, but had also been lost. His broadband, uncoded broadcasts back to every region where there might be listeners were public property. He was not out there for riches or material rewards.

There was enough interest and excitement about the rediscovery of the Three Kings to attract the best and the worst of spacefaring humanity. There was only one problem. While the reporting probe contained the samples and the report and vast amounts of data, nowhere inside could they find star maps or location data or the beacon system that would allow them to get there in a hurry.

This was the fourteenth solar system Ishmael Hand had reported on in the two and a half centuries since he'd launched himself into the unknown, but it was the first and only one where the location data was lacking. It wasn't like Hand to have any such lapses, and he certainly gave no indication in his report that he didn't expect a horde of expeditions to be heading out to the Three Kings straightaway. Nor did any of the data suggest damage or instability in Hand's ship and cybernetic parts. Not even His Holiness in Exile and his monastic group understood what might have caused problems with Hand at this key moment.

And yet nowhere, absolutely nowhere, in *any* of that data, did it show where the heck the Three Kings were, and at no point was there enough of a star sky given that would allow the position to be deduced.

Hand, as usual for him, wound up his broadcast report with a long string of prayers and chants from the Bible and other holy books, but then he stopped in the middle and added, "You know, if I wasn't sure this was the

Three Kings I'd never have named them that. I *still* considered naming them something else, but there's much to be said for tradition. Nonetheless, beware! The three perfect names I would otherwise have bestowed on these little beauties are Paradiso, Purgatorio, and Inferno. But which was which would only have confused you secular scientists anyway. God be with you when you arrive on these, though, for nobody else will be, and your lack of faith might well be the death of you! *Amen!"*

And that was the end of the report.

The Three Kings had gone from legend to reality, but were now more maddeningly desired and more maddeningly out of reach than ever.

Still, they had been discovered not once, but twice, even if centuries apart. By hook, by crook, by luck, faith, or perhaps destiny, somebody would discover them again.

Or solve the mystery of Ishmael Hand.

Those in space now divided neatly into two types of people. There was the profane group, the pirates and raiders who made a living from a bit more knowledge of the colonial worlds' positions and assets than most others. And there was the holy group. Not just Ishmael Hand and the Catholic priests and nuns who followed him and his kind, but the others as well, the evangelists and teachers of every conceivable faith who could put together a ship and who were as determined as Ishmael Hand to return the truth of God to the lost colonies.

And finally someone had found a way to the Three Kings, or so he believed. The eccentric former physicist turned iconoclastic evangelist Dr. Karl Woodward had, it was said, discovered the way to Paradise. He had fitted his great ship for a rough ride through a natural wormhole, something considered suicidal for anything save robots and scouts, and he had vanished shortly after. Others tried to follow, lured less by the promise of theological perfection than by the riches of Paradise, but whether any had managed to follow him all the way wasn't known.

What *was* known was that the route hadn't been left around for others to follow, and nobody, not Woodward or his people, nor anyone who followed, had returned.

The Three Kings of Ishmael Hand seemed as elusive and mythical as ever. . . .

I:

SCIENTISTS DIE FOR LOVE

In twenty years of exploring strange worlds and seeking out some kind of indication that possibly humanity wasn't alone, Randi Queson had never found any signs of any alien civilizations, past, present, or future, but she'd found a number of human ones. Perhaps it was because only human beings were both adaptable enough and insane enough to settle even the armpits of the universe that they were surviving at all.

This was a particularly ugly place, all gray and white, with constant winds whipping a fine sand against any exposed parts of the body. In most places where there was this kind of sandblasting there had at least been great natural carvings out of the rock, but the ugly pillars and squat, black, twisted forms created here were more reminiscent of a ghastly entryway to Hell than of the kind of unique beauty that would have drawn tourists and preservationists back in the old days when space-ships had been plentiful and space travel relatively cheap.

But there was water here; not on the surface, but not far underground, and in great quantities, filtered by the rock and sand base into a mineral-rich freshness that would nourish almost anything you wanted to plant. And so humans had come here, in better times, to set up vast enclosed hydroponic farms and draw the rich water and its minerals and make it explode into life. Just by standing there and staring down at the flat plain with the ruins of those great automated farms, she could imagine how it had all looked at its peak, even though it was before her time.

Just so much junk now.

Highly automated surface farming was impossible now; they'd manufactured no spare parts here, nor had they the means and materials to innovate beyond a certain level. When the pumps went and the power supplies finally wore out and the spare parts for the robotic monitors were gone, there had been nobody to bring them more, nobody to trade the rich and probably exotic high-demand delicacies they'd raised here for what they needed.

"There are some places even people can't manage after a while, huh, Doc?" a man's voice commented near her.

"Perhaps," she responded. "But I wouldn't put it past some remnants to have made it here, perhaps in caves or underground. They knew what was happening, and they had time to plan. I don't know what shape they'd be in after all these years, but I wouldn't be shocked to find some pockets here and there, people living in sheltered areas and somehow getting by. It wouldn't be much of a life, but back on Old Earth and in several worlds out here we've seen people get by with less. In deserts so hot and dry they'd boil your brains, and in areas so cold that you'd swear nothing could find enough food and warmth. Keep that in mind, all of you, when we go down there! We don't want any ugly surprises, and we're not exactly in the business of giving poor stuck farmers a ride."

The man chuckled. "You're all heart, Doc." He turned and looked at the rest of the team, all in environmental suits with helmets on to protect against the elements, and waved them forward. All of them were armed. "Everybody spread out and be at the ready! I don't think we're gonna find anybody down there in those ruins, but you never know who or what's gonna pop up from where. If they're around, though, they'll already know we're here."

"So what do we do if they come out and welcome us as liberators and shit like that?" one of the team asked.

"Keep it friendly and businesslike," Queson told them. "If there's anybody around, they know where everything of interest to us is. It's a lot easier to have it given to you than to take it. If nobody is stupid then they don't have to know until the very last moment that we're not leaving with anybody we didn't bring. Understand?"

The tall, thin man in the rust colored e-suit who moved to take the point nodded, still chuckling. "All heart for sure," he muttered as he checked the charge on his pistol.

The fact that no alien civilizations had been discovered didn't mean that there wasn't a lot of alien life, and they all understood that. Any world that was habitable by humans tended to be inhabited by *something*, and the more water present as a liquid the more likely that was. Much of the life that had been discovered wasn't very smart, but it was astonishingly dangerous. All the more dangerous because until you met it you often didn't know anything about it at all, and after you met it you hoped you could figure it out before it got you.

They weren't there to be gotten, but to get.

In the old days, they would identify themselves as being in the salvage business, and salvage was in fact what they did. With few factories capable of the quality of work that used to be available before the Great Silence had cut off the children of humanity from their roots, this was how you did things. Groups could make a living finding one of the lost colonies, hoping against hope that it had failed and that everyone who'd lived there was long dead, and then stripping it of everything of value before anybody else found it and selling it as best they could.

Most of the salvagers were pretty tough people. Some of them wouldn't care if the colony they found was dead or alive, desperate or thriving. The bigger, more civilized, more developed worlds needed this stuff, and tended to look the other way as to where it came from. The philosophy professors called it "mutually beneficial amorality"; others retained their immorality by pretending that everything that came in was from ruins of the dead, and they prayed for the souls of the departed as they bought their property.

This group was a varied lot, as all such salvager cooperatives had to be. In the old days, you just had to be brutish and amoral to be a pirate; now you needed high technical skills of varied sorts to do this sort of thing. Only the soul had to be piratical, or dead.

Take Randi Queson, Ph.D. Nobody else on the crew knew why she'd chosen this life, or even whether she had chosen it or had been forced into it. They all knew that she was very smart, very knowledgeable, and totally pragmatic about the job. That was all they needed to know.

Yet, in a sense, beyond the ship's crew and maintenance, she was the most important person aboard the *Henry Morton Stanley*. You could hire a captain and a crew, and much of the salvage work was automated, but only she was knowledgeable enough to know what was valuable and what was junk. She, and the chief engineer, Jerry Nagel, who could say if some particular gadget or gizmo could be put back into service or whether its parts were potentially golden or simply fried goo. That was why both had to be down on the surface with the exploration team, and why the rest of the team's main job was protecting the two of them.

Queson was in fact the only one aboard who knew the irony of being a member of a ship's complement named after Henry M. Stanley. Stanley, a British-born American newspaperman who set out to find David Livingstone, a famous explorer and missionary, found him, wrote a book about it, and became a legend. What was not as well-known was that he then went with his exploration experience, his maps and charts, to European powers, most notably the King of Belgium, and created one of the nastiest and most immoral colonies since the days of slavery, the Belgian Congo. Stanley'd gotten famous for Livingstone, but he'd gotten rich by exploitation.

Livingstone, a godly man with a love of Africa, died, nearly a saint, bringing medicine and Christianity to the natives he loved, and who loved him, while sending back the maps that the Stanleys of that time would use to rape the continent.

The ship was not named for David Livingstone.

Nagel signaled to the rest of the team and they approached the first of the vast series of structures that had once been a great farm supporting a town that was clearly intended to become a city. The cold wind continued to swirl and howl all around them, like some sort of ghostly presence, or perhaps the pain that dreams feel when they die.

The buildings seemed to go on and on; long, boxy affairs with high-pitched roofs facing the maximum sun. A mass of greenhouses, perhaps, although they did not, had never, depended on that sun for very much.

Still, much of the structures had been designed to be, if not transparent, then nearly so. Now, they were nearly opaque, sandblasted over decades without any attempt at maintenance to clear them. Here and there there were jagged holes in the surface, like the remains of great rocks thrown through plate glass.

Only this wasn't glass, it was a synthetic material designed to withstand far worse than this miserable planet could normally dish out. Rocks, even huge ones catapulted by who knows what, would have been very noisy and created a lot of vibration, but they wouldn't have penetrated that stuff.

You needed to *shoot* these holes in those panes. Nothing less would have done.

"What do you think, Doc?" Nagel asked her, standing in front of one of the holes now. "Civil war? Riot? Revolution? Or maybe early raiders?"

She examined the wound in the building pane. "Hard to say. Not raiders, though, I wouldn't think. Hard to tell with all this dust and sand piled up, but the curvature on the edging here indicates that it was blown *out*, not in. I'd bet you'll find some missing shards if you dig enough in this pile. Bring up one of the big searchlights. We're going inside."

Two of the crew floated in an obelisk-shaped remote light. About a meter and a half high and slightly thicker at the base, it was not heavy, and very, very useful.

A tap on one symbol at the base brought the entire thing to light, giving a bright but diffuse lighting to a large area. Other settings allowed different kinds of light as required, at different intensities and, if needed, it could be brought to bear on any point with the greatest accuracy and illumination that any spotlight ever made could manage. They moved it inside, and the two leaders followed.

Inside wasn't as bad or as beaten up as they'd assumed. In fact, it looked relatively intact, although any remains of plants once grown there appeared to be either missing or turned to dust.

Nagel examined the hydroponic rows one by one. "Pretty worn, showing their age and heavy use, but still more than serviceable," he proclaimed. "With the exception of the broken panes, we could probably dismantle this down to the flooring and do pretty well. It ain't sexy but it sure looks profitable."

Queson took her personal light and took a close look at the holding membranes for the plants. It was a familiar design, pretty standard about two centuries earlier, and still very much in use back in civilization. She went close, opened her kit, and took scrapings from the whole area, including the holes.

"What's the matter, Doc? See something you don't like?"

"Probably nothing," she responded, continuing to take samples at random points in the complex. "But either this went *before* the silence or there should be some remains of *something* here. We know there's nothing intrinsically caustic in the atmosphere, so if one of us were to drop dead here and be left in place, we'd find a skeleton, certainly, or at least identifiable parts of one depending on the exposure to the elements, and probably clothing or parts of clothing and personal stuff."

"Yeah, so? I'd be surprised to find any bodies around here. Whoever wanted out sure seems to have *gotten* out, and this don't look like anyplace other folks would be living. Most of the complex is automated—you can see the mag tracks and signs of robotic tending. We'll probably find the robots themselves, power depleted. I hope so. *Those* would be the most valuable finds yet."

"Yes, well, that's what I mean. In conditions far more primitive than this, and less protected, there's always the remains of plant matter of some kind. Dried remnants of vines, that sort of thing. I don't know of anything we grow in this kind of setting that would leave not a single trace behind."

"Maybe it *was* raiders," he suggested. "I mean, they'd strip the food out of here just like we would if it had any. Or, this is one of—what? Seventy, seventy-five buildings, each around a kilometer long, just in this valley? And the last one out at that. Maybe it never got put online. Maybe it was down for maintenance. Unless we find some kind of record we'll never know."

"You're right, of course," she sighed, wondering why she just felt that something was very, very *wrong* here. She couldn't shake it, and in this business you lived longer if you trusted that kind of instinct. "Still, I'll feel better if we find more normal things in the others. I really wish we knew what went on here."

"If you ask me," came the deep, gravel voice of Sark, one of the ground detail, "anybody who'd come and live on a hole like this place in an armpit like this had to be nuts from the start."

"I've seen worse and I've seen it work," Queson told him. "Back in those days they even had means of controlling weather and climate on a planetary basis. They didn't do that here, but I think that was the ultimate goal. Take a place with all the elements but in the wrong places and forms, prove it and mold it, then eventually create out of an armpit, as you call it, a garden of beauty and plenty. Some of the best worlds we still have were created that way by these kind of people. This one just failed, for some reason."

Now she badly wanted to know what that reason was, too. Not just because she had to weigh any threats against the salvagers from all this, but also because it was another chapter in the story of humanity. She hadn't gotten her degrees to go into the salvage business; she'd gone into the salvage business to provide a means to satisfy her curiosity.

"Tag this building and prepare it for dismantling," Nagel signaled to the salvage team through the intercom. It would take a few hours to fully analyze the site, but then less than two to salvage anything of and in it that might be of value. The robot deconstructors were very efficient once they'd been told what was what.

"Going into the next building," Queson told them. Even as they progressed, slowly and methodically from building to building and throughout the site, business would be going on behind them. "Achmed, take this sample case back up to the base and have it fully analyzed," she added, speaking to one of the nearby team. "Then return to us."

The big man took it and frowned. "Yes, ma'am, Boss Lady," he responded with a slightly mocking tone. "Um— you don't think there's anything dangerous here, do you? I mean, like germs and stuff?"

"Possibly. I shouldn't worry about it. If it can get through these suits we're already infected anyway."

Achmed took the case and hurried off, never sure when she was kidding.

Nagel chuckled. "I love it when you're so fatalistic."

"He deserved it. His faith says to accept what happens as the will of Allah. It's one of the most fatalistic religions we have. I'm doing him a favor, allowing him to test his obviously wavering faith."

"Maybe he's just worried where he's going if his fears pan out," the engineer noted. "That's why I keep a hard-nosed atheism inside. The alternative is so much worse than obliteration I find a lack of faith one of my dearest comforts."

They went through a connecting tube, seals pretty well loose from all the wind outside beating against it and the lack of maintenance, but serviceable to get where they needed to go. From this point, the buildings went in three directions, and they'd have to decide on a route.

The eerie light of their personal torches revealed pretty much a carbon copy of the first building, as they expected. This building, however, still had all its panels in place and so was very much the way it would have been abandoned.

It looked as clean, even sterile, as the first would have been without the hole.

Nagel checked his instruments, and sent three small probes down the wide aisles. He checked his screen and saw nothing he didn't expect. Even as he was recalling the small probes he said, "Nothing at all here. The stuff's almost too new, even with a lack of power and maintenance. You think they built these but never got to actually use them?"

"That's been my thought," she responded. "But, then, what was somebody doing running out through that last one and blowing a hole in it rather than simply exiting via the door? I don't know. I'd almost prefer the crumbling rot of ancient vegetation and a dead body or two to what we're finding. Something here just isn't *right*."

"I agree. Still, we've got a long, hopefully boring examination of all these buildings, and sooner or later we should turn up something.

"I'd almost prefer that howling wind outside to walking blindly through here," Nagel added, sounding uncharacteristically nervous. "I don't like going down dark corridors blind."

"Not blind," Dr. Queson said from in front of him. She put her light on a wall plaque at the far end of the greenhouse, near the connecting tube to the next unit. He walked over to it and stared. The characters meant nothing to him; whatever language it was in was way different from the one he knew. Still, it was very clearly a drawing of the entire complex, and, right near the end, in one of the two units farthest out, there was the drawing of a stick figure inside a circle. The message was universal.

"You are here," he said, nodding. He looked over at the far end, which extended to and actually inside the cliffs beyond. By that point the greenhouses were twenty across and it would be easy to get lost without maps like this.

"It's gonna be a *week* before we get to the living quarters," he commented.

"Why wait that long?" she responded. "Looks like a

standard layout. We should be able to pinpoint the master control building and get any records that might be there. We might even be able to get some power going again. It would make looking through this jungle of empty greenhouses easier and more tolerable. In fact, if you see the finely etched maintenance keys along each unit, and trace them back, I'd say that the control center was about . . . *here*." She pointed to a section almost dead center and embedded in the cliffs.

"Long walk," he noted. "Want to bring in the shuttle?"

"It's a good hike, that's for sure, but we've already seen the problems the shuttle has in flying low under these conditions, and it should be all inside. I'm not in the shape I used to be in, but this is eighty-six percent standard gee, and I think the exercise would do me good. Besides, I'm more curious to find out what's going on here than to keep walking through deserted buildings for days on end."

Nagel sighed. "Okay, agreed. Sark, you take over here. Buzz if you find something out of whack, otherwise do a survey and mark 'em. We'll see about turning on the lights."

" 'Bout time," Sark grumbled. "Why didn't you do that in the first place?"

There were several possible answers to that one, not the least of which was that there simply wasn't any safe place to put down the shuttle close to the cliffs, between the density of the greenhouses and the tremendous, swirling winds with their sandblasting effects, effects which were magnified close in to the cliffs.

"Stay with me and move fairly quickly," Jerry Nagel cautioned. "We still don't know if anything's inside ahead of us."

"You worry too much," she told him. "Anything here is long dead." But she wasn't foolish enough not to heed his caution.

Each of the greenhouses was connected by a flexible

tube along which metallic flooring had been laid so that humans and robotic units could walk between without having to go outside. The seals had held remarkably well considering the constant buffeting from the outside winds, and the flooring was rock steady.

There had been some initial worry that some of the robotic devices might well still be present, might even view them as invaders or interlopers, but orbital and close-in scans showed no sign that the power grid was active. It was cold and dead, save only well below and inside the cliffs where the fusion reactors were in the process of cooling down. It would take them another few hundred years for reaction to cease completely, though, so turning the lights back on shouldn't be a problem. The real question was, why was everything turned off?

They walked for some time, stopping only to check that there was still a plaque at each entrance/exit tube showing where they were and where they had to go.

It *was* eerie, particularly after two hours, to still be walking in those great, dark halls beside empty racks that were designed to be the nurturers of abundant life. Here and there they found signs that once these places had in fact bloomed: not residue, but a wall on which hung protective clothing, rebreathers, and the like used when checking chemical mixtures, testing radiation levels, or doing maintenance on the automated equipment.

Still, there wasn't the least sign of wear and tear on any of the equipment, rails, robotic arms, you name it. Not even marks and rings where water and nutrient excess would have flowed down into drains to be reseparated and reused. In a sense, the place had the *feel* of being used but the *look* of being brand new. It didn't really make sense.

Before they could safely salvage any of it and take it aboard their ship, though, they would have to solve this puzzle.

The maps held up; like everything else they saw, they

looked so new it was as if they'd been put up yesterday. Sheltered from the outside violent weather, they
hadn't faded or lost any luster. It was a tomb, but it
was an eerily new tomb, one so fresh it didn't even seem
to have any remains around.

Still, in the protective suits and with no interior lighting, it was one hell of a long walk.

"Nagel? Doc? You okay?" a high, reedy feminine voice
asked.

It was An Li, the operations controller when people
were on the ground, the first officer of the *Stanley* when
in flight. She was one of only three people who *never*
left the ship while it was in search or salvage modes.
No matter what they might find on the ground, it could
not get to the ship, now in geostationary orbit well above
them, nor to the ship's controls. An Li could dispatch
anything from heavy weapons to food and drink, assume
control of any of the machinery below, including the
salvage tug and its heavy robotic equipment, and do
whatever was necessary to protect the crew on the
ground if possible and the ship above in all cases.

Queson wasn't the only one who thought that An Li's
choice of positions stemmed more from the fact that she
was fifty-eight centimeters tall—and then only when she
wore thick work boots—and weighed at best thirty-six
kilos. But at that control panel high above, she was the
height of a constellation and the weight of a neutron
star. In orbit and on station, she had *all* the power.

"We're fine, Li," Queson responded. "But if we have
to go much farther I'm not so sure." *Maybe I'm getting
too old and out of shape for this*, she thought, feeling
the distance in her back and legs. She was never one
to work out hard and regularly on the long space hauls.

"We'll pick a real low-gravity planet next time," the
officer promised with a chuckle.

"You want to rest?" Nagel asked her, suddenly aware
that she was breathing hard.

"No, I'm all right. I'll rest when we find some sign in this spook house that something was ever alive in here."

"Like those, maybe?" Nagel responded, shining his light on the floor and stopping to look.

She came over and stared. Clothes. Standard work uniforms like you'd find even now on hundreds of worlds—synthetic, automatically form-fitting, utilitarian, along with synthetic-rubber–soled work boots. There were several sets on the floor, spaced out in an unnerving fashion, as if each had once had an occupant who had simply, well, dissolved. As if they'd been balloons, pumped up with air, and suddenly punctured.

Randi Queson studied them, and particularly the areas around where the head would have been. One figure clearly had earrings, kind of crudely placed on either side of an imaginary head, as if they'd fallen a small bit to the floor as the head had ceased to exist.

Nagel picked up a work glove and shook it. A ring fell out and clattered as it landed on the smooth floor. He stepped on it, stopping its roll, and then leaned down and picked it up.

It was clearly a wedding ring.

One of the other phantoms also had a ring in a glove, this one a school ring from some far-off university or other. The cuneiform around the institutional crest was the same as on the signs in the greenhouses, and so far still unfamiliar to any of them.

He looked at the anthropologist and frowned. "There aren't two explanations for this coming to mind," he noted, sounding a bit nervous.

She nodded. "They were in these clothes, and then they weren't. It happened fast and it was complete. Organic matter, animal and plant, was completely consumed. Nothing else was touched."

"You ever hear of anything that could do that?" he asked her. "I mean, come on! I've used a particle-beam disintegrator and there's always *some* residue, no matter how slight. Nothing is converted so efficiently that it leaves *nothing* behind!"

"There may be something there, but if so, it's so minor it'll take a full lab analysis to find it. Queson to Control."

"Yes, Randi? What did you find?"

"The question is, what *didn't* we find. Anything back on that sample I sent?"

"Um, yeah. Ground lab says nothing. Brand new. No vegetable matter of any kind, nothing carbon. They don't have full facilities there, but they're pretty good."

"They're good enough," the Doc responded. "Whatever got this station consumes everything organic, and I mean *everything*. Run that through the computers and see if you can find anything that efficient and that selective all at the same time in the records. Any luck on the writing yet?"

"Oh, yes. Turns out to be one of the Sanskrit family of languages in its original alphabet. This was either an ethnic or national extension, that's for sure, not just a commercial one. Most of them used one of the widespread alphabets for centuries, but a few kept the old stuff for cultural cohesion. This was a really nationalist group, since the signs have no translations. The computers say it's probably Laotian, possibly Thai— Siamese, but it may be an east Indian regional one. Impossible to get any closer than that unless you find the history records, though. It doesn't *quite* match anything we have."

"But can you read it?"

"Oh, sure. If you find anything more than directional signs and shit like that, we can make it out. You sure you want to go farther in without some kind of backup, though?"

"I think it's pretty unlikely that anything that got them made it through the years after it did," Queson told her, hoping her logic held. "First, it was probably some sort of thing they either brought with them or that mutated, since anything that efficient with our kind of plants and animals had to know us. It eats, therefore it has starved for generations because of its own efficiency. Any such organism would have turned on its own species to survive. Unless the ultimate survivor learned to eat sand or metal—and it clearly didn't from the looks of this— it would finally croak. Still, this means high-level sterilization of any salvage and a Class A containment situation for everybody and everything down here until that's confirmed."

"That's affirmative. You hear that, everybody? Class A containment. Any violators get left down there and outside. And as for you, Doc, and you, Nagel, I want your helmet cameras on and audio key permanently open. I'm recording from this point if you're going to go any farther in."

"Acknowledged, switching to permanently on," Nagel responded. "This might cut power by a third, though."

"Well, then, keep an eye on it. Remember, the more in you go, the more distance you have to cover back."

Queson gave a low moan. "Don't remind me!"

Jerry Nagel stood up, shined the light around the ghostly greenhouse, and sighed. "God, I *hate* this part of the job!"

"Well, as you pointed out, our shares of something this big are going to be enormous," Queson said resignedly. "And even with all this, in this day and age, it's a hell of a lot safer than robbing banks. Still, I wish we had an archaeologist on the team. Going blind into ancient graves is what they get off on, and they're never happier than when they're digging up and carting off some old graveyard. Come on, let's see what's what."

Finally, they made the cliff. At this point the complex ceased being a greenhouse or processing area and instead became a small self-contained city built inside the protective rock.

As they expected, the amount of clothing absent owners increased with every step now, and often was so dense you couldn't help but walk on them even though both salvagers felt, somehow, that they were stepping on bodies.

Now they were on instruments, using the "You Are Here" signs only as confirmation, as they followed the dark halls and walkways towards the central energy core.

There were, at least, some pictures along the wide hallways and in many of the large offices and stores that were built, multilevel, around the control center. Both Queson and Nagel had expected to see exotic faces in some kind of ancient-looking cultural garb, but the fact was, the folks looked pretty ordinary. Beaming faces, mostly dark complected but with Oriental cheeks and eye structure rather than Indo-European, making it likely that the original guess was right. Something like Laotian, Thai, Vietnamese, or perhaps Malayan was at the root of these people's ancestry. They certainly had a sameness about their racial features that made it clear that they were either picked to a standard or had remained cohesive when having children long before these people had come here.

"Vegetarian, most likely, and not enamored of synthetic foods," Nagel guessed from the three-dimensional photos that seemed so real. "That would explain the huge greenhouses. Funny, most of these racial-purity-type colonial projects were also selectively technophobic; I don't see any signs of that here."

Queson nodded. "A couple of the pictures show they had babies the old-fashioned way, and I don't see much attention to livestock. You're probably right. Some form of Buddhist sect, I would suspect. Affluent, well educated, setting up a colony so they could practice their specific faith, whatever offshoot it was, and keep away from the culture polluters while enjoying the benefits of modern life where it didn't conflict. Makes sense."

"Except they chose this hole. As you say, they clearly had money, so what the hell were they doing picking a cold, rotten desert like this?"

"Oh, I don't know," Queson replied. "They were here for the long haul, and for religious and cultural reasons. They probably took it because nobody else wanted it, and it had enough underground water and a heavy enough atmosphere to sustain them. Their ancestors way back not only lived in dense jungles but in valleys carved by glaciers from mountains eight or more kilometers high. If they indeed had any Laotian blood in them, then their distant ancestors picked up and walked ten thousand or so kilometers from ancient southeast Asia on Old Earth up to the frozen Arctic, across frozen ice bridges eighty kilometers across, and down another two continents back when they were hunting prehistoric mammals with spears. These people were technological enough to grow fat and lazy without a challenge. This was it."

"Yeah, I'll take fat and happy to dead and consumed," Nagel commented. "Look at where their faith and high dreams took 'em. What a waste."

"Maybe. I'm reading fifty-two percent power, though. If we can't find the light switch and get going, we're going to wind up a kilometer short and with no protection."

Nagel nodded and stepped up his pace. It was getting easier and easier to just ignore the density of empty clothes and just make sure you didn't slip on them.

They'd had this discussion before, and would again. Nagel believed in nothing but the moment, and attaining by any means available the wealth to indulge every pleasure; he thought it was stupid to do anything else. The universe, after all, was going to end someday, going to go out and die, and then everything, everybody, and the sum total of all human achievement would be absolutely meaningless. To him, and many of the others, such a philosophy was the easy way to justify just about anything they felt like doing.

Scavenging dead worlds was a way to accumulate great wealth without having to dig mines or commit more daring robbery against the living. It could be dangerous, as now, but never once in his experience in the salvage business had a dead man ever shot him.

Randi Queson stopped and shined her light at a doorway that was, like almost all of them, wide open. It had been standard procedure when the power went down for all the locks to spring open and all the doors to slide open unless tagged specifically for security. That way, you could always get out. It was a much larger entrance than most of the others, and had all sorts of signs and pictographic symbols as well.

"Jerry, I think we've found the control center."

He came over and looked. As with many of the important stores and offices in this part of the complex, there were lots of empty suits stacked up around the doors. Clearly there had been great panic at the last moments here, but it was also clear that they knew what was coming for them. It seemed clear, from the direction of most of the clothes, though, that whatever they were running from had begun right around here.

"Everybody's running away," she noted, feeling a tightness in her chest and breathing very heavily.

She could hear his breathing, too, and took some comfort that it was as labored as her own.

They walked cautiously into the control center office. It was a large place, clearly the center of administration as well as the central power plant. The inner wall, however, was transparent, a shielded window down to the power plant and reactors far below. She checked her suit monitor. Radiation was well within tolerance, although higher than it should have been.

The window area, and the whole inner office complex,

was also notable for its near lack of empty clothing. Whatever had come for them, they were running from it, running from *right here.*

The control board and manual override stations were still active, as they'd suspected. The screens were dark, but unless they'd shorted out or been damaged somehow they should come on when an operator assumed control. That would not only give them a view of the power plant area at various levels but also access to the bank of screens on the inside corridor wall that probably would allow them to examine any greenhouse or, perhaps, any public area in the whole complex.

"I wonder how long this stuff's been sitting here, running on standby?" Nagel mused. "Maybe a century or more. Control, can you still get us?"

"We're all eyes and ears, Jerry," An Li's voice responded. "Give us a scan of the panels and the control system. We'll see if we can access an operator's manual. They almost certainly used a standardized system, and if we can translate the stuff for you then we can show you how to operate it. Both of you, do as much scanning of hardware as you can, will you? And if you see any manufacturer name, symbol, serial or model number, or whatever, focus in."

They did as instructed, and finally An Li called, "That's enough. They're Kalnikoff Systems units, almost certainly fifteen oh fives. That makes the power station almost certainly a colonial model five five six three Kaminichi Power Systems unit. Yes. No problems. And in that condition we might be able to do a ton of salvage. That's fairly recent stuff for colonial kits, no more than a hundred and five years. You just can't get those any more. Expensive to chip it out and move it, but it might well be sold in place. Then it would be the buyer's problem."

"Quit adding up the hypothetical profits and let's see if we can get some of it back on line!" Queson snapped. "The sooner we do, the sooner we can access and upload the records and find out what the hell happened here. And the sooner Jerry and I can get out of here and back to warm food, showers, and a bed!"

"Only one? Hmmm. . . . Never would have thought it of the two of you."

"Can the comedy," Nagel grumbled. "Something killed a shitload of people here, and I'd really like some confirmation that it isn't going to suddenly show up and dissolve me too."

"All right, all right. Are you sure you want to bring it back on line, though? Somebody deliberately shut this thing down before they panicked, or maybe *while* everybody was panicking. Sorry, but if something's shown up and started eating or dissolving folks right and left, do you take the time to lock the door and turn out the lights before you run like hell?"

That brought them both up short. Nagel looked at Queson in the eerie near-darkness, illuminated only by their lights, by a few other lights showing shutdown status on the command consoles, and by the soft glow from the power plant even in its most dormant stage beyond that protective picture window, and she looked back at him.

"Maybe we ought to take a closer look at the rest of this room," she suggested, and he didn't argue.

An examination through various light filters didn't help. The only one that registered much was infrared, and that only because of the residual energy coming from the close proximity to the well-shielded reactor chamber. The lights, though, showed that at a point where the undershielding extended underneath the fifteen-centimeter-thick floor, there was some *buckling*.

"Jeez!" Jerry breathed. "That's *impossible*! We go to space with shielding pretty much the same as this, and the interior of *Stanley* is made of this same calrithium compound. What kind of pressure short of a black hole would distort it so much?"

Randi Queson walked over close to the window, and, for the first time, looked down deep into the central power core and shaft.

"Jerry? I don't think we can salvage this power plant."

"Huh? What do you mean? I—" He suddenly saw her just staring down and went over to the window and saw what she was looking at.

"Holy Mother of God," the most faithless of men breathed as he looked down.

II:

RESEARCH AND RESCUE

Behind the window was a vast area that must have been impressive under any conditions. Always lit by its own glow, the shielding material was actually designed not only to trap radiation but to convert it into harmless light that did good rather than harm.

It was likely that the entire complex had been built into a natural cavern, although there were signs of some enlargement by laser construction trimmers. Still, the opening went down so far that it was only barely possible to see the reflected surface of a relatively warm body of water below, perhaps a vast underground sea. The water almost certainly wasn't that warm, but it was liquid and that was good enough for anybody looking to develop a planet.

Rising up from the ocean to beyond their own viewing level was a huge core complex, roughly cylindrical but with walkways, robotic service tracks, and monitors all about. Catwalks and thin bridges containing magnetic

tracks for the robots went in at various levels, allowing for service without obscuring the view of the entire
complex. Bumps, hatches, burl-like bulges off and on
through the structure, all provided access to various parts
of its internal circuitry and systems, and around the outer
walls of the cavern were oval dishes that captured output
as required and transformed the energy into useful
forms and sent them on to storage elsewhere in the
complex.

It was a magnificent site, and all they expected to see,
but what was about halfway down the center shaft
between them and the dark waters below was not. It
required magnification to bring into proper view, and, even
with that, it wasn't clear what they were looking at.

Both knew, however, that they were observing the most
dangerous thing they'd ever seen.

It looked for all the world like some kind of cartoonish
mouth, swallowing the shaft at that point like some kind
of carnival sword swallower. You had to stare at it for
a few seconds to realize that it was actually a mass, much
the color of the surrounding limestone, and without much
in the way of features, but a mass nonetheless of gigantic
size wrapped completely around the shaft at, or perhaps
from, that point. It hadn't been immediately clear that
it was a living thing rather than some kind of poured
support, but the more they looked at it, the more they
could determine slight undulations along the outer skin
or whatever, and the clammier it appeared.

"Well, you guessed that the last one would eat up all
the others," Nagel whispered, although he didn't really
know why. They were talking over a radio inside sealed
helmets, after all.

"Yes, but why is it still alive, let alone so huge?"

"Maybe it isn't through digesting things yet. After all,
it ate all the food for an entire city, plus the plants that
grew it and even the people who would have consumed
it. You ever seen anything like it?"

"No. Sleeping off a big feed, maybe, but I don't think it ate the place recently. No, it's getting the warmth from the shaft, but it's not feeding on the energy. If it could do that, why attack the colony? There's no sign they even *had* any big weapons, so it wasn't self-defense. That leaves hibernation. It came up from the sea attracted to the warmth, and after a while it found things it could eat here. When it finished, it went to the warmest point and went to sleep."

"How about letting it stay asleep and getting the hell out of here and back to the ship before it decides it wants a midnight snack?" Nagel said nervously.

"I doubt if we'd be worth much to it. Still, it would be totally instinctual. I agree. I think we ought to get out and leave the power down as it is. In fact, I think we ought to lift off when we get back and wave goodbye as we blast off."

"We'll see about the rest, but I agree about the first. Let's go."

They backed out of the place, and walked briskly down the hallway back towards the corridors to the greenhouses.

"We can't get close enough in to pick you up from there right off," An Li reminded them, "but we think we ought to extract as soon as feasible. At least until we can figure out what to do next. Let me run some figures and we'll see what's possible. In the meantime, get back into the greenhouse area quick so we can get individual tracking. It's a little too hot in the cliffs for what you put out."

They needed little argument, and stepped up the pace.

"Jerry? Are you sure this is the corridor we came in on?" Queson asked him.

"Probably not, but it's to the greenhouses," he responded. "I—"

He stopped abruptly, looking ahead into the darkness. His helmet light streamed ahead and caught what appeared to be several figures standing at one end of the corridor, near the first tube into the greenhouses. He was keyed up enough that it took him a moment before he realized that they were environmental suits quite similar to their own.

"Jerry! They're not empty!" Randi exclaimed, approaching the nearest one.

Sure enough, as her filters popped into place, she could see inside the helmet of the yellow suit in front of her. It was the ghastly face of a partially decomposed human head.

"There's another one like that in this blue one," Nagel told her. "Huh! Looks like all but one of them. Wonder why they weren't consumed?"

"This thing appears to be able to penetrate only organic material," she told him. "Remember how perfect everything else was, even the clothes and boots? These are sealed suits. I bet you'll find a tear or some other failure in the empty suit."

"Yeah, but if that's the case, how come they died?"

"Where do they go? What do they eat when the emergency rations in the suit run out? What about water? Recharge and it's got you. It might even have engulfed them, just waiting for the air to run out or the power pack to run down. God! I don't know how horrible it is to be dissolved, but I'll bet you the ones it got had a cleaner and easier death than these poor people!"

"That's us if that thing wakes up," Nagel reminded her. "Let's save the funeral for another day."

As they went on, Queson commented, "Actually, death by oxygen deprivation's supposed to be kind of peaceful, like drowning without the panic. You hallucinate, you feel you're floating, and you slowly go out like a candle in a gentle breeze."

"At least that solves the mystery of who shut everything down. They knew they had enough protection to be able to handle it. Must've been hell, though. I can't imagine anything close to that size being all that fast. Makes you wonder why they didn't lower the emergency doors, too. There's a set at each entrance and exit and each new corridor or section. You could even seal off a greenhouse and get enough air, water, and, if you're in one with the right stuff growing, even food. Why shut down the control center but not take the time to get people where they had at least a slight chance, maybe keeping the power levels up a bit? It still doesn't make sense."

"It's always a mystery until you know the facts," Queson replied, breathing hard now. At this pace, she was rapidly approaching her own personal limit.

"You okay?"

"No," she admitted. "But I will be once we get out of here."

They went through three greenhouses without any more incidents or discoveries, but then they got a call from On High.

"Hey, you two! Heads up!" An Li called. "We've got you on our tracker now and we're trying to work on as quick an exit as we can. But I have to tell you we're monitoring some movement behind you. It's still inside the cliffs, but we're getting really odd fragmentary radiation readings from there now, distinct from the core."

"That—*thing*?" Queson asked her, feeling her stomach knot up.

"Nothing that big. Smaller, faster, and somewhat indecisive. Like whatever it is is trying to figure out where you went. Randi, I've got your readings right here and I know what condition you're in, but you've got to keep going and step it up! If you can make another three or four greenhouses and stay roughly in the middle of the complex, we may be able to chance it, come in, and get you off the roof from outside! But you can't stop and you shouldn't stumble! My blips have merged and are now coming down the same exit you used. They finally picked up your scent or whatever they use."

Jerry Nagel unsnapped his pistol and with his thumb set it to maximum power without even stopping. She took hers out but was in no shape to set it. Its average power level would just have to be enough.

"You really think these little pistols can do much?" she asked him.

"Save your breath for moving! I have no idea. I think not, since that window in that far greenhouse was shot out, so they had a few things here and couldn't dent it, but who knows? Better than rocks. Stay along the far wall there. If anything comes close to us we want to be able to get outside and quick. Whatever that thing is, it's carbon based, a child of water, and loves the heat. That's three things that aren't outside."

"Yeah? If that's so, how come *these* people didn't all get outside?"

"They had sun suits and walking shoes on, not ones like this," he reminded her. "The only ones with *these* were doing what they could close up. I suspect they were moving to get out but time ran out on them. Let's not make the same mistake!"

An Li broke in. "Whatever it is is now just a greenhouse and a half behind you. You're still at least two, three away from any point where you might be picked up. Any of those isolation doors have a manual trigger? Just a thought."

Nagel cursed, wondering why he hadn't thought of it. The power-down had opened all the doors except ones that would be exempted in the control room or were subject to a manual override, just as the airlock doors on each compartment of the spaceship made said parts little independent biospheres for a while.

Sark's voice came over their intercom now. "Red handle, always to the right of each interconnect, facing the location map," he told them. "We just tried one and it works, but you may have to shoot out the cover. Side angle, low power works fine."

Nagel waited until Queson was through the tube to the next unit, then followed. Immediately he looked for the map, then the opposite wall on the right. The thing was pretty clear; he just hadn't noticed it before. He took his pistol and shot, and there was a tremendous flare and sparks flew everywhere. The emergency switch turned almost molten, but the door didn't drop.

"Damn it! I was on high!" he realized. "Come on! I apologize, but we're gonna have to run the length of this thing and through to the next one!"

Randi Queson tried, but her lungs felt like they were about to burst and her back was an increasingly concentrated single mass of severe pain. "I don't think I can make it, Jerry! You go! You can always find another frustrated old professor someplace!"

Jerry stopped, turned, and sighed. "I ain't got time for this, Doc," he said, then he yanked on her arm and began pulling her along. It was sheer agony, but screaming and cursing at him seemed to give her some extra energy.

The places were huge enough as it was; now, like this, it seemed as if the corridor was actually growing longer as they moved towards the far end.

"Guys, if that energy surge was Jerry's gun then they're about to come through the tube into where you are," An Li warned them. "We're picking up the rest of the team now. If you can't make the next greenhouse and close that door behind you in the next five minutes, then get outside and try and climb up on the roof. There are ladders at both ends of the buildings and in the center, both sides. Wind's really bad, but the suits should be able to take it. Once you're up there, keep moving until we can pluck you off. Understand?"

"We're gonna make it through!" Jerry almost yelled

to her. "C'mon, Doc! There's the connector! Get on through!"

Somehow, Queson made it, although she felt as if she were going to faint once she reached the other side of the connecting tube. This time Jerry dialed down his charge, angled, and shot the protective cover cleanly off. He then pulled the lever, praying that, somehow, it would work.

It did, and fast. The door shot out with amazing speed and they could hear the building shake as it went *chunk!* sealing off the other side.

"Well I'll be damned!" he breathed. "The thing was spring loaded!"

Randi Queson was breathing so hard the noise almost blocked off the intercom, and she was partially slumped, but she slowly seemed to be getting her wind back.

He knew that they weren't anywhere near safe yet, but he felt he had to give her a minute or two to catch her breath.

Something went *bang!* really hard against the metal blast and protective door they'd just triggered.

He jumped. "I thought you said five minutes!"

"That was five minutes ago," An Li pointed out. "Jerry, you've got to keep moving. Get to the far end as quick as you can, then exit and go up the *next* greenhouse ladder. Understand?"

"But there are doors right there!" Queson protested, pointing. Then, suddenly, she realized just how close things were.

Even a human being wearing very little or nothing at all could stand it long enough to get out one set of doors, pry open another set, and get back inside, and what-ever this creature or creatures were, they appeared to be made of much the same stuff as humans, even if put together differently.

Both doors were closed, though, and would require something like Jerry's crowbar assembly to open manually. That thing they'd seen wrapped around the core was more like a giant slug or worm of some kind, though. Not the most likely creature to figure out crowbars, and unlikely to have really great physical strength in any one part of it. Even if it, or something like it, could get outside from the other greenhouse, one with the same door problem, how long could they stand it out there before the sandblasting and cold got them?

There were still noises coming from the other side of the fire door.

"If I didn't know better I'd swear that somebody who knew what they were doing was laying out tools to try and open that door," Jerry muttered.

She nodded. "Too much we don't know yet. I'm better. Let's get going!"

She really *did* feel a little better, more clear-headed, less in pain right at that moment. Adrenaline and shock, most likely, but she'd take them while they were there and gladly accept the consequences when they wore off. It would mean she was still around to suffer.

They got most of the way to the next interconnect when they heard a major metallic racket at the other end and the sound of something big beginning to move.

"Oh, my god! Those damned things can *think*!" she shouted, and started running with an energy reserve she would never figure out the source of. Jerry was right behind, and they got into the next greenhouse and he once again triggered the door.

"Now let's go outside," he told her. "I think the odds will be a lot more even there."

An Li couldn't believe her instruments. "*Jesus!* Whatever those are, they peeled back the door! How come they couldn't do *that* when they ravaged the colony?"

"Maybe it learns," Randi Queson responded. "Maybe it's been digesting not only their material selves but also whatever information or skills they might have had. I don't know. That's why we call alien lifeforms *alien*. I only know I want *out* of here!"

Jerry was at the door. "Ready?" he asked her. "Keep the gun handy and kick yours to high. If they're that bright they might well have figured out this move!"

He pulled on the bar and the door half opened, letting in the fury of shrieking wind and blowing sand and pebbles. He drew his pistol again and stepped out, then she followed.

They weren't outside yet, or at least they weren't in the four- or five-meter range of visibility the blowing crud allowed them.

"Here's the ladder!" Nagel called, pointing.

"You go up first and I'll watch your back," she told him. "Then you watch while I come up slower." She sensed his hesitation. "Go ahead! I have no intention of being a martyr, and I intend to be around to razz you for years about the time you turned into Sir Galahad."

"Just for that, I *am* going up," he told her. "Don't watch me, though. Watch those doors!"

She waited, gun in hand, until she heard him call, "On the roof! Easy climb up, but watch it once you're here. There's a pitch and the small rails here are pretty damned short."

She could hear noises inside even through the storm and the helmet insulation, and she needed no further urging to get the hell up on top.

It *would* have been easy in a lesser wind and without the bulk of the e-suit, but it really wasn't that hard, it just took longer than she thought. *Everything's longer than I think now, it seems*, she reflected, but she soon had his hand to help her the rest of the way up.

"Slow and steady down the catwalk," he told her. "Can't see much or hear much, but what's inside has to come out here to get us, and I don't think they like that idea very much."

She sighed, but decided to walk sideways so she could see both out and back while keeping her balance. Speed wasn't the overriding factor here now, just keeping from falling off while making forward progress.

"If I could be absolutely sure that they couldn't get to me, I'd sure love to see what was chasing us, though," she told him. "This place is getting creepier and creepier and we still don't know a damned thing!"

"I know it's dangerous, it's smart, and it's not alone, somehow," Nagel said. "That's more than enough for me. Li, what's the plan?"

"It's tricky, but on manual Cross thinks she can hover the shuttle off the back end of the unit you're on and hold it steady long enough for you to at least get a handhold if not aboard. If you can only get a hold, hang on, she'll fly you back a ways from all this, then you can get in from the ground. Best we can do. Clear?"

"Clear," Nagel responded. "Keep the weapons armed on that thing, too! Our company's not that far away and it's suddenly grown a whole set of smarts."

"Cross, you got that?" An Li called.

"Got it," the pilot responded.

Gail "Lucky" Cross was a very good pilot in an era when human beings didn't have to be any such thing. She enjoyed it, practiced it, played with it, and that ability had paid off more than once. How could you figure out just how to tell a robotic pilot what they were propos- ing to do here? Or trust it to do it right?

Cross was actually a robotic engineer, the chief of salvage operations for the *Stanley*, and the one who would do the instructions and supervise the salvage operation once it was crunched and the method deter- mined. She had hair so short she sometimes seemed bald, was twenty kilos overweight and had a voice that was almost dead even between a very low soprano and a foghorn, and swore like a sailor. She was a Character with a capital "C" and she loved it.

Still, this would be as close and exacting a job of piloting as she'd ever done, and nothing for which she or anyone could have practiced. With the wind and minimal clearances it would be a job nobody else would consider doing, too.

Which was, of course, why she was clearly having the time of her life.

"Move on back, you mothers!" she shouted, taking over com control. "Ease back! I'm totally manual here and it's bucking like two dogs in heat!"

"Moving back towards you," Nagel told her. "Sounds like our friends are right below us inside the greenhouse, so we've got to do this on one pass."

"You got it. I won't be there when you arrive, but you tell me when you pass the last ladder and hold up there. I'll have two hooks out and it's gotta be fast and dirty!"

There *were* noises below, as if something was pacing them and pushing things out of the way to make sure they kept up. They *couldn't* be part of the slug or whatever it was; too small and too independent, Randi reasoned as they made their way back along the roof catwalk. And they had some use of *tools*. Whatever had consumed the others here couldn't have imagined tools; otherwise they would have had no problems penetrating the full body suits of those others. A third player? Something else as well? Something that survived, perhaps, or was working *with* the slug? It made no sense, but this job had gone sour from the start and all she wanted now was out of it. Later, in safety, she'd worry about the questions and look for answers. The crew wasn't about to abandon this mother lode of salvage unless they were forced to; they would address the questions when circumstances allowed. Most jobs had to be financed with mortgages on the ship and ground-based prior salvage in the yards left back home. Come home empty, and you lost both.

"We've passed the last ladder," Nagel reported. "Now, come and get us!"

"Stay close, arms up!" Cross ordered. "We may not get two passes! If anything, this damned wind is kicking up more! Just listen to my count! I have you on my scope. Five . . . Four . . . Three . . . Two . . . One . . . *Now!*"

Out of the swirling dust cloud came a dark but familiar shape, an egglike oval with a ring around its center and an aircraftlike tail rising seamlessly out of its back. It was going to and fro so much it almost disoriented the two stranded on the roof; even with the help of the entire system, Lucky Cross was having a really rough time, now even rougher as she came in low enough to the greenhouses that a severe downdraft might well bring the shuttle crashing into one of the roofs.

She stopped about three meters over the edge of the rooftop, two cables dangling from one side. The cables, with large mechanical hooks, whipped about like snakes in the wind, and threatened to either not come close enough for them to grab or, worse, to suddenly whip into them and knock one or both off the roof.

"Grab the nearest one!" Nagel shouted to Queson, although both were on intercom and shouting wasn't physically necessary. "Go ahead! I have a better shot at either! I need you to go first! *Now!*"

"Gang, I think that'd be a neat idea," Cross said to them. "I'm battling this son of a bitch with everything I got, and on top of that it seems like something's outside and slowly climbing up that ladder!"

That did it. As one of the cables whipped around, Randi Queson grabbed it and suddenly found herself flying in air, in a big and not fully controlled circle, holding on dearly with both gloves.

"Jerry! Hurry up!" she screamed. "I can't get the hook on, and I'm not sure how much longer I can hold on!"

"Coming as soon as I can get a line, Doc!" Nagel responded. "I don't want to take you out when I leap! Here we go! There you go! C'mon, c'mon. . . . *Holy shit!*" Nagel turned and jumped at that, got the cable, and tried to just hang on. *"Lift off! Lift! Go! Go!"* he shouted.

They felt themselves suddenly yanked backward, and Randi almost lost her grip, but managed somehow to twist some of the cable around her arms and hold on. Cross quickly moved out from the greenhouses and towards the rocky desert beyond before slowing to a near stop and lowering down.

"Get off on the ground, both of you!" the pilot ordered. "Then I'll put down on the surface just long enough to allow you both to get in the hatch. You hear me?"

"Yeah, yeah," Nagel managed. "You far enough from those buildings?"

"I'm already five kilometers out. That should be more than enough."

"Yeah, well, you didn't see what I saw. Okay! Let's do it!"

The shuttle dipped to only a few meters above the ground and first Randi and then Jerry dropped onto the surface, fell, rolled, and managed to get back up. The shuttle seemed to rise and vanish for a moment in the rapidly building storm, but managed to come back around and put down about forty meters from them. With their last strength, both rushed for the shuttle, and Jerry Nagel beat his partner into the open hatch by only a few seconds. They tumbled on top of one another as the hatch closed and sealed.

Cross didn't wait for anything more than confirmation they were inside and then lifted straight up, then out at a steep angle, trying to get above the storm.

"Back on automatic now. You two okay?"

"Yeah, I think so," Queson responded.

"Well, get out of those suits and into the inner chamber as soon as you can. 'Scuse me, but I have you on deep disinfection just in case. The suits, too."

Jerry was already deactivating his suit and there was the hiss of air as the helmet seal was broken. He lifted it off, put it down, and then began to climb out of the rest. Randi felt drained, sick, every combination of misery, but she managed to start the same process. He helped her with the last of it, seeing her distress.

She couldn't help but notice, though, that there was something different about him. The cockiness was gone, the cool confidence, the boyish sense of adventure. He looked scared.

"What did you see back there, Jerry?" she asked him, stretching to try and get her back in place and swiveling her neck to try and ease the pain and strain.

"I—I'm not sure," he told her. "Maybe when we look at the video we can see if it was my imagination or what. If it wasn't . . . I don't even want to think of what we'll do next. C'mon, let's go into the decontamination chamber. I need to lie down badly."

"You aren't the only one," she sighed.

She really didn't want to get out of the chamber, which had her lying, naked, on a specially contoured bedlike couch while all sorts of radiation and diagnostic streams and such were played all over her to determine any alien or unusual organisms not present before and, if found, to try and deal with them. It meant lying there, only turning on one side, then the other, then on her stomach and then on her back, but mostly just lying there in a nice, warm, safe cocoon.

She didn't bring up what Jerry might have seen again, or anything else. She was just too damned tired to care now that she felt safe.

A soft bell sounded, and Cross's voice said over the internal intercom, "Okay, you two. You're as clean as you usually are, for whatever that's worth. Come on in and join the crowd."

She groaned. "Do I *have* to?"

"Yeah, you have to. We're waiting for Li and the Captain to decide what the hell to do next. We've set back down on the Salvage One central complex, but we'll have to see how long or if we stay here. In the meantime, you're free to go to your quarters, take a shower if you want, get a change of clothes, then join us in the conference room."

"I just want to take some painkiller and sleep for a week," she groaned.

"Yeah, well, you might get a nap, but we got some real work ahead of us now. There's too much money lying out there to just leave it, but you ain't gonna believe what we got to do to get it now. Nice, easy pickings! Hah!"

Now she really *was* curious, but still not curious enough to override the thought that whatever they had seen or discovered would be just as valid after twelve hours of sleep as it would be now.

Still, she welcomed the respite, and she certainly could use the shower, she thought. At least they didn't seem to think that *this* complex was in any danger. Otherwise, the whole thing would have lifted off the moment they were all safely docked.

Still, as she made her way to her quarters, she couldn't help but wonder how safe those colonists had felt where *they* were, apparently until the very last minutes.

Maybe, she thought, I'm not going to be able to sleep all that well after all. . . .

Later, a bit refreshed, having eaten something, sitting there with a cup of coffee and under some powerful muscle relaxers from the dispensary, she was better prepared to at least join with the rest of the team in deciding what came next.

The entire ground party was there, which was most of the salvage crew. There was Jerry, smoking one of those foul things he liked without regard for who else had to breathe it; Achmed, eating a pastry; and Sark, looking like he'd just climbed out of his suit and with a three-day growth of beard, slumped in a big oval chair with his eyes closed. Lucky Cross had on nothing more than a robe and sandals and was drinking very strong-looking stuff. Cross was the only person Queson had ever known who mixed powerful alcoholic drinks by color. This one was a pastel blue. It was in a beer mug, and she wasn't exactly sipping it when she drank, either.

Five people in the whole ground salvage crew, but this five was all that was needed to handle even a major demolition and recovery like the colony back over the desert and against the cliffs. Once these big machines went to work, you only had to make sure they were doing what they were told to do.

Randi looked over at Cross. "Okay, Lucky, did *you* see what Jerry thinks he might have seen but won't tell us about?"

"Nope. Too busy battling those fucking winds to pay much attention to suit monitors. What *did* he think he saw, anyway?"

"As I said, he wouldn't tell me. There's no playback here?"

"Nope. It's all up top at that moment. So, Jerry, you want to tell us about it or keep us in suspense?"

"Yeah, Nagel," Achmed rumbled. "What the devil could scare *you*, anyway?"

Nagel reached over, picked up his beer, and swigged it, downing maybe half a liter before he paused. Then he gave a loud, ugly belch.

"Oh, Jerry! If you can't mind your manners go outside and play!" Randi told him, not really grossed out but knowing that Jerry was putting on a performance, either to deflect questions or to show he wasn't as frightened as she'd seen him. She wondered about that most of all. Was it unusual, or had she simply seen him for the first time with his guard down? It sure wasn't down now.

"All right, Jerry, if that's how comfortable you are, want to tell me what you saw when I was being lifted off?" she asked him.

He shrugged. "I still want to see the video, considering the situation and the visibility," he replied, "but, if you must know, I thought I saw a kind of man climbing up the last part of that ladder."

"A man? And that scared you?"

"Well, it didn't make me feel great," he told them. "I said it was a *kind* of man. All I saw was an arm and a head, but it had the usual requirements. Except that it wasn't right. You remember the texture of that worm thing, whatever it was? Kind of an icky translucent character, like clear glues?"

"Yes. You mean—"

He nodded. "Yep. It was a man made out of that stuff. Not covered by it, *made* of it. Kind of like a man sculpted out of stiff water or fluid ice."

The ship-to-surface intercom opened at that. "Hello, everybody," An Li's voice came to them. "I just overheard the description and it's basically what we saw and what he said in the debriefing. Take a look. First, real time. Look real sharp!"

The holographic projector over the table in the center of the room showed some static, then suddenly became a three-dimensional replay, without sound, of those last awful moments on the roof, all from Jerry's point of view. He was watching the shape of the shuttle emerge from the storm, then helping Randi position herself to grab the first cable. At that moment he seemed to hear or sense something and turned, and he looked back at the ladder. A right hand, then more of an arm came up as something was climbing the last rungs of the ladder. Then, quickly, there was a figure partially visible, and then Jerry turned and took a running leap and grabbed the second cable even though he wasn't fully in position for it.

"*Oooowee! Superman!*" Cross noted approvingly. "That's one hell of a leap, there!"

The video cut out at that point. "Any more and you'd get very dizzy very fast," An Li warned them. "Did you see it?"

"Yeah, we all saw it," Sark commented. "Not much to see, though. So fast I dunno if I was seeing what I thought or what he told me to look for."

"Okay, here we go again, only this time we'll hold each frame for one second."

At sixty frames a second, that gave them a good five minutes to look at the very short video, more than enough. In fact, it was almost maddening waiting for that hand to appear, then slowly, ever so slowly, advance, exposing a little more of the person or thing behind it as it climbed the ladder. Jerry had been a good observer, though. It was a very human hand and arm made of something no human had ever been made of.

Now, with agonizing slowness, the head began to emerge, and Randi Queson was suddenly aware that it had become so quiet in the room she could hear her own breathing.

The picture was grainy; the sandstorm wasn't the best environment for clear pictures, but it wasn't so bad that the details couldn't be made out, particularly when isolated and enlarged as An Li had done.

You could see the hair almost to individual strands in some frames, yet there was one thing about it that was very unusual.

"That hair's fixed, like a sculpture," Randi noted, breaking the silence.

"Yeah, or more like gelatin, some kind of clear gelatin," Lucky Cross added. "Weird, 'cause the figure's animated just like a human. Look at how the hand grabs and the muscles implied on the arm flex."

The living sculpture, as they began to think of it, continued to slowly emerge, until they finally saw the full face and part of a shoulder. The other hand was just about to come up to grab the other side of the ladder nearer the top; you could tell that by the very natural climbing motion it was making, much like any of them would look climbing a ladder.

The face was also a living sculpture; the eyes were made of the same stuff, but did give some odd sense of looking around, and the lips parted a bit, revealing some teeth. But that was all they got before it suddenly ended.

Everybody sat back in their chairs. Sark looked over at Cross, grabbed the glass with some of the pastel blue stuff, and took a swig.

"Back home, my people would have considered that a demonic being," Achmed said. "Although I am a rational and logical man and well traveled, at the moment I can think of no other explanation myself."

"Well?" An Li prompted. "It's not like we can take samples and do analysis of this. We need some input, people!"

Jerry shrugged. "Nice to see I'm not nuts or given to panicky hallucinations. I have to assume that if the whole thing climbed up on the roof it would be a copy of a human being in full, probably including his dick and pubic hair. That's what it is, though. There was no muscle inside that stuff. It just knew exactly what a man looked like and was copying everything but the coloration. Since there was more than one, I'm sure of that, we got to assume that the second one was either below or climbing up behind him. I have to admit that it was the teeth that shook me. I mean, why bother?"

"Because whatever it is knew precisely how the human body worked and should look," Randi said, thinking. "I think whatever is required for consistency simply is made, maybe faster than the eye can see, as required. Did you notice the features on him?"

Nagel nodded. "Yeah. Kind of east Indian or South

Asian, like the people who built this place. It was copying one of them for sure, as close as it could, but it just doesn't have any pigment. Or, at least, it doesn't have any way to color the various parts of people."

"Okay, so they're alien organisms who can mimic humans," Randi said. "So the next question is, why?"

"Huh?"

"Why mimic us if you can't fool us? They're absolutely related to that worm or whatever. Extensions of it, maybe, or offspring, or maybe just smaller relatives."

"Yeah, but, if they can do *that*, how come the scenes all over the colony?" An Li put in. "How come they couldn't get through any inorganic substances before and now they know how to throw the switches and force doors open?"

Randi Queson was thinking. "Maybe they didn't know when they attacked the colony. Maybe they learned. Unless we can access the records from the control room we'll probably never know for sure, but I've got a scenario in mind that fits. Maybe it's all wrong, but it's at least a working hypothesis."

"Shoot."

"Suppose those new greenhouses were just being put on line. Until then, this creature, whatever it was, was happy and dumb and living somewhere in that sea down there eating who knows what? Then they ramped up the reactor power to power up the new complex, and test things all out, and that was enough of a jolt or enough warmth that it got attracted to the core. Who knows if it was that big or lots of little ones or whatever? It probably bided its time. Maybe it ate one of the service supervisors in there, at a quiet time, night shift, or whatever, when it might be assumed that he or she fell in. Maybe somebody *did* fall in by accident. Anyway, it got a sample, and somehow this thing used that sample to adapt to consuming and converting our organic tissue. Little by little, it figured a way in. That buckling was probably some kind of structural mistake or sloppiness that developed over time, but the settlers hadn't bothered to fix it because the radiation levels weren't triggering any dangers and they had other things to do. Heck, replacing some of it might have caused a temporary shutdown, so the maintenance boys went against the political boys and you know who always wins *those* arguments."

"So far so good," An Li replied.

"Well, it used that to extrude into the control room. I think that, once it came out, it did it with as much speed as it could muster. It simply consumed everything and everybody who fit this new food model."

"You said 'extrude,' " Cross noted. "You think it's able to come through the keyhole?"

"Probably, yes. It's certainly a shape changer or it wouldn't have that human copy ability. I don't know what stiffens it, what powers it, or whatever, but I think it can flow almost like a thick liquid. Probably not a keyhole, but those buckled plates in the floor didn't allow all *that* much room. But they didn't have much time to do anything, and they had no real defense. I think we're dealing with a big single organism, but one that can spin off parts of itself and, although unconnected, use them just like we use arms, legs, whatever."

"But how does it *learn*?" Sark wondered. "And where's its brain since it does? And why did it take so long to learn stuff?"

"Maybe it didn't," the anthropologist replied. "If it, and lots of extensions of it, wiped out this colony in a matter of a day or so, a colony that had no heavy defenses or even a lot of light arms, it had a ton of experiences and new knowledge. But think of how that must have been incredibly confusing to it, even bewildering. This thing adapts. It's the most adaptable creature I've ever heard of, just judging from what we've seen. But 'alien' is a very good term to remember. We don't know its evolution, we don't know its composition, origins, or makeup. Does it reason or just copy?"

"It figured out how to override the fire doors," Nagel pointed out. "I'd call that some good measure of reasoning, particularly since the fire doors weren't tripped in the first place. How could they have seen that? They had to figure it out."

"A point, but we don't know how they did it. Still, I'm willing to admit to a level of reasoning here. They didn't come for us when we were well in and exposed. They had to know that we were part of a larger group, and they held back and followed us. Only when it looked like we were on to them, or were going to get out fast and clean, did they try for us. That shows cunning. Also, we ran ferrets through every square millimeter of that place before we went down, yet they showed nothing organic, no life, and nothing moving. That meant that they were all within the control room area, maybe inside, where our instruments and ferrets wouldn't be able to tell them from the residual radiation."

"Yeah, we didn't send any ferrets into the core area because of the reception problems and the fact that it seemed normal," An Li agreed. "So, it hid. It watched our little toys scramble around, then it watched you two without showing itself even after you found the main body of the thing. It's smart and it's sneaky. But if you look close at one side of the face, it also has problems with the sandstorm. Otherwise, it would just have gone out the side door and waited for you. It came through the fire door rather than going around, so we know it has weaknesses."

"The question is," said Randi Queson, "did it learn what it did by observing and then over years digesting and correlating and meditating on all that it saw, or does it, somehow, have some or much of the knowledge of those it consumed? Even if the former this thing is one of the most dangerous organisms ever found. If the latter, it's *the* most dangerous organism."

"You know, according to our charter, if this is a reasoning, sentient organism previously unknown we can't disturb it, let alone hurt it, so long as it stays on its own planet," An Li pointed out. "This can make salvage really sticky in a legal sense."

"Okay," Achmed growled. "So how do we kill it?"

III:

SALVAGE OPERATION

There wasn't an awful lot of sentiment among the crew for respecting a new lifeform. There just wasn't much love lost for a creature or creatures who had killed so many humans so wantonly and who had then tried to get at them. There were some, including Randi and Jerry, who wondered about the safety of continuing, and whether or not it was worth the potential cost even if doable, but the general sentiment was, if it could be done, let's do it, and if this thing gets in the way, let's deal with it.

"I'm not at all sure what would kill it," Randi Queson commented. "Something certainly can—if it eats, it can be gotten—but without a lot of experimentation on it who can tell? I doubt if shooting it with anything we have would do much. The industrial stuff, maybe, but not any sort of slicer and dicer. We'd simply make a big one into a few littler ones who'd recombine and be even angrier. We can probably incinerate it, if we're sure

we do it completely, or totally and completely disinte-
grate it, but if we do we'd better get *all* of it or it'll
just come back."

"Seems to me the best thing to do would be to poison it," Sark suggested. "Get the whole damned thing
at once. Let it gobble up its own doom."

"That's great, except that it probably wouldn't work.
Any poison would probably be ingested by one of the
smaller bits, and if it was *very* slow acting the thing
would probably adapt to the new substance and either
expel it or figure out a way to eat it. Fast and it's not
going to be able to infect all the pieces. As we said, if
you miss even one, we're potentially toast."

The problem was fed to the ship's master computer,
which came up with a compromise none of them had
considered.

The lifeforms all burned food for energy in a range
that made them show up on sensors the same as people.
That meant they could be located. Doing anything to the
large mass in the core would be impractical, maybe
impossible with what they had available, and would
certainly take better lab work than they could do even
if they could figure out how to safely get and contain
a tissue sample of the creature or creatures. They also
had mass, but couldn't come through walls or floors or
solid rock, and certainly they still had problems with
inorganic substances overall.

The obvious solution was to use the big industrial
salvage lasers to sever the greenhouses from the main
complex and then create a molten rock flow that would
cover and seal in the cliffside complex, core and all. Then
it would be a matter of sending in small disassembler
robots with full torches and dealing with the small ones
that might be left outside. From that point on, and with
a constant watch on the cliffside to insure that there were
no more holes and that there was no breakout by the
main mass, they could methodically and safely disas-

semble the greenhouses. The profit would still be huge; it just wouldn't be as huge as if they could have reclaimed the interior complex and the reactor. Humans would be placed in harm's way only when absolutely necessary, always fully armed and fully suited up, and with cover.

"The computer believes we could do this operation in six weeks or less, that the profit on the enterprise would still be in the millions, and that it's the most likely compromise," An Li told them. "Of course, it assumes that we can contain the thing and deal with any small ones left outside."

"And if we can't?" the uncharacteristically nervous Jerry Nagel asked her.

"Huh?"

"If those things can't be dealt with and or the big one figures a way out? What then?"

"Then the only solution would be to abandon everything in place and use the shuttle to lift survivors to the ship if possible. If that happens, we will all be dead broke and unable to return home unless we find money for new equipment and a new salvage job. And if we just say goodbye right now, we've got no credit and nothing to trade, so even if we find something else, which probably wouldn't be nearly this profitable, we couldn't pay for maintenance and repairs, recharges, you name it. Cap says, though, that she can't order this one since we're safe up here. You got to decide down there."

"I can kill anything except my bills," Achmed growled. "Let's go do it."

"I say so long as I don't face no thirty meters of morphing worm, let's get the stuff that's just lying there and get out of here," Sark added. "The little ones, they *got* to burn."

Cross joined them. "I just can't be no grasshopper, sittin' on a farm workin' fixin' some guy's milking machines," she said, "or flyin' over pissing pesticides.

Let's do it. I'll yank your shit-ugly necks out in time if I have to."

Nagel sighed. "Well, that makes Doc's and my votes unnecessary. So let's get to work, see what we're dealing with here, and I'll start running scenarios through the computer. Luckily the greenhouses are of only two types, both known prefabs, so it's going to be easy to create a deconstruct model. The wicked part's going to be getting the smelter in place to turn that cliff into a lava flow."

Queson nodded. "And I'll coordinate with the ship. We're going to need a much more exhaustive ground survey extending down as far as our instruments allow. We've got to know how far that sea extends under the complex, and beyond, and where any weak points to it might be other than the cave in the cliffs."

In the meantime, Cross flew in over the complex and dropped a dozen or so ferrets, small robots no larger than a man's fist that nonetheless had a great deal of instrumentation as well as continuously broadcasting cameras and the ability to both hide when need be and move up walls and even along ceilings in most cases. They'd been used in the initial surveys and found nothing, but now they were not so much hunting as guarding, simply searching for signs of any sort of life. If they found none, they took up positions between the cliff complex and the greenhouse area where work would be done in order to insure that nothing at all snuck up on anyone or anything working there.

Queson suspected that the creatures only reacted to organic life, which was why neither the initial ferret survey nor their own walk into the complex had triggered any alien actions. It was only when they were stomping around in the control room, looking down at the mother thing or whatever it was, that the thing had become aware of them even through their suits. If that really was the case, and it wasn't simply noise that did it, then they might get lucky and trap the whole thing inside the cliffs.

The only thing that worried her was the inability of the orbital survey equipment to get a good sense of where that sea began and ended. The lay of the land wasn't conducive to accurate underground mapping; something was throwing off the information. There were some indications, though, that the sea extended very deep down under much of the complex, and that, in fact, it was the reason why the colony was here at all.

"It's very deep down," she explained, "particularly out this way. It could be a vast complex of flooded caverns hundreds of meters down below this very hard rock. That would mean that we're talking maybe not being able to pen that thing in there."

Nagel looked at the readouts and nodded. "If these holding tanks are filtered by this system under the greenhouses rather than from a central supply, those things could ooze out of every faucet—at least, if they could get through all the twists and turns." He paused. "No, I'd say not, though. To open the valves in the filtration setup is going to require power. So long as we keep 'em powered down, it shouldn't be possible for anything to get up through there. It's designed to purify the water and keep the crud out. I'd say our friend qualifies as crud. Power would be required to bypass the system. Otherwise, forget it."

She nodded. "I hope you're right. I don't see any faults or openings through the rock there that would allow another route."

They worked through the better part of a day getting their settings right, running simulations, making sure that this operation was as safe and as feasible as it could be made to be.

Another worry was that it was going to take a lot of power they could ill afford to use to get the smelter in the right position and then to use it at full power for as long as it would take. If nothing went wrong, there would be enough to do the whole job and still get it back and into operation for what it was intended to do. The tricky part of that was the phrase, "If nothing went wrong . . ."

Both of them could find a thousand ways things could go wrong, but, using what they knew, the vast majority of computer simulations showed that everything would work out quite nicely.

"There's nothing left to do but to do it," Jerry Nagel said at last.

Lying on the plain was the complete salvage complex, detached from the mother ship and then landed and anchored on the surface. It was basically a rectangular structure but with the front and back ends tapered outward, and its length was divided into three sections by a series of inverted U-shaped structures that at first glance seemed built into the rectangle but which were actually simply attached to it. The shuttle sat in a cradle at the front end, just beyond one of the "U" structures, providing both an independent on and off system and a primary control for the entire thing when it took to the air or space. For ground salvage work, though, each of the parts as it deployed had its own independent control cabin as well. It was where everything was housed, including the crew, and where all the work of salvage was based.

Achmed moved into the control seat of the central structure and strapped himself in. Normally the job of the Smelting Section was entirely automated, but in this case they felt that someone had to be there, to take manual control if need be. The computers were smart, but they hadn't been programmed nor tested for this kind of thing. The smelter was not intended to move any great distance, just to be able to move beyond the salvage modules so it could exercise its great heat and power without risking anything else. Now it was expected to go a very long distance, then rise not to fit into a structure but to hover independently while it did its work.

The robotics would be relied upon for the needed precision, but it had been decided that it would be easier for Achmed to handle the operation directly than to try and explain it to the computer in such a way that there were no slips. All of the cliffside complex had to be sealed, yet not enough to dissolve sufficient base rock to burn through into the caverns below.

Once the job was done, all survey equipment would be directed into determining the firmness of the seal. Once that was done, smoldering lava or not, the other units would be coming in to begin salvage work on the greenhouses, starting with the farthest ones out. *That* at least should be doable entirely by remote control and, after the first one was completely done, by robotic control, but this equipment was never to be depended on a hundred percent. It was always best to have a human being overseeing the thing, ready to take over for the unforeseen.

Randi Queson had seen pictures of earlier days, the state of the art in this, when master engineers were fitted with direct implant jacks and could be plugged into machines like this and become one with the machines for these operations. Although some of the military ships had them even now, the operations to implant the jacks required sophisticated surgical machines that needed constant maintenance and upkeep due to the incredibly tiny tolerances required. The expertise and technology needed had been held close to the vest by the old System Combine and the specialized guilds who each guarded their programs.

Another major part of human knowledge lost for the most part, the few jacks left kept going by cannibalizing others that had failed for parts. She wasn't at all sure it was a big loss, not like a lot of the other stuff, and many others agreed with her. *We've had to give up our metamorphosis into machines and learn to become human again,* she thought.

Still, at this time, for this kind of operation, she wouldn't have minded being able to use those jacks just for this.

"Power at point nine nine nine forever percent," Achmed reported. "Clock on, tied to power reserve. Detaching unit aft."

The inverted U of dull blue-gray coloration came to life and there was a series of *chunk! chunk! chunk!* sounds as the connecting pieces detached and slid back into their recesses. A light on the tiny cab centered atop the structure flashed yellow, and the two side lights flashed red and green as the section slowly lifted off the main structure and then turned, cleared it, and lowered itself to only a few meters off the ground.

"Moving out. Lucky, you coming?"

"I'll wait a few minutes," the shuttle pilot responded. "You'll be a while getting *that* thing over there, and I don't feel like waiting around in this crud."

"Fair enough. Punched in, navigation is on automatic. Ride is steady. Some slight buffeting by the winds at the cab level, but nothing that isn't being compensated for. Estimated arrival time at current very slow speed is sixteen minutes."

"Hell, I'm gonna take a crap and I'll still beat you there. Hold off at least one klick out, though. We don't want any of them things gettin' ideas."

"Never let me stand in the way of a woman going to the bathroom! Go, in more ways than one!"

Queson was no pilot nor, even less, a salvage center controller, but she drew the chair at the center control room while everybody else would be away. Achmed would be operating the smelter unit, Jerry and Sark would be backup on the shuttle, and Cross would be flying. That left the anthropologist/geologist, the latter a field she'd added late in life because it was actually marketable, to monitor everything. In one way it was the best seat in the house; her monitoring screens showed every lens view, every ferret, the cabin view from Achmed's lofty perch, the fore and aft shuttle views, the surrounding security perimeter established around Salvage One, as well as the maps, monitors of lifesigns, and just about everything else. It was, in fact, too much information; while it was useful to the master computer and the ship above, in most cases she had to pick a view and stick with it. She knew that if anything unusual showed up, the system would automatically switch to that view.

She felt the whole complex shudder and then there was a big banging sound for a moment. The shuttle was away.

"Overview of target complex," she said, and the whole thing, as photographed from high above, came on the screen. "Show infrared and lifesigns."

The reactor showed as a nice, steady glow, but there seemed to be nothing else of note within the structure. "Active overview," she commanded.

Now she could see the smelter unit, represented by a simulation but looking probably as real as a current picture, with Achmed's small lifesign at the top, and the shuttle closing in on it rapidly, three dots showing inside it.

"Li? You on?"

"Yes, Doc, I'm here. What's the problem? You're the only one down there who can sit this one out."

"Yeah, I guess so. I sure don't envy any of them being out there. I dunno. Maybe it's just what almost happened to me there, maybe it's my anthropologist's self saying that we're trying to seal off the first apparently intelligent creature we've met out here, maybe it's a hundred things. Mostly, though, I just feel like we're underestimating this thing. If nothing else, it's going to take several minutes to heat up that rock so that it becomes useful. Those things were *fast*. I don't like not knowing about those caverns below, too. Too many unknowns."

"Yeah, well, that's what the face of poverty will do for you. Take risks. The bigger the risk, the bigger the payoff, too."

"Yeah, maybe."

The shuttle now did a slow flyover of the cliffside above the complex, and checked the openings and interconnects to the first rows of greenhouses in the complex. They, of course, would have to be sacrificed to the rock seal as well. It wasn't what they wanted to do, but it was necessary.

"Twenty-six, move forward to interconnect with the cliffs and hold on the ceiling," Queson ordered, and the ferret moved with lightning speed down the last big warehouse and into the interconnect. "Pan."

This was the area where they'd emerged, the one with the only bodies left on the planet as far as could be determined.

"Hold it! Lock onto the floor and pan."

"What's the problem, Randi?" An Li asked.

"Take a look. Bones, some remnants, dumped out and all over. Those are the bodies, but where are the e-suits?"

"Huh? Even if they took the suits, why didn't they consume the remains?" An Li asked, even as she confirmed the video.

"I have no idea. I don't know what the hell we're dealing with at this point," she responded. "Queson to shuttle. Watch out below. They've dumped out the e-suits, which means that they're wearing them."

"*What?* Hey! Everybody hear that?"

"I don't believe it," Achmed responded. "They're just animals. You just went down the wrong corridor. At any rate, I'll melt their slimy little asses in a few more minutes and there's nothing they can do about it."

Suddenly all sorts of alarms went off on the main

board, causing Queson to almost jump out of her seat. She looked around frantically, silenced them, then sought what had triggered them. It wasn't hard to figure out.

"What the hell . . . ?" Lucky Cross said, amazed.

The reactor was clearly being powered up inside the cliffs, and, eerily, like some kind of ghostly march, one by one, row by row, the lights and general power in each of the greenhouses was coming on.

"Animals my ass!" Queson called to him. "Damn it, it knows how to work the control center! It's powering up! Stay above your targets by a fair distance! It knows you're there and it's moving to try and stop you from doing whatever you're doing. It may not have figured us out yet, but it sure as hell knows we're up to something nasty for it!"

"I am in position, power at ninety point two percent!" Achmed called to them. "Clear?"

"All ferrets back to safety distances, shuttle in hover mode well over you, Achmed!" Randi Queson told him. "Do it! Do it *now*, before that thing figures out a way to stop it!"

"Engaging on target at forty percent power," Achmed responded coolly. "Going up five percent per minute."

Queson looked away from the general view and to the monitors showing the ferret views from just inside the safety circle, as close as they could safely risk to the smelter's actions.

"Fifty percent. Surface rock going into the red, six hundred degrees surface at the mark. *Mark!* Fifty-five percent. Seven hundred degrees, accelerating nicely."

Two distinct and large patches of *something* came out of the entry tube and into the now well-lit greenhouse. They looked like large two-meter-by-half-a-meter puddles of water to Queson, only they were *moving*, moving under their own power somehow, and leaving no wet trail behind.

She watched, even as Achmed's status report came

through the audio, and a much more precise account of its progress was being posted on a parallel screen.

The two things, whatever they were, came up to where some of those eerie, empty clothes were lying and they flowed right *into* them. It was as if some sort of invisible balloon inside them suddenly inflated, and now those clothes were once again inhabited, this time by living sculptures in that translucent watery material. A man and a woman, so detailed that it was as if they were reincarnated on the spot. They actually looked at one another, nodded, then got up on two legs inside their work shoes and walked over to the door. The male took a pair of utility goggles from the tools hanging on the wall and put them on quite like anyone else would, then pressed the door latch which, with power restored, at least for a short while, slid back. "He" stuck his head outside, carefully looking back up towards the cliffs, then withdrew back inside, took off the goggles, and closed the door. The pair were so humanlike in every movement that they actually looked, well, if not angry then certainly pissed off, yet there was an air of puzzlement, too, like they were trying to figure out what the hell to do about things.

"I've got primary melting at seventy-five percent," Achmed announced. "White hot around the edges but nothing major. I'm going to hold at this, both to save power and to allow it to spread as an even flow. Surface rock temperature is at fourteen hundred thirty-four degrees Celsius. That's a rather nice temperature for a nice, slow magma flow."

"We've got flickering on the lights," Cross reported. "I think we're into the cliffside interconnects."

"Yeah, well, that central worm can drop down into the sea below, and it's got some offspring running around looking and acting just like us," Queson warned them. "We're not out of this yet!"

"We've got the laser cannon on manual and are

covering," Jerry Nagel's voice came in. "We're open wide, maximum heat at a three meter square spread. I—"

At that moment, the audio from all sources suddenly began blasting out very bizarre sounds that were stepping on and breaking up everybody else.

"What the shit is *that*?" An Li managed through the direct to ship link that was the only one not affected.

"It's—it's *music!*" Randi responded, confused and amazed. "Some kind of Hindu or Buddhist chanting against some exotic instruments."

"Damn! That's one smart worm! Can you get through to the shuttle or Achmed at all? This link's only good to the base where you are unless the shuttle activates its emergency communicator, and I suspect that's not a good option with all the other power, particularly weapons, on. *Damn!*"

Queson set the intercom on full scan. It scanned tens of thousands of frequencies in the blink of an eye, but it just kept locking on different south Asian music or eerie, rhythmic chants.

"It's got a repertoire, but no signals ground-to-ground are getting around the jamming," she reported. "I'm getting video, but no audio, but I suspect that's the next thing to jam. Lucky's got her keyboard active but either it's being jammed, too, or she's really rusty actually typing out anything. It's mostly garbage."

"How're your keyboard skills?" An wanted to know.

"Rusty, but competent."

"Pull it out and send, 'Do you want to abort?' That gives her a yes or no. She should be able to manage that."

Queson turned and found the release and brought out the keyboard. It was a last-ditch antique transmitting on an equally ancient frequency, but it was often the only way to get through in high-interference regions.

The screen responded, "N. I thr trblnhyt = "

"No trouble. Your keyboarding is awful. Stick to yes

or no." Clearly Lucky was typing with a finger while trying to check on a dozen other things at once and going off the keys without realizing it.

The smelter was doing its job on the rocks, but it wasn't at all clear that the solution was working. Magma wasn't something that could easily be predicted or controlled, and the models were based on standard assumptions. The fact was that, at this point, the whole face of the cliff was melting like some surreal painting, and the base of the complex where it connected to the first row of greenhouses was heavily engulfed in billowing smoke. The four connected directly into the cliff were on fire, even though they were nominally fireproof.

"Ha! Let anything try and get out of there now!" Achmed cried in triumph. "Powering down, still have thirty-one percent, more than enough to get back and mate with the main unit. There is no question that the linkages are sealed!"

The main board in front of Randi started going wild. She looked up at the displays, but so much was going on at once she could barely make sense of it. Small dots, small units or something, were outside the greenhouses but well away from the action. Two—no, three small blips. Yellow . . . red . . . green. . . . Why?

Suddenly she realized that the colored blips had numbers in them. They were e-suits, powered up and therefore registering on the universal transponder frequency. Red, yellow, green. . . .

Suddenly the vision of the partially decomposed suits came into her mind. Yellow, red, green. . . . *They were using the suits to move about outside and away from the fire!*

"Lucky, you'd better cover down there! Three things in powered suits heading out and away from the complex! They could be coming my way!" she warned.

"Huh!" the pilot responded, surprised. She hadn't really

seen these things in action. "I'll be damned! Think we can shoot 'em?"

"Fire will take them out, or full power disintegration," Queson told her.

"Yeah, but those suits can take a lot of shit. Stand by! I'm going to swing around and see if I can spot the little buggers."

"Watch it!" Li cautioned from above. "If they have power in those suits then they have short-term weapons!"

"Ah, c'mon! They're fuckin' *worms*, aren't they?" Cross came back.

"Worms that can figure out what the suits are for, operate them, and, more important, worms that have figured out how to recharge the batteries in the past day or so!" Queson reminded her. "And if they can do *that*, then you better damned well figure they can shoot."

"Well, I'll keep the hatches closed. Nothing they would have could penetrate the shuttle," the pilot responded, a bit chastened. "I think we can put a few energy bolts down there where they'll do the most good!"

Queson looked at the board. Something else was going, too, something that was only readable by a faint yet enormous heat signature.

They'd awakened the big one, the one wrapped around the power core! The sucker had oozed down into that underground sea and was now moving around the molten area. The ground was so thick and the interference from the greenhouses and the smelter operations so prevalent that only the size of the thing made it obvious that it was more than an intermittent anomaly.

"The mother creature is free in the water," she reported. "I think it's coming my way. What the hell do I do?"

At almost the same moment, Cross called, "Where the fuck *are* the little bastards? I don't have them on visual at all!"

"Try the emergency transponder frequencies! They show up here!"

And, at just about two seconds after she said it, they suddenly vanished from her board.

"What? Where?"

"Damn it! *They're listening to us!*" Queson almost screamed.

How was that possible? How could such a creature, however smart, learn enough of their language to understand it? Or to power up and operate all those complex gadgets, including knowing just how to turn the emergency beacon off? Hell, even these colonists hadn't spoken the language the crew of the *Stanley* was using!

"Good God!" she swore, almost as if speaking to herself. "I think those things absorb the knowledge, the intellect, of the people they ingest! They've got the collective knowledge of every colonist who lived down there!"

"Oh, c'mon! That's *impossible!*" Nagel put in. "Anything that adaptable and that smart wouldn't be sleeping wrapped around a radiation core!"

But that was exactly what it might do, several of them realized at once. All that collective knowledge couldn't get them out of this hole. All it could do was frustrate a smart entity or entities, now knowing all the wonders of the universe out there but being unable to get to it. It would make sense to put the power on minimum, use it as an alternate energy source, and then just go to sleep, hibernate, dreaming great dreams of potential conquest, waiting, waiting for somebody, from somewhere, to stumble over this outpost of Hell and give it a ride to the stars.

This wasn't something they were prepared for, nor something they could deal with. There was only one course they could follow, and they all knew it.

"Everybody back! *Now!*" An Li ordered. "The captain has issued a full abort! Lucky, drop the hunt and cover

Achmed. Get that smelter and all of you back to the ground base. Ain't no way we're gonna salvage anything except maybe our lives here."

Randi Queson looked at the heat shadow that came in and out on the board, twisting and turning, sometimes too faint to make out, other times very clear if amorphous in shape, and it was very clear that the thing was trying to figure out how the hell to get to the base and her. Only the fact that they'd feared that the weight of the base would break through the crust and so chosen a solid basalt outcrop for the anchor site, and the fact that the creature couldn't stand that weather out there unprotected any more than they could, were saving them.

But what if you had the brains of a thousand or more colonists and their collective knowledge of everything from geology to conventional biology to use? It—*they*— would figure something out. She knew it.

"Screw the smelter!" she yelled. "Pick up Achmed from the cab and get back here *now*! Otherwise it's going to be here waiting for you!"

"Belay that!" An Li cut in. "There's no way we can make up for the loss of the smelter. You come up here without it, we won't be here. Understood?"

"You mercenary bitch! Next time *you're* comin' down!" Queson said, disgust competing with fear as her dominant emotion.

"It's all about money, honey," An Li replied. "Always was."

"Calm down, ladies!" Achmed called. "I'll be home as quickly as I can! Nothing's going to get up here to me, so relax! And I don't think that the Big Bad Worm can undermine the base. It may be the fastest learner in the universe, but it's pretty soft and at least as much water as we are. Not to worry! Allah is merciful! He will protect me!"

"Allah pays as much attention to you as you do to

Him," Nagel responded. "Just get your big smelter over there and show us you can mate!"

"Jerry, I think we all ought to switch to a private frequency," Cross commented. "If this thing can listen, let's put its ears out! Randi! Li! Achmed! Listen up! Private fourteen, full digicode! Got that?"

"Wait!" Queson called. "How do I do that here?"

"Fourteen full, aye!" Achmed responded, and the whole communications system went very, very dead.

Queson looked around for something, anything, to order a change, and nothing was obvious.

She looked up at the main display. The thing was almost engulfing the plateau, but so far below that it still registered only as a faint shadow. On the other hand, the three dots, no longer color coded, showed up quite close to the base now and proceeding towards it on the ground. They'd minimized their energy signatures to a remarkable degree, but this close in they couldn't hide from the scanners any more.

They didn't have to.

She was all alone, and about five minutes from possibly having the worst kind of visitors.

IV:

NEITHER COMMAND
NOR CONTROL

Randi Queson was never more frightened in her life
than at this moment. At the same point when they'd
all switched frequencies without telling her how to do
it back at the base, she was getting the distinct impression
of being surrounded by what was surely an alien intelligence of tremendous malicious potential.

She frantically tried to figure out the frequency shift.
It would be easy to just scan for the active ones if this
were a conventional switch, but this was a security switch
to an encrypted and secure channel that wouldn't even
show up on any monitors even as gibberish. That
required more knowledge of this master control board
than she had, simply because she'd never had to do it
before and nobody had thought to teach it to her.

She was always "out there" in these operations; Cross
or occasionally Sark or Achmed would handle this.

She tried opening all the common frequencies, thinking

that surely An Li above would have them scanned, but instead of the silence she expected she got ear-splitting screeches that forced her to cut the audio. For a second she was confused as to what the sounds were, and then it hit her: *the standard frequencies were being jammed!* Damn! This thing, whatever it was, was one quick learner. Must be nice to eat your education instead of having to work at it.

She looked back up at the area scan visual and saw that all three small dots were now stopped at the bottom of the base, a bit spread out, as if assessing the situation and figuring out how the heck to get in. She knew that the security seals were locked down, but she couldn't underestimate this new intelligence.

Even as she frantically looked for loopholes in the defense perimeter and decided to check out a couple of hand weapons from the locker outside she also felt a sense of regret that what was possibly the first human contact with an alien mind was in this sort of situation. She would love to have a conversation with it, learn something about it, see if some kind of equilibrium could be reached, but she also knew, deep down, that it would have no percentage in doing that. If it got to her it would simply absorb her and all that she was would become a part of it. If it couldn't reach her, then there was really no percentage in it talking at all, except, perhaps, to deceive.

It was smart enough to do everything else, she thought. Why not some good old human trickery?

She looked at the board and saw that Achmed and the smelter were almost halfway back, shadowed by the shuttle. Whatever this alien was going to do, it would have to do it in the next fifteen or twenty minutes or it would be too late. The smelter would dock from the top, affording Achmed access through the top hatch that otherwise was sealed, since there was no other use for it, and the shuttle would settle in its cradle and lock down, activating the forward lock. Theoretically, she was sealed in and totally protected.

Theoretically.

She went to the locker in the ward room and pulled a long-burst disintegration rifle and a wide-mode side-arm. Theoretically, either one would be sufficient to vaporize any of these things.

She retreated back into the command and control center and shut the door.

Every door on the base unit was a total seal, so that even the unexpected, fires and floods and who knew what else, could be isolated. The C and C was particularly well protected, since it could control the entire unit if the shuttle wasn't mated. It even had its own bathroom, food unit, and water supply. The only point now open to the outside, via its own separate channels, was the air supply, and she quickly switched it to self-contained and heard the rebreather apparatus come on. It could recirculate things for weeks if need be, and she only needed a quarter of an hour.

Now she had to wait, rifle in her lap, to see if the rest of the team could get back before the alien or aliens figured out a good move.

In the meantime, the control center suddenly started feeling like a cold, silent, and lonely tomb, an office in the City of the Dead.

Curse you, you bastards! You didn't all have to go on that junket and leave me here all alone!

The tracking board indicated that the smelter was well on the way, covered by the shuttle, but there was no longer any sign of the three non-company spacesuited figures. That meant that they were somewhere close, probably at the base camp, trying to figure out a way in. They wouldn't find the cracks or vents that they'd used to ooze into the colony, not here. Anything like that would have meant that the base couldn't have withstood space and the descent. The air vents would be the only way in, and those were up top and pretty well exposed for the shuttle's guns to take out. Cross would know to just blow away anything up there, unless, of course, the damned things were already up and inside before Cross was close enough to act.

The board showed that the shuttle had detached from shadowing the smelter and was now circling the base unit.

Good for you, Lucky. So where's the critters?

The radio suddenly came to life. "Doc? What the hell happened to you?" An Li's voice came to her. "Why aren't you over on the security channel?"

She had never felt so relieved in her life. "Li! You bitch! Nobody ever showed me how to switch it!"

There was a sigh on the other end, then, "Well, screw it now. Are you locked down?"

"Yes, yes! I'm just waiting for company!"

"Stay there. No sign of our friends yet, and I'm getting signs of your big, big worm just about surrounding the plateau. Wait until they're inside and you get an all-clear from them on the internal intercom. The aliens won't be able to tap that. In the meantime, I'm gonna keep the others on the secure channel so nobody's hand is tipped. Just stand by. I don't want to broadcast anything useful."

It sounded sensible, even reassuring. Why the hell did she have this paranoid feeling in her belly, then?

Maybe it was the absence of a sign of those three colorful suits. That and the extreme intelligence the aliens had shown up to now.

"Li, tell me how to dial up the security channel from here. I want to coordinate with them."

"That's kind of moot right now. Just sit tight."

"Li, tell me the way to dial in! Now!"

"I said—"

"You're not An Li, are you? That's an excellent imitation."

"Don't go nutty on me now! We're almost home!" the voice said, sounding *exactly* right.

"I want you to do it before either of the units docks with this base. If you don't, then I will know it's fake. Then I will have to use the panic button and create a near instant vacuum in the rest of the base, which, if it doesn't finish you off, will at least seal the entry ports so that the others will be protected. You understand me? I'm *not* going to be absorbed."

"You're crazy, Doc! You know who this is!"

"If you can't tell me the procedure, then, yes, I know *exactly* who this is."

There was dead silence, and she could understand why. The creature had never absorbed one of the crew. As smart as it was, by hook or crook, it had never been in this control room before and thus had very little idea what it actually looked like, much less of the commands needed to switch to an unknown proprietary digital frequency.

It wouldn't even know that there wasn't any such thing as a panic button creating such a vacuum.

"So long as the truth is out," she said slowly, sitting down in one of the command chairs, her stomach almost in convulsions, "would you like to talk?"

For another moment there was silence, and then An Li's voice asked, "To what purpose?"

"You're highly intelligent. Probably a lot smarter than any of us. Did your kind evolve here or just become stranded here until those unfortunates landed and built their colony and somehow woke you up? Were you this smart *before* or only after you killed them all and stole their knowledge?"

"Dialogue is irrelevant. No one is dead. All have become part of us. The many have merely become one. You will know this when you are a part of us, and we will know you, and you will become immortal with us."

She started to protest, but then realized that, from the

thing's point of view, it probably was right. From its vantage point, it simply incorporated their minds and mass into its own, and this was the proper way of things. To her, the colonists were dead. To *it*, the colonists were all right there.

The base gave a shudder, then came a series of vibrations that shook the entire control room.

She thought for a moment that the alien was doing something, then she turned and looked at the scanning screen, amazed at her own composure at this point.

The smelter! Achmed was sliding the thing back into its grooves on the base unit and then locking it down. Next he'd be opening the hatch from up top. If they'd managed to ooze in through the air vents, then he'd get a sudden and dramatic welcoming committee!

She didn't know much about the settings, but the small cameras showing the entire perimeter of the base, so useless in trying to find the suits, now showed the shuttle. It hadn't docked as yet; Cross seemed wary, and was checking over the entire structure from stem to stern.

Suddenly a heavy bolt of energy shot out from the shuttle to a blind spot between two ground-level cameras and something jerked and then dropped into view on the ground itself under the base, writhing and smoking. A second expertly placed bolt caught the blue environmental suit full. It shimmered, glowed white, and for just a moment there was the sense of a human or humanoid body shape in the midst, then it winked out, leaving only white powder that was quickly picked up and dissipated by the wind.

Damn! Lucky had caught onto *that* one, but where were the other two? Their colors should really stand out if they were hovering in the blind spots, so obviously they weren't. They also had clearly turned off and adjusted every element to be as invisible to sensors as possible. So where were they? Even if the creatures had gotten inside somehow, it was very unlikely that they could have brought their suits in with them without access to the controls in this room, and *that* she was going to deny them.

An alarm sounded behind her, and she turned, startled, to see the diagram on the main screen showing a complete dock and lockdown of the smelter unit and the opening of the topmost hatch. That meant Achmed was coming inside. If the things weren't already here then he was safe, but if they'd somehow gotten in he wouldn't last long at all.

Outside, Cross was laying down a weak fire field around the entire base unit and under it as well. That was what was causing the slight vibration she felt now, and it puzzled her. As it reached a stronger level, though, two suits popped out from under the base in one of those spots a scanning camera would leave blind for a few minutes, and she realized that they'd somehow dug a shallow pit in that time and covered themselves with the fine dust. Cross saw them, too, and came around near ground level and sprayed them with a series of bolts just strong enough to blow the suits but not strong enough to threaten the ground on which the base stood nor the base itself.

"Still there? How do you like it now?" she asked the thing.

There was no reply, but she wished she had better control of the cameras and a better understanding of the master board now. She needed a closeup on those two suits, or at least a second look, for she'd sworn that one of them, at least, had its helmet blown clear off and that there was nothing in it.

Cross angled a burn on the side and Queson realized that one of the things, now in its flowing, plastic state, was crawling up the side of the base. From being open to exposure of the hostile elements, the thing suddenly found it very hot as Lucky Cross fried it with a heat ray, the safest powerful weapon she could use directly against the side of the base. An outer skin designed for atmospheric entry would not find even a full-power heat ray much of a jolt, but anything open and exposed on the skin would find it a different story.

Still, was that the one from the empty suit or from the other one?

Damn! she swore to herself in frustration at the lack of communications. These things could split. *Who said one had to be the size of a person? There could be one sitting right there on the shuttle dock airlock or even inside via the air vents and if they zap a third creature out there they won't know it. They'll feel safe to come in.* Hell, if it was already inside it would already *be* Achmed, and would know everything about internal operations anyway.

Damn it! How was she going to know if it was safe?

"I'm gonna turn back to the old channel now," Cross's voice came out of nowhere. "They ain't got no fuckin' radios any more, not that would it useful. You okay in there, girl?"

"Sort of," Randi responded. "Trouble is, that thing did a nice imitation of An Li that almost had me fooled, so I don't know who or what I'm talking to now."

"Good point. Look, check this first. Is there any way, did you give it any way, to get inside other than through the air ducts?"

"No. Haven't touched a thing, I'm sealed in here."

"Okay, if you check you'll see that any breach of the air filtration would cause a major alarm. Did that alarm go off? It shoulda been loud, and even if it somehow got silenced, it should have lit up on the board in there."

She hadn't thought of that. "No, no alarms. But you should know that," she added suspiciously. Cross had duplicate controls in the cabin of the shuttle.

"True, but you never can trust nothin' anymore, can you? Look, I haven't docked yet, so if this is me on the squawker then it's the real me, right?"

"Yeah, okay."

"Put your palm on the plate and then instruct Emergency Gamma Two. The computer will do the rest."

She looked over, put her hand on the flat identification plate, and said, "Emergency Gamma Two."

"Switching to alternate emergency frequency, encryption level maximum," the computer responded.

"There. Still hear me?" Cross asked her.

"Yes."

"Welcome to the club. Sorry we had to leave you in the dark, but we just couldn't risk giving anything away and we wanted the fuckers to surface."

"You shouldn't have left me like this!" she almost shouted, feeling on the edge of breaking. And it wasn't over yet.

"Can't do much about the desertion. Didn't figure on this going so far," Cross told her. "Who'd have thought the sons of bitches would be putting on and using fully charged e-suits? And that big bastard, it's tryin' to figure out how to undermine our safe plateau, there, and we may have just accidentally given it the general idea. If it doesn't take us easy, then them colonists had to have some pretty powerful machinery to carve out that base from the cliff in the first place, let alone move and construct that base. If we can melt this cliffside, then it can surely figure a way to cut through the solid rock holdin' the base up. Just like us, though, it'll take a lot of time to get that stuff powered up and over to where it can do much good. That means keepin' us here as long as possible. Hang on."

Queson could see the main board suddenly come alive. Cross was running some kind of diagnostic, including one on the smelter.

"Sweet Jesus! That goop's 'bout *coverin'* the damned thing! Son of a bitch!" Cross swore. "Lemme fry what I can!"

Nothing at all that seemed out of the ordinary was

showing on the internal cameras, but on the schematic on the main screen there were hundreds of low-level fuzzy blotches. As Cross opened up on them, the cameras showed thin layers of the living alien protoplasm or whatever it was peeling off like dead skin and dropping, smoking, to the ground below. Some of it was trying to get away, to flee the wide beam, but if there was any more of the stuff on the thing then it was out of direct reach of the heat beam.

"Shoulda thought of that earlier. Jerry came up with it just now," Cross told her. "Damned thing would have enough residual heat that it would provide a rough and uncomfortable but potentially life-preserving ride. Spread itself so thin and with such consistency that you couldn't even tell it was there on visual!"

"Does that mean that Achmed—?"

"That's the big question, ain't it? Depends on whether he kept everything totally buttoned up and nothin' came loose. The thing isn't pressurized and uses basic air exchange unless it's outfitted for an alien mix, but it's tight because of the insulation."

"And all that means?"

"It means it beats the hell out of us."

Yeah, thanks. Back to square one. "There's no quiz you can give it now that it can't pass if it *did* get him," she pointed out. "We could have him go back out, but he could leave just a small part of himself behind if he's now part of *it* and it wouldn't do any good."

"Seeing him would tell us what else we have to deal with," Jerry Nagel put in, taking one of the comm links. "They don't seem to have the ability to assume the color and texture of real people, at least not yet." He thought for a moment. "Listen, do you have an e-suit in there?"

"No. Not that I know of. You know where we have ours."

"Yeah, yeah, but hope springs eternal. I thought you might have put one on before you built your little fortress.

That's bad. We can't get to you without coming inside, and we can't do anything drastic in there without making it maybe impossible for you to ever get out. Hmmm. . . . This is going to take some thinking."

"Try not leaving me alone next time!" she shot back, anger almost edging out fear.

"Sorry, doll. Had to be there to see if the problem was getting solved. Next time you and Sark can cuddle."

"Fuck you, Nagel. Just get me out of here!"

"Just tell the computer to show you the forward view, under, shuttle and watch. Lucky's just told Achmed to come back up into the bubble on the *other* secure frequency, the one we were using."

"Shuttle, forward, under, on main screen," she instructed, and the schematic changed to the view forward of the shuttle craft, which was nearly stationary and hovering just above the smelter blister.

Achmed did not appear to be there.

She could hear Cross in the background talking to Achmed and insisting on a security check, and Achmed's familiar grumbling, accent and all, and protest that he was in the shit can, but Cross wasn't in the mood to be patient for long. She gave him two minutes to get his ass back up in the control chair inside the blister.

"Jerry, what if he doesn't do it?" Randi asked, worried. "Right now some kind of thinking goo might be running around looking for a way into this place. If it finds a way, I'm toast."

"Or worm, anyway," he responded, trying to keep the tone light although she could hear his concern. "Hang on. We're not gonna let them get you."

There was a pause, and then somebody else on the shuttle, probably Sark, said something. Queson looked at the screen and saw a figure emerging partway into the hatch leading up into the blister atop the smelter and waving. It *looked* like Achmed, but it was only a face, shoulders, and one arm, and then it was gone back in just as quickly.

"Achmed! Get your fat ass back in there *now!*" she heard Cross roar through Jerry's headset. At the same time, the appearance was replayed on the monitor and the image of Achmed increasingly blown up.

"Jerry! The face!" she almost shouted.

"I see it. Looks like a death mask."

Which, in a way, it was. Clearly trying to improvise on the fly with whatever was at hand, the thing that had consumed Achmed, probably inside the smelter as it either hovered or traveled back, had tried putting some kind of powder or light brown grease on the face to make it look human. It probably knew that the ruse was unlikely to work, but there hadn't been much time and it was better than nothing.

"Okay, so it's got Achmed and it's inside," Nagel sighed. "Close everything up tight, Doc, including going entirely on internal air. Sit tight. I don't know any other way of handling this."

"What are you going to do? My god, Jerry! I don't dare ever to crack that door and you don't, either! You're going to have to leave the base, and me, here and get the hell out! You saw the way it hid as a thin coat on the smelter! I'd be paranoid to even pick up anything in the place!"

"Sit tight, sit tight and just relax," Nagel responded soothingly. "This thing may be a smart and supernasty organism, but at the bottom, the least common denominator, it's just an infestation problem, and those we've got policies for. It's not going to tolerate extremes because no matter how fluid it is, it's carbon-based and organic just like us. It doesn't like wind and it doesn't like extreme cold and somehow, I suspect, it breathes in something. Even cockroaches, who can withstand what would be lethal radiation for other creatures, breathe and have their limits. Critters come with crew and pressurized container cargo. They don't ride on the outside of space-ships. At least, from what we've seen, *this* one won't. I admit I wish you had a suit in there with you, but you ought to be able to manage if you're totally sealed, totally on recirculating air, and just sit tight and let us do the driving."

"What are you going to do?"

"Infestation handling 101," he responded. "Standard by-the-book procedure. You forget, and *it* can't do any-thing about, the fact that we have the master controls for just about everything right here. Stand by and strap in. We're sealing out suits here, and then we're going to dock and take control. I'm just more than a little fed up with this alien bastard."

The shuttle pivoted, then slowly glided over the top of the base unit until it reached the depression that was its dock and integration spot with the base unit. Just as it came in to land, Cross gave a wide heat burst that covered the entire dock area. Stuff started curling up and burning under it, and more began to ooze away from the landing area.

Damn! That thing had covered half the base exterior!

Not exactly, but it had managed to hide in that part that was out of the wind, showing that it could with-stand at least the daytime temperature. Now, though, it backed away, shocked by the unanticipated fire and also knowing that it only had to wait. When the shuttle docked, it would be right there on top of it, looking for a way in.

It wouldn't find it. Cross had activated the spacefaring mode; that thing was sealed very tight indeed.

As soon as the docking occurred, Queson saw all the lights and controls in her lower room flash and then things began to move of their own accord. Displays that were incomprehensible showed up on the screens, and the schematic was back on the main one, doing a full diagnostic.

"Doc? You strapped in that chair?" Nagel asked.

"Yeah, Jerry. Good as I can."

"Then sit back and assume launch position. We're going to go to orbit. Sit tight and trust me on this one."

The whole base shuddered, then came to a kind of life of its own. She could feel soft vibration, and a few storage areas and loose items began to jiggle and rattle.

"Lucky? You got control?

"Yeah! There were a few spots it was workin' on, but the son of a bitch can't get around the failsafes. Going up, count of ten . . . nine . . . eight . . . seven . . . six . . . five . . . four . . . three . . . two . . . one. . . . *Now!*"

One of the smaller screens showed the view from the underside of the base. Now as the vibration rose to maximum and a few things in the control room started bouncing around, the base unit lifted up from the plateau and rose steadily if with agonizing slowness into the air.

Cross rotated the combined craft and much of the exterior coating of the creature was suddenly full into the wind. It peeled off and dropped to the ground with amazing speed.

Now the whole plateau was visible, and both Queson in the main unit and the trio in the shuttle gasped as they saw how much of the region around the hard, flat rock had been undermined with what looked like water-filled tubes or punctures. That thing had been preparing to engulf the whole damned base if need be! That would mean . . . Just how huge *was* the main body of that thing?

Now it was all a speck, and then even the plateau, the base, and all fine detail merged into the usual high-altitude view and then was completely obscured by the clouds.

The sky turned increasingly dark, and within another couple of minutes they were a hundred or more kilometers above the deceptively peaceful-looking world below.

It was unlikely that any of the goop, exposed to the

vacuum and extreme cold of space, could have survived anywhere on the exposed surface of the unit, and there was nowhere it could hide from those extremes. Inside, though, was a different story. Inside, what had been formed from the ingestion of Achmed was as warm and comfortable as she was in the sealed control room. She wondered, though, how it liked being weightless. Such a fluid creature would find it most unpleasant, she suspected, unless it was pretty well concentrated in one anchored spot.

Cross put them in a parking orbit well away from the *Stanley*, perhaps only halfway to the main ship, and turned to that problem next.

"Okay, Doc, relax and don't get nervous about what you hear or feel," Nagel told her. "We're gonna find out just how well insulated the backup control room really is from the rest of the ship."

"You mean there's some doubt?"

He tried to laugh off the comment but knew he needed some amplification. "Not between it and the rest of the base, no, any more than there's any doubt that we're well insulated here. If not, we'd be dead here in one fashion and you'd be dead in the other."

"How can you be sure I'm not? That this is really me?" she asked him, irritated by his tone.

He paused a moment, then said, "Because there's no privacy once we're docked. Period. We can see you, even do an analysis of your composition, just as we can with what remains of poor Achmed. It's just that what we're gonna do may test the mechanical integrity of these systems and, well . . ."

She finally understood what he was trying not to say. "The blister should have been totally insulated from the outside, too," she managed. "It shouldn't have been able to get in to get him."

He sighed. "Um, yeah. Somebody's been skimping on the maintenance bill."

"Well, what about the maintenance *here*?"

"Don't worry so much about that. If it could have gotten in it would have by now. Just hang tight."

Alarms started going off all over the board. "What are you *doing*?" she almost shrieked at him.

"Just hold on! Busy right now! Just stop up your ears if it's too noisy!"

The computer's voice now came from the control panel itself. "Passwords approved. Decompressing main quarters unit."

Now she understood. Lucky had commanded the immediate decompression of the whole base unit except for those with their own separate systems. It was the emergency decontamination he'd talked about, the one that was supposed to even kill the roaches and the rats.

"*Ooooeeee!*" Cross exclaimed, looking at a view Randi couldn't share. "Lookit how the goddam things explode! Sounds like fireworks!"

"Sounds like bacon frying, but I'll take it," Nagel responded. "Pressure down to ten percent . . . five . . . that's the last. We've got a vacuum inside. It'll ice down pretty quickly. How long you want to keep this going?"

"The hell with the icing! Half the shit that means anything to me is ruined anyway!" Cross responded. "I want every little bit of that thing dead, dead, dead!"

Nagel thought of Randi. "How you doin', Doc? Still warm?"

"So far, yes," she told him.

"Good. The only place any of that goop is likely to find any chance of survival is against the inner wall of your unit. That's why I wish you had a suit. As it is, we're gonna have to risk bringing you one. Shouldn't be a problem if I'm fully suited up— remember, it couldn't get those last folks in the colony, or at least by the time it got to them it didn't bother, and whatever's left, if anything, in the base has got to be small bits, not something that can break or harm an e-suit. The problem's not with me or Sark bringin' you the suit, it's you."

"Huh? What?"

"Think of it, doll. We're gonna have'ta use the emergency supplies to repressurize the interior or we're gonna kill you when you open the door. Any environment safe enough to risk you in is an environment safe enough for any bits of that thing that are left to survive in as well. That's not to say that there's any of it left—I don't think Achmed knew enough about the engineering behind the base quarters to do anything, and this thing's not space savvy, but a risk's a risk. You understand that?"

She let out a deep breath. "Yeah. So either I get safely into a suit and out of here or I get absorbed or liquefied or whatever and you burn me."

"That's about the size of it. I'll be coming through with a torch. Sark and I will cover each other's back. There's no airlock to use into the base command center, so there's no easy way to do this. You ready?"

"No, but if we don't do this I'm never going to get out of here."

"Not to mention the captain won't allow us to dock with the *Stanley*. Okay, we'll start repressurization in, oh, ten minutes, just to give Lucky's paranoia a chance to get going. Then we're coming down through the airlock from here. It's still gonna be pretty damned cold, but it'll only be for a few seconds if we're lucky, and it won't be absolute zero, anyway. You stand by and wait for instructions, but when I want you to act, you have to *act*, and fast. Still, we're gonna take your pressure down during this period so breathe easy but don't move around a lot. If anything of this thing's left, the cold and low pressure might just make it slow and sick."

"I'm ready," she told him, but she wondered if she really was. Maybe it hadn't been so smart to actually *speak* to that thing. Was this really Jerry? Was everything true or not? They were up there; she could see them, but she couldn't see inside the very place where she was. Could this thing somehow anticipate and survive what had been done if it *was* as she'd heard? Even if Jerry and Sark came down, might they be taken on the way? How fast did it take to absorb a human and sort and classify and make use of his memories? There had been an awful lot of people in that colony, and they hadn't had a prayer.

But she couldn't stay here forever, either. The captain and An Li would rather they all died than not recover this huge and complex unit, but they were not about to let it dock with the *Stanley* nor anybody else to board, either, unless they were sure it was safe. To be sure, she'd have to be out of there.

She had to risk it. She knew that. And if some of that thing got to her, then Jerry or Sark would just have to take her out completely as quickly as possible.

"Stand by," Jerry Nagel told her. "We're repressurizing to a three-kilometer height, which is what we have you down to. Breathing all right?"

"It's a little hard, but it's tough to say if it's the pressure or my nerves."

"Good girl. We're almost to you. Okay, we're repressurizing the airlock to shuttle norm. All seals on the suits check out. Opening the hatch."

There was a sudden terrible sound like a great wind, then a *thump*.

"Jerry? What was that?"

"Relax. We opened the hatch and Sark let a blast loose in there to take care of any surprises, even though there shouldn't have been any. We're okay now, let's see if we did anything."

He opened the airlock hatch full now and stepped inside. She could hear him and Sark breathing.

"Looks good. No sign of goop. A little ash where we burned the area before docking, nothing serious. Okay, closing lock, depressurizing to three klicks. Lights on full inside. Jeez! I feel like I'm breaking into my own house here! Ooookay . . . Guns charged, opening inner lock on green *now*."

There was the sound of heavier double breathing, then Sark said, "Inner hatch closed and sealed, pressure back to normal inside. Nothing's getting outta here through *there* unless it's with us. Jeez! What a mess! Home Sweet Fridge!"

"Nothing useful in the lounge," Jerry noted. "Want to burn it?"

"Maybe. If anything's alive it's gonna be against that bulkhead, though, or along the ceiling seams. I'll settle for that."

There was the same whooshing sound, longer this time, and then it cut off as Nagel yelled "Hold it! Hold it! We don't want to start a fire! The cure would be worse than the disease at this temperature!"

"Doc, you still with us?" Sark called.

"Yes, I'm here. Let me get up and get to the—*ungh!* Suddenly I can't move! I—oh, shit! Forget it."

"What's the matter, Randi?" Jerry Nagel called, uncharacteristically using her first name.

"I'm embarrassed. I had myself strapped in, right? Forgot to remove all the straps. Felt like somebody was pinning me down!"

"Just relax. Go up to the door panel. If you press the control on the right of the identipad you'll be able to see through the door somewhat and that should give you a look at us. Don't mind the look of the place, though. It's a real mess."

I never knew you could do that with this door, she thought to herself, but she tried it and discovered that he was right. So long as you kept your palm on the plate for more than ten seconds, a kind of see-through window opened in the door. Clever, and useful for the kinds of emergencies this room was really designed for.

She gasped when she saw the outer room, even though

she'd been warned about it and even though the view "through" the door was less than ideal. The room had been a common meeting place, a place to relax, to plan, to just joke around. Kind of a living room for this communal base unit, really. Now it was all discolored, much of the furniture and wall decorations were oddly misshapen, and half the lights were either out or cocked at odd angles. Debris was all over the floor from the rapid decompression, and some very solid things had shattered from the cold.

She saw the two figures in the room, completely suited up. One was holding a heat rifle at the ready, the other had a similar weapon on its belt but was now fumbling with a standard e-suit.

"Got this one from the shuttle spares, so it should be okay," Jerry told her. "Now comes the hard part. I'm coming right up to the door now, and I'll turn on my internal light so you can see I'm not made of gelatin." He came straight to the door, the light went on, and she was very relieved to see the old familiar face. Just to emphasize who was what, Jerry Nagel winked and stuck his tongue out at her.

"Satisfied?" he asked her.

"Yeah, okay, if it's not you we're all lost anyway. Now what?"

"This gets tricky. To unlock and unseal the door you're going to have to do it manually and with the full palm authorization. The thing is, while we've got equalized pressure in here now with you, it's still about forty below, and I'm not about to turn the heat on. The only way we can do this is for you to open the door, then get back and away from it as quickly as you can. It'll still give you a real cold blast. I'll toss in the suit and close the door again from this side. Turn on the suit's internal heater from the outside and wait until you have something that won't freeze at the touch, then get suited up fast, full seals—set it for 'vacuum' even though we've got air here—and make sure all the systems work. We'll cover your exit here. Lucky's gonna take this back down to a vacuum as soon as we're all set, and that should do it. Then we go back up and ride the shuttle section in to Mother. Got that?"

"Yeah, I think so. Palm on, got a green, now I'm punching in the security code."

There was a hiss as the very tight vacuum seal on the door let loose and pressure equalized.

"Okay," she said, "Turning the latch now, then getting back!"

She turned the big security latch and could feel the cold creeping in even before the door opened. There was a frigid blast, and then the suit was tossed in and the door reclosed. She felt suddenly like she was trapped in a refrigerator, although the safety systems in the command and control center popped on blowing warm air back in.

She pulled the latch back down, worried that she might stick to it in the cold and relieved when she didn't, even though her hand felt slightly frostbitten from just that little touch. Now she examined the suit, reached in, powered it up and turned on the internal heating. It wouldn't be warm until she sealed it up with her inside, but it wouldn't freeze her toes off, either.

For a moment she got the paranoia back. What if some of that stuff had gotten into the suit? When she got in and sealed it . . . But, no, she *couldn't* think that way. If she did, she'd never get out of here.

Put it on, put it on, seal it up, check all systems. . . . *God it's cold!* Verify power and working heat, then verify she was at vacuum setting. She heard the seals go tight, knew she was now in a smaller biosphere but as isolated from the outside as anything in the C and C. It *was* starting to heat up, and the internal readings said she should be comfortable, but she just kept feeling the cold.

There was no longer a secure seal on the door, so she went over, unlatched it, and opened it. Jerry turned his helmet light back on and smiled, and she did the same so he could see that nothing had crept in at the last minute. They both turned and looked at Sark.

"You, too, Sark. Lights on," Nagel told him. "This is nightmare city right now."

Sark grumbled but turned on his internal light. Unless the thing had learned more nasty tricks, it was Sark, looking nervous and pissed.

"Okay, Lucky, decompress the unit, and, for good measure, we'll do the C and C room now, too," Nagel called to the pilot. "Just in case."

"Got it, lover boy," Cross responded. "Come on home to Big Sister and we'll see if Mama will take in the prodigals. . . ."

V:

STANLEY NEEDS LIVINGSTONE

Before the Great Silence, what the *Stanley* crew had managed would have garnered applause, awards, instant fame and glory, and even poor Achmed would have gotten a statue at the very least. The Earth System Combine would then have dispatched a military unit including a battleship capable of turning a planet into dust to the system, and *then* if dialogue was irrelevant, and they couldn't be talked out of it, the threat would be totally vaporized.

That was something governments on a wide colonial level were good for.

But there wasn't such a government, hadn't been such a government or colonial empire for almost two centuries now. There were still some massive naval vessels and even combat groups, but they were responsible only to themselves and their officers and, although they claimed to still police the spaceways, they were often hard to tell from the pirates and private armies that prowled the region. A report would be sent to the nearest naval group, of course, since it would no more want that creature to get out of its planetary prison than anyone else would, but whether or not it would be considered enough of a threat to waste precious energy on was problematical. They hadn't been there.

At least no other salvagers would be tempted to try because of the potential profits. *That* was what Sark and Nagel had been doing while Achmed had sealed the cliff entrances. Planting and igniting enough thermite bombs to reduce all those greenhouses and all that potential salvage to bubbling, hissing primal goo.

They had reason to be proud of themselves, too. They'd stopped possibly the greatest threat to all humanity in its tracks and they'd done whatever they could to keep it there. A half dozen dirty old salvagers and a beaten-up old salvage ship. All that with the loss of just one of their number.

And they *would* have felt proud, if you could have spent proud, or gotten some reward for being noble. Instead, they were going back to Sepuchus, a dirty, smoky little planet that was the current headquarters of the Kajani Salvage Works, the company that had chartered the *Stanley* to go get that dead colony's physical remains and bring them back to be recycled and remade into new things once again.

That was what the crew had been hired to do, and *that* was what they most definitely had not done. The lease on the *Stanley* plus the time and the expendables was substantial. The crews were the least of the expenses, though; they drew no salaries, and worked for a percentage of the wholesale value of the salvage.

If the Kajani family could eat the expense, they would still take a huge hit on the expenses and the extensive base unit repairs and have little new to sell; if they couldn't, then a venerable old company would be bankrupted and taken over by creditors. Either way, the crew of the *Stanley* would get absolutely nothing, and might well be black carded by the guilds, branding them unreliable and therefore unemployable. There were more crews than ships these days.

There would be no gold, no laurel wreaths down the metaphorical Appian Way for saving humanity. *That* hadn't been their job, either.

"I really think that we made one and only one big mistake back there," Jerry Nagel commented over coffee in the *Stanley*'s cozy lounge.

Randi Queson looked up from examining her scientific notes and responded, "Yes?"

"I think we should have just brought the damned worm back. Keep it in the base unit, all sealed up, and then drop it on the first bank that shows up."

She sighed. "And you think that just because it would absorb the bank that it wouldn't foreclose anyway?"

"You've got a point. Too much alike to begin with, banks and worms."

"Have you thought what you might do?" she asked him.

He shrugged. "I'm an engineer without references at this point. Never had any big scores and now I've got a major blowout. Still, I'll make do. The one thing that we're always short of is people who know how to fix things. God! Who would have thought in the romantic days of interstellar colonies we'd be an economic basket case slowly breaking down? One of these days, or years, or decades, we won't be able to fix it anymore. When the machines die and can no longer be fixed, people like me will still be around making do. Sark? He's muscle. Even in the age of machines you need occasional muscle. He'll make do as well, as somebody's personal bodyguard or in some private army someplace. Lucky'll wind up crop-dusting some dirtball, and people like An Li always seem to come out smelling like a rose sooner or later. What about you?"

She sighed. "Going over my notes here. I've got enough to keep them going in academia for a while here, from biology to philosophy. I'm the only known human being who ever had any sort of conversation with an alien intelligence, at least as far as we know. That should be good for a position in some minor department someplace, lecturing on the rights and wrongs of containment and whether or not it's really true that you can't have a dialogue with a unified intelligence. It'll drive me nuts after a while, but it'll be good for eating and sleeping money for a couple of years, anyway. At least it's Li who'll have to face the Kajanis, anyway. Better her than me, and she sure as hell deserves it. We're just the hired help."

Jerry Nagel nodded and looked up at the ship's chronometer. "Well, it's been nice working with you, anyway. It's about two hours until we have to get out and walk."

That wasn't literally true, of course. In two hours they'd be in orbit, and then they'd have to wait until An Li went down and filed the official reports. The entire account of the mission would already be there by now, of course, downloaded as they'd come within range, but face-to-face reporting was the last of it. As team leader, Li would have to find them some kind of quarters and arrange for some sort of holding position until the crew could be taken to various civilized destinations. That wouldn't take long; there were always ships, big and small, coming in and out of Sepuchus, shopping at one of the sector's biggest salvage yards for whatever they needed.

The account would be part of the public record, as tradition dictated, so it would spread as well. That would both help and hurt them, but there wasn't much they could do about it.

"You know, I've got a virgin fifth of bourbon, really good aged stuff, private label, in my cabin," she commented. "I was saving it for a little celebration when we got back and could total up the shares. Not much I can do about that now, but even coming back flat broke and a failure again it's at least an *occasion*. Want to break a seal and have a few toasts?"

"Real alcoholic booze, huh? No funny pills, no virtual mindblasts, just good old-fashioned good-going-down-make-you-puke-later stuff? You know, you're a real throwback, Doc."

"Well, we may as well get used to it," she responded. "Just in case this is an omen, the spare parts aren't there anymore, and it's sooner than we think, that time when you can't fix things anymore. . . ."

An Li was not a very happy person going down to the surface, nor was she much happier coming back. The chewing-out, screaming, cursing, and threats she expected; par for the course. The accusation that they'd failed to do the job because of cowardice was unacceptable. They'd seen the records and the data, the same that she'd looked at before okaying the abort. There was no way that those greenhouses could have been salvaged entirely by automation, and the loss of Achmed was proof that when you put people back into there, well, sooner or later they would be gotten. It was very easy to second-guess from afar, and long after the fact.

There were twenty-one vessels in orbit with the *Stanley* at the time she was getting her ass chewed. These included nine capital ships, three large military vessels, and several slick yachts clearly used to move purchasing agents to the wares they needed as quickly as possible, which meant that their employers were desperate and would pay through the nose.

The cost of repairs on the base and the consumables would be stiff, but she'd done the math, and they'd brought the ship and base back intact, when common sense had said to leave that base and smelter and disassembly unit behind. *That* loss might have broken the company, but not a simple failure to reclaim a site. She would almost wager that more than enough to cover the *Stanley's* bills was being paid out just today by those various orbiting ships looking for vital parts to keep going.

Poison the ocean indeed! she sniffed, thinking of the exchange. Like *that* would have stopped them from becoming translucent units of a greater whole.

Well, she'd get the crew put up at Canyer's Guild Hostel about a hundred kilometers south of here. That would at least have them out of Kajani territory, so any funds that *might* be dropped by or on behalf of the crew wouldn't go back to those bastards.

What *she* needed was a room, a hot bath with real water, and maybe a few patches of squibs to send her into another and more pleasurable state of mind for a while. Canyer's had mineral baths, and even if she would have to tap her private account for some privacy, it was available.

She looked around the place for the last time and sighed. *We, too, are in the funeral business,* she thought sourly. *In this day and age, it's everyone for themselves and if it takes grave robbing, then so be it.* These days what was left of civilization maintained itself by robbing the failures of the past and by cannibalizing the rest. *Eat. drink, and be merry, for tomorrow* . . . Nobody thought much about tomorrow, herself included. Not in this day and age. No money, no job, you did what you had to do. She'd worked her way up to here from a start in a navy brothel, and she'd do it again if she had to.

Those Kajani bastards! Did they think she'd have let such a threat as that thing in the sea stop her from a profit even if it had cost the whole damned ground crew? She'd authorized the shutdown because it was impossible to salvage without even her becoming a part of that thing. "Dialogue is irrelevant." What a stupid worm that was! It wasn't enough to imitate, you had to *learn* from your victims. She'd have sold out the whole damned human race except for her own private places if that thing had been smart enough to make a deal.

And this *would* have been a hell of a great base for taking over the rest of the race, too. Everybody came here eventually, everybody who could. Three of the biggest salvage yards in the remnants of the empire were right here. Hell, that destroyer up there . . . How long would it take the worm to have taken every soul down to the rats and roaches on the damned thing? A few days? Less? And then it goes back and takes a planet destroyer, and the rest of the battle group, and there's *power*. That's what *she* would have done, but *she* didn't have to spread her knowledge over countless cells. It was nice, compact, and in one place for easy correlation.

Trouble was, I needed to become the worm, not the other way around, she reflected bitterly.

Canyer's Guild Hostel looked like the kind of place that put up working stiffs between jobs on a junkyard planet. Cobbled together from every conceivable kind of old building site, it seemed less a large building than an assemblage of junk that had somehow come alive from the weight of salvage all around and under it. It could have been described as ball-shaped, triangular, oblong, rectangular, starlike, and flowing adobe and been pretty well depicted correctly. The only assurance was that, because it had been put together by the same sort of people who might need to stay in it for a while, it was pretty damned stable. No two rooms were *remotely* alike.

Getting the crew set up wasn't a problem; the guilds owned the place, and if you had a valid card they couldn't refuse you, even if you couldn't afford to stay there. Salvagers, like other skilled workers in guild or union organizations, took care of their own because, God knew, nobody else would.

There weren't many different guild facilities on a dump of a world like this. Salvagers', engineers', longshoremen's, and entertainment were about it. "Entertainment," of course, was always there except on the Holy Joe–type worlds, and, buried deep, even on a couple of those. The folks who lived in the entertainment hostels didn't exactly do Shakespeare. They were more like a service industry.

The odd thing was, she was a card-carrying member with some experience in three out of four. Engineers required more than on-the-job training; when you were dealing with the complex cybernetic spaceships and robotic design and reprogramming, well, you needed an education for that.

But she'd run tugs to and from orbital freighters, she'd been on and then led salvage teams, and she'd begun, actually had been born, in one of those entertainment guild hostels, so she had the other three. She might have had the fourth one, too, if she'd ever had the time to learn to read and write. That was a luxury in an automated age, even one that was falling apart. She'd never felt the need nor figured out the sense of knowing those skills.

She set up the crew and signaled them to pack up and come on down, and suddenly felt empty, almost drained. It took her a moment to realize why.

For the first time in a *very* long time, she was absolutely on her own. She'd done the last thing she had to do. Oh, a few added debriefings, and some soft soap and maybe fancy moves when the leasing company digested the fact that the *Stanley*'s rent hadn't been paid, but, otherwise, she was done.

She had a week or two, she knew, before things began to get ugly. Word didn't exactly travel instantaneously around the known galaxy anymore; it took time for these things to get back to the leasing people, for somebody to figure out the score, and maybe for some enforcers to be sent out to see what could be done, if not to collect, perhaps to make examples for the future.

Avoiding those types wasn't a real challenge, either, for the same reason as it took for word to get around. The distances involved in this kind of life were vast. The *real* challenge was the DNA sample they had of her, but even that could be fudged, if it came to that.

What was required was what she didn't have: money.

She wasn't worried about the others. They were a guild crew and had been properly hired; *she* was the one with her ass on the line, putting her neck on the chopping block thanks to a talkative young marine who'd seen this whole deserted colony while on his last patrol and who wanted to show off just where he'd been.

She knew now that she should have left it to the marines, but the money potential had been *so* huge that it had been worth the risk. She *still* would take such a risk again for such a possible prize. Those who didn't take those kinds of risks remained insects, grunts on the ground or in the brothels doing the same monotonous and degrading shit until they either died or killed themselves leaving no permanent marks on the landscape of history.

It was time to find her own room here, take a shower, dress for optimism, and go on over to a bar.

She didn't want a place close to the guild billets; it would do her no good to run into everybody she knew or try and pick up another broke guildsman. Hocking what little she had left, she got herself more than presentable and took a taxi over to the Hotel Center where the buyers and sellers of all sorts of junk congregated.

Most of the time she always hated being so small. A hundred and forty-five centimeters put you well below most, and even if your body was very well proportioned, forty plus kilos didn't make for an imposing figure. You had to do that on look, on bearing, on how you moved.

Her entertainer background was always the most useful to her when not in space, although much of it came
as naturally to her as her height or weight. *She* hadn't
been designed as an entertainer in some genetics lab,
but the odds were her mother, or maybe her whole
lineage, had been.

That's why she'd liked space so much, though, other
than that you were on your own or the equal or boss
of the rest of your fellow workers. If you were in a
weightless area you could move a ton of ore just as easily
as someone twice your size, and even if you were piloting
a tug, the tug became an extension of you and made
you just as powerful as anybody else in one.

Now it was back-to-basics time until she had enough
to break away again and guarantee a disappearance into
another more equalizing position.

The dumb-clever name of the Prefabricated Inn showed
up between two of the five central hotels in the business district. It looked like the right kind of place,
although she didn't remember it from the past.

She paid the taxi with her card and then got out and
looked around the place as the little vehicle, itself res-
cued and rehabbed from the junk pile, buzzed off.

It hadn't been too long ago that she'd been a *guest*
in one of these, after she'd taken the prospectus and
proofs to the agency reps and gotten financing for the
salvage trip. It had been, in many ways, the fulfillment
of a lifelong dream: Here not because you were doing
escort duty, plying business information, or giving other
forms of personal service, but because you were a *guest*,
a *paying* guest who *belonged* here. Being called "Miss"
and "Ma'am," having the service types try and solicit
you, walking into places like this bar like you were about
to sign a billion-dollar deal.

Well, she was dressed pretty much the same now, and
had the same look, so maybe she'd be remembered. If
so, nobody would be looking for her as just another

escort on the make. She just hoped she could find a mark quickly and easily in this place.

She couldn't afford to be sitting around one very long otherwise, and it was a long, long trip back to the hostel if she didn't score.

Young, old, male, female, it didn't really matter so long as they had some money. Even information wouldn't be all that valuable now. Not until she could clear the decks and her obligations and take chances again.

The place wasn't a dump like the world it was on, but it was a prefab model that some designer had tried to disguise as something interesting while only making it something more plastic. It probably *was* something from the salvage yard—even the fancy hotels in this area were assembled from true surplus projects—but, for a bar with some limited food service, it looked and smelled pretty clean.

It wasn't all that busy, though. Oh, there were a few dozen men and women, mostly business types, sitting around talking in low tones to each other, and a few young people in military uniforms over in one corner accompanied by a man and a woman who were clearly both from the escort services and doing their usual fine acting to their paying clients. She recognized the guy— Yuri, his name was—from old times, but she gave no acknowledgment nor would he to her if he saw and recognized her. It was part of the code.

You knew you were in a first-class establishment, though, because there were real people doing drink service. Usually it was all automated: you gave your order into a hidden speaker, it arrived on a robot tray after being mixed by some barely concealed bartending machine, and that was that. Nobody *needed* to wait tables, or be waited upon. It was all ego, all part of making you feel like you really were better than other people. Not like the escorts. Cybersex could be far more intense than real sex and very, very authentic, but it turned out that you paid a real price physically for doing a lot of it, and it got cold after a while, too, because you knew it was fake and you knew just how it would wind up. Until people became machines they needed other people.

She had always wondered about those who *did* merge with machines. It was a one-way trip; you could be switched to other mechanical devices but you'd never be human again. Like the woman who was the captain of the *Stanley*, for example: a brain and spinal cord in a charged fluid bath whose thoughts controlled every aspect of that big ship and whose thought processes and calculating abilities were augmented by a gigantic high speed quasi-organic super computer. What would make somebody do that? You really didn't live much longer, overall, unless you were employed by people willing to put in constant maintenance. Even then, even if you got to live a few extra centuries, what did it matter? You might feel superhuman and all powerful, but you were really just a part in a big hulking ship that went where others told it to go, and you could never touch or feel other human beings, never really come down here, even to a dump like this, and enjoy life.

But you sure were anonymous if you wanted to be. After all that experience, An Li realized that she never knew the captain's name, nor anything about her past except that she'd been a woman. She'd been nothing but a disembodied voice, the captain. She was up there now, unable to move out of orbit until somebody with the correct codes allowed her to do so, and then only to where those signals told her to go.

One thing was sure—you had to be crazy or desperate to become like that. Little more than a slave to some corporation, forever locked in a cold vacuum of space, looking down on what you could never again share.

She could never do that. She thought death far preferable to that kind of life, but because others thought differently she and the rest of humanity could still travel on working ships requiring no crew and no skilled bridge. It wasn't the only way to travel through space, but it was the most cost-effective, the most *efficient* way to do it.

"What would you like, ma'am?"

She was startled out of her reverie by the question. She looked up and saw a young, dark, curly-headed man in a kind of uniform wearing a barely visible headset and microphone.

"Oh, give me a half carafe of the house chablis," she responded.

"Yes, ma'am. Coming right up."

She wasn't used to being waited on, and she couldn't see the appeal of it. Hell, with the all-automated system she'd have ordered when she wanted to and had a quick response. Now she'd been interrupted, would have to wait until this boy got the wine from probably the same kind of machine they had in the lower-class places, have him bring it when he had the time and noticed it was up, and then she'd have to pay him or even tip him. It seemed not only archaic but so . . . *unnecessary.*

She decided to keep to something mild and controllable. Any of the fun drugs would just siphon precious cash while impairing her, and hard booze was murder on somebody her size. Wine was low-alcohol, and she could sip it.

She looked around, and settled for some reason, perhaps past experience or just plain instinct, on one guy who was sitting at the end of the bar near the route to the rest rooms. She wasn't sure why her senses were attracted to him; certainly he looked less like he belonged here than she did. Maybe that was the reason—he just looked like a fish out of water. Rumpled clothes that looked like they'd been slept in, but of an expensive designer-type cut and look. Gray and black peppered hair that went in all directions at once and looked not only uncombed but perhaps uncombable, and a full but very nicely trimmed beard and mustache of the same middle-aged mix that fit his face quite well but which also marked him as an anachronism. Nobody who traveled between worlds had beards these days. Too much trouble. And the fact that the thick facial hair got a lot of attention when the rest of him did not told her that the look he had was the look he deliberately cultivated.

And he smoked! She wasn't sure *what* he smoked, but the pipe was clearly visible when he reached inside his coat for something. People who smoked were just about flaunting their wealth and position, particularly these days.

What was a guy like that doing on a world like this drinking beer alone in an overpriced bar?

She decided to see if she could find out.

The method wasn't subtle nor innovative, but it usually worked if a guy liked women. Sitting as he was on the stool just in front of the rest rooms, it was fairly simple to go by him fairly ostentatiously to get a feel if he noticed you, and, whether he did or not, when you came out (assuming he was still there) you were simply stuffing something, maybe a small makeup kit or anything that would make a real clatter on the floor, and you just dropped things near the guy. Most people were polite enough to notice and even help, and it broke the ice.

This guy was no exception. In fact, she felt his eyes on the back of her neck as she went in, and, after five minutes or so, when she emerged and dropped the small makeup kit so that it opened and scattered small stuff all over the floor, he was fairly quick to slide off the stool and begin to help her retrieve things.

She gave him the patented smile and thanked him for helping. It didn't take a minute to recover and put away the dropped materials. "Thanks," she said. "I do that a lot, I'm afraid, after I've been offworld for a while and then get back on. Different gravity or something, I guess."

His eyes, an odd blue-gray unusual in any company, widened a bit and his bushy eyebrows rose. "You've been in space as more than a passenger, I take it?" It was a throaty baritone, one that wouldn't carry all that far but had a kind of friendly, relaxed texture to it. The accent was definite but unplaceable; he was from someplace she'd never been.

She nodded. "Just got back from saving the universe and getting canned for my trouble. We weren't getting paid to save the universe, we were getting paid to salvage a dead world."

He was definitely interested, possibly hooked. "You were with that group that ran into that thing that ate a whole colony? I heard about that."

"Everybody has. All it's done is make me and most of my crew unemployable around here. I shoulda brought back some of the damned worm and let it eat my creditors. Trouble is, the worm would then know what they knew and it would *still* come after me for the money." She looked around. "Pardon, but I'm standing and my drink's over there. Care to join me, Mister . . . ?"

"Norman Sanders," he responded. "Thank you, I'd be delighted for the company."

It was as easy as that. It still amazed her after all this time, but it *usually* was as easy as that.

"You know," he said, sitting down opposite her, "this is quite a coincidence. I was actually thinking of getting in touch with you, or at least one of your party, when I heard the story. Might not pay much to these hard-bitten salvage types, but it might well make a great production."

"Production?"

"Yes, that's part of my work. I'm a producer. Actually, I'm a writer, but you have to be officially a producer or they rank you lower than the janitor."

"A producer of what?" She honestly didn't know what the guy was talking about.

"Comedies, dramas, extravaganzas. Whatever they'll pay to watch. Go in, pay your money, and become one of the crew of—what was the name of your ship?"

"The *Stanley*."

"Ah, yes! Become one of the crew of the *Stanley* as it explores a bizarre and sinister world of the dead. Feel what it's like to be pursued by a voracious monster! And, if you survive and get away, *this* time you'll be a hero. It's a natural. I write it and get a real producer to finance it—piece of cake with all the clearances in hand—and then we use some classic virtual actors and a few real ones and we pump in the adrenaline and it's a natural. Fine tune it, pump it up, and sell it to the bored and stuck masses on a hundred worlds, particularly the young folks, and we got a hit. And based on a true incident, hell, it's critic proof!"

She tried to follow him. "You write—plays? Books? Cyber experiences?"

"All of the above," he responded with a smile and a shrug. "It's a lot more complicated these days in some ways, but the professional storyteller remains the oldest profession of humankind!"

"I thought something else was the oldest profession," she noted.

He chuckled. "That's what they all think! But, listen, it wasn't just animal lust that got the first whore in bed with the first man. No, ma'am. It was because that first man, and first woman probably, and maybe even the first whore, all had *fantasies*. The fantasies came first, then the act, then more storytelling afterwards as the first man tried to explain it away to the first woman. It doesn't matter. We storytellers sometimes get shot but we generally don't starve. One of the earliest tales is of Scheherazade, who was supposed to be executed for something or other but got to telling stories the king found fascinating. She knew when she ran out of stories she'd lose her head, so she kept telling them, a thousand and one, until the old king forgot or dropped dead or whatever. And thousands of years later and on worlds hundreds of light-years from Old Earth, they still remember *her* name, the storyteller's name, while nobody knows who that king was."

"So you lie for a living, so to speak?"

"Well, not really. I *entertain*, or I'm at the start of the entertainment chain. Without me there's nothing to watch, nothing to see, hear, or experience. It's not a lie if you *know* it's not the truth, but it entertains you. You mean you never saw any of the big productions? Never walked into a cyberworld story or even had a favorite story or poem you read as a kid?"

She gave a wry smile but decided not to mention her lack of reading skills. "No, not really. I've done some cybersex stuff and I've heard a lot of stories in my time, but I never was anywhere where you could see the kind of stuff you're talking about. The most I ever saw on that score was a play once, with one real actor interacting with a bunch of cyber characters on a stage. They all looked and sounded real enough, but it was kind of boring. The language was so weird you could hardly follow it, but it *did* get bloody now and then."

He shrugged. "Sorry about that. That's kind of a lowbrow, low-budget cousin to the kind of things I do. Still, we might be able to put together a package that would make us all a little money. What do you say about that?"

"I can use it. They're gonna be coming after me real soon for the ship rental. How much are we talking about?"

He gave a low, apologetic cough. "Well, not much up front, but once we get a script and studio deal and then start production there'll be more. Most of it would be in royalties, percentage of the net, after the thing's released and the money comes in. That *can* take a while."

"How long's a while?"

"Oh, a year or two. Sometimes more, sometimes less. But it goes on and on."

"I don't have a year. I need some money in days, or weeks," she told him honestly. "The kind of people who'll be coming to look for me to collect don't like waiting around."

"Huh! Too bad! What kind of money you talking about? That you owe, that is?"

"Rental of the *Stanley* for sixty days, which is sixty thousand, and repair of damages and losses to equipment, maybe another twenty or so."

He whistled. "Eighty *thousand*? That's a bit steep for what you'd get up front on this deal, although you might well make much more than that down the pike. Wonder if they'd accept your percentage in payment?"

"If they would, it would solve everything, but, truth to tell, if they didn't I'd be a dead woman, and I don't plan to have to stand there while we find out. No, my best bet is to try for a smaller amount and just screw it. For under ten grand I could become somebody else. Somebody they wouldn't recognize even with a genetic scanner."

Norman Sanders leaned back thoughtfully in his chair and said nothing for a while. Then he reached into his inner coat pocket and removed what appeared to be a small jewel case. He opened it, and carefully removed a *huge* gem from its custom holder inside, then leaned forward and held it out to her.

"Ever see one of these?" he asked her.

It was, apparently, a natural gem almost as large as a hen's egg, colored in a translucent emerald-green color with a clearly visible center of some different substance that, when viewed from different angles, seemed to form pictures or shapes of some sort. She had never seen anything like it.

Staring into it, she was startled to see that the pictures inside seemed to congeal into images of strange,
bizarre landscapes peopled with real, familiar figures from
her own past, glimpsed only fleetingly. It was like
watching tiny bits of past experiences in her own life
against a backdrop of lavalike motion creating the shapes
and swallowing them almost as fast as the act of creation had made them.

"I—how does it *do* that?" she asked, mouth agape,
watching the increasingly personalized visions, many of
which were becoming quite disturbing.

"Nobody knows. It comes from your own mind,
though. I don't know what you're seeing, but it wouldn't
be what *I* see, or what anybody else would see in it.
It's a Magi's Stone, sometimes called the Magi's Gift.
There are fewer than a thousand known, and they all
pretty much look alike and do that sort of thing, although
some are colored more like rubies, others sapphires,
running through the gamut of gem colors. It's quite rare.
In fact, there are a lot of folks around who'd kill for
that thing, even though they couldn't sell it. They're all
registered, their owners known, and the insurance boys
would make the ones after you look like teddy bears
when they hunted for it."

She couldn't take her eyes off it. "Where—where did
it come from?"

"Nobody is really sure. The name comes from the
general belief that it comes from the Three Kings. Ever
hear of them?"

"Who hasn't? Paradise, the Joys of Heaven. Three
worlds nobody knows the location of that will give you
your heart's desire. Never much believed they really
existed, though. Maybe now I do, sort of. But if this
thing's so valuable, how do you dare carry it with you?
Particularly on a world like *this*?"

"Well, because I'm fairly well armed in spite of what
you see, and in its case it's so booby-trapped that it

would kill anyone trying to get it. Better hand it back. I know it's endlessly fascinating, but the images get darker and darker as you look, and eventually—"

She suddenly gave a cry and dropped the stone onto the table. He was prepared and quickly reached out, grabbed it on the first bounce, and put it back into the case, closed it, then put it back in his pocket.

"There was—*something. Somebody . . .*" she managed, in something of a whisper.

"Yes, I know," he replied.

"Something that *knew*, and instead of *me* seeing *it* through that thing, *it* was seeing *me!*"

"Oh, yes. He always shows up, sooner or later."

She stared at him, genuinely shaken as even the worm had never bothered her. *"He?"*

"Well, I call it a 'he,' but it's probably not a he, or a she, but more of an 'it.' I just feel more comfortable calling it a he, that's all. Gives you the willies, doesn't he?"

She nodded. "Is he—*real?* I mean, is he actually *looking* at me when I'm looking in there, or is it just an illusion, like the personal visions?"

"Nobody knows. He doesn't show up all the time, or at any given interval, either on this one or in the others, but he's always around somewhere. That's why you don't stare too long. They've never been able to synthesize these, not the real ones. Some neat-looking imitations, but nowhere near the real thing. You know the real thing the moment you look into it, whether he shows up or not. They've never figured out what triggers the images in the mind, either. Best guess is some sort of natural force or radiation, but they've never been able to measure and identify one. They can't really get inside one, either. The word is that they tried when the first batch was discovered. Every time you try and cleave it, and I mean *every* time, it shatters into a million tiny fragments, nothing more than powder, that analysis shows have some unusual chemical bondings, but nothing so alien as to explain the effect or give away its secrets. There are, however, people who won't look into them. Not just superstitious types, real smart and powerful people. They think there's a possibility that the thing works in some unknown, alien way as a receiver and transmitter."

"How's that?"

"That while you look at it, the thing's reading all your memories and broadcasting them in some way, through a medium we can't understand, to *his* data banks."

She felt a slight chill. Just the idea that that . . . *thing* inside there that she'd touched on some plane for just a few brief moments was doing some kind of mental readout made her feel more violated than a physical rape. It was that disturbing a sensation when she'd connected with it.

She began to understand just what the Doc had been feeling locked in the C&C talking to that worm.

"Why did you show me this, Mr. Sanders?"

He gave her a wry smile. "I thought you might be tempted to do a little prospecting."

She stared at him. "Where? And with what?"

"I've been using some of my off-time for several seasons looking for just the right combination of people to do this sort of job," he told her. "I told you I was going to look you up if we hadn't met here, and I meant it. You and your people seem almost uniquely qualified for this sort of thing."

"And 'this sort of thing' is what, exactly?"

He took a deep breath, then said, "I am almost positive I know how to reach the Three Kings. No kidding, no joke, no fake theatrical gimmicks. I'm too rooted in reality to believe in all that paradise guff, but I *do* know this: just a handful of these Magi's Stones and you could buy yourself your own paradise. There are other things as well that are associated with the Kings that could be worth even more. It's not a salvage job exactly, but that's why I came here. Salvage people might be able to go get these riches, figure out what was what, and do something nobody else has so far managed to do: get back in one piece."

"I was wondering about that," she told him. "Everybody's heard of this magical realm, and there are all sorts of stories about wrecked ghost ships being discovered with treasures from them inside, and even one in good shape with nobody in it, but I never heard *anybody* who claimed they'd been there and come back, even the drunk and stoned braggarts of the universe. It's a deathtrap, if it exists at all. And now that I've met your little buddy in that green hellstone, I think the Kings are probably a scam. Not *our* scam, maybe. *His* scam, maybe. Send pretty little baubles to the barbarians so a few would come and become his pets or lab experiments or something like that. That's a one-way trip, mister."

"Perhaps. But the stones are real. The artifacts are real. The detailed scouting reports from the Three Kings' discoverer, with the locations unfortunately damaged in transit, were real enough to prove that these are real worlds. Moons, most likely, from what I can tell. Big, planet-sized moons around a massive gas giant. Three of them warm enough and with atmosphere enough to support life as we understand it. I'm pretty sure I know how to get there, and I'm just as sure I know why nobody's made it all the way back yet, at least why *most* ships are wrecked if they try. You have to get there using a wild hole. No wormgates, and a wild and totally uncharted and unpredictable ride there and back. Not many ships could take the punishment, and even fewer captains could. But nobody since the first scout so long ago has been a cybernetic ship, a *living* ship, and I think your captain, the *Stanley*'s captain, is uniquely qualified to do it successfully. She's ridden a couple of wild holes before. I looked up her history. And you, you and your current crew, they've met an alien intelligence and they beat it. You all beat it. You know salvage, you know value, you've got the guts, and you're virtually unique in having outthought and outfought an alien mind. If this ship and crew couldn't make it in and out, then I don't know who could."

"You can can the flattery, but I'm beginning to see your point here. The question is, first, why should we chance it? The odds were almost nil that we got back in one piece this last time. The odds on *this* one are much, much smaller."

He gave a Cheshire Cat–type grin. "You've got only two choices. You all find whatever little menial jobs you can and dream of what might have been, or you do this and maybe wind up owning a world or two. *You* are certainly holding the bag if nobody else is. You won't get the money for that ID change here. It would take months driving a tug to make that kind of money, and on a place like this, one of the universe's assholes, selling yourself would bring in even less. You don't even have passage to anywhere the syndicate goons won't find you in a matter of days anyway. You know what's going to happen. If you don't kill yourself or make them kill you, they'll take you back, jack into your brain, and make you a conspicuous slave to feed their egos, with decades of public exhibition and humiliation as an example with no way out. But you'll make them kill you first, if you can, won't you? I've heard excerpts of the conversations you had ship to ground on that ghost world. There's only room for you in your universe; you'd have let them die if they'd tried to get out without bringing back all the shit, or if there was any chance of bringing up the worm. If the computers had given you any odds at all of success you'd have tried to salvage that anyway, even if it meant all their lives. Excuse me for being blunt, but you'll do it because you've got nothing left to lose."

All at once she hated him. She'd killed once for not

much more of that kind of smug assholery than he'd just given her. The problem was, in *his* case, he was trying to make her do a deal on his terms, and in that she almost admired him for that same insulting toughness. It was so much like, well, *her*.

"So, if we *could* make a deal, what makes you think I could get the others?"

He smiled broadly. "Let's all meet for lunch tomorrow in my suite at the Stellar. I can be *very* persuasive."

"I'll have to think about it," she warned him.

He nodded sagely. "You do that. You think about it a great deal." And, polishing off his beer, he got up and left, saying no more.

VI:

A DEAL WITH THE DEVIL

They had all come.

Somehow, that had surprised An Li, although it didn't seem to surprise Sanders at all. She had an idea that very little surprised the slimy weasel.

Just overnight, she'd discovered a lot about him. That he was, in fact, a rich producer of thrillers, and that a percentage of the net was a joke in his industry about akin to saying "when pigs fly." With some good accounting even the most successful productions somehow never saw a profit; nobody, it seemed, ever had produced a single thing that had made one single penny. Funny about that. Buy cheap, make a fortune, and, through creative bookkeeping, keep said fortune. Show business sounded like the same sort of thing as the kind of folks who'd loaned her the money for the earlier expedition, only Sanders and his types were always legal. What a racket!

She'd also fingered his traveling associates, a young, muscular guy and a woman with a face and body to die for. She hadn't put them together until she saw them both at Sanders's hotel suite, setting up things for a working lunch, as it were.

All the time she'd spent sizing him up as a mark, and they were already on her tail and reporting to the boss on her movements. He dangled his bait and she'd taken it, thinking she was conning *him*.

The penthouse of the Stellar was sumptuous, even for Sepuchus. There probably weren't but one or two like this on the whole planet, and they were here only for the kind of people who were outfitting a city or a fleet. Its sheer opulence was testament to what a knowledgeable designer could do even with salvaged parts.

The table was real polished wood, not synthetic, polished so perfectly that you could use it like a mirror, and the chairs were firm but plush, made of wood and natural fabrics. Sanders himself had not yet made an appearance, but they expected him to emerge from behind massive bronze doors at some point. The two assistants were now acting as host and hostess; the man, who seemed barely out of boyhood, introduced himself as "Jules, Mister Sanders's personal assistant," whatever that meant, and the sexy young woman with more than ample everything and a voice that was higher than An Li had ever heard before said she was Mister Sanders's secretary, Suzy. Neither spoke or revealed very much, but they didn't have to. The few present who hadn't seen these types in their natural habitats still knew what they were. Randi Queson had tired of rolling her eyes, Lucky seemed amused by them, while Sark and Jerry Nagel betrayed their hormonal directions even as they pretended to be strictly business.

An Li had already briefed them on the basics, but left out the Three Kings part for the moment. She had also warned each of them that, if they had anything at all in their wallets, they should grip them tightly in Sanders's presence.

There was a buzz at the main door, and Jules answered it. It turned out to be a small army of men and women dressed in white pushing carts full of what had to be food into the room and towards them. They proceeded to set the table and then place the food on it in containers that preserved the proper temperatures. It looked and smelled wonderful.

An Li wondered how much it cost to tip this kind of mob to do what two machines could have done just as well, but she kept quiet. Any man who could waste this kind of money just feeding his ego by showing off human service was somebody who certainly should be listened to.

Suzy went over to the bronze doors, knocked on one, then opened it just a small bit and said something to whoever was on the other side. In a moment, Norman Sanders strode out and towards them, wearing a genuine crimson silk dressing gown. It was one of the most breathtaking of all the examples of opulence they'd seen, but, An Li thought with some satisfaction, he *still* looked like an unmade bed.

"Good day, everyone," he said cheerfully, if a bit sleepily, taking a seat at the head of the table. He waved his hand at the steaming items on the table. "Go ahead! Be my guest! Dig in! I never eat much for breakfast. Never feel like I'm started. Some coffee, maybe some eggs Benedict, that's about it for now." He suddenly realized that most of these people hadn't seen real food in their whole lives, and the one or two who had probably had forgotten the look of it.

"Omelettes there at the end, with lots to put on them if you like, and those over there are crepes, and those are breakfast meats. All real, I'm assured, with one or two minor exceptions. There's apparently some farming done here, in very limited amounts, just for the hotels and the bosses. Those are teas and juices, and over there are various sandwiches if you'd rather lunch than breakfast, with, I think some onion soup in the tureen. Go ahead, dig in, eat, get joyously full, and then we'll talk."

He was as good as his word, and the food was as rich as he promised. In fact, some of the food didn't taste all that good to them, with one notable exception. They'd been on the artificial and reconstituted stuff so long, some forever, that they had no appreciation for the taste of real things.

The exception was Randi Queson, whose only real regret was that she hadn't much of an appetite. She hadn't been sleeping well, even with some help from a medical computer. She kept having nightmares about cold, alien voices dismissing the human race as irrelevant.

Still, she managed some old favorites she'd neither eaten nor been able to afford in a very long time.

During the whole thing Norman Sanders said little except pleasantries and "Pass the coffee," but they all sensed his mind going behind that dull, cherubic bearded face as he carefully watched each of them in turn.

And when they had regretfully watched the ample leftovers being cleared and taken away after none could manage any more, An Li couldn't help but wonder where those leftovers went. Not anywhere she knew could use them, that was for sure.

Leaving only coffee and tea, the army of cooks and waiters had left with the remainder of the food, and it was again only them. Suzy took a seat on a divan across from the table and said nothing; Jules stood by the table to pour anyone's coffee or tea but otherwise to stand impassive looking at them all. Clearly neither was going to be a central part of this forthcoming discussion.

Finally, the producer stuck a big cigar in his mouth, which Jules promptly lit. After puffing on it a bit and beginning to fill the air with thick and unpleasant smoke, Sanders began to speak. As he did, air filtration clicked on, drawing the smoke up and to his rear, out of their own nostrils. It was a nice touch.

"As Madame An has most certainly told you, I am Norman Sanders. I already know who you all are, and I've gone over what you accomplished and I'm impressed. I'm not much of a man of action, and I draw most of my courage from good whiskey, but that's why I'm looking to hire people. That's what a producer does, you know. He's kind of an entrepreneur. He finds a project, gets control of it, then he puts it into action by hiring the best people for the job and giving them the best tools he can within a budget that will be adequate but realistic. For that, he gets a share of the payoff, sometimes the biggest share. It's not fair, maybe, but if he does his job right he's doing something others can't do. I realize that this isn't cyberspace, we're not talking about jacking in customers in a safe and secure place to experience the thrills of whatever we dream up, but the basics are the same anyway. I didn't come here looking for any of you, but synchronicity seems to have put me here looking for just such people at the time when those people show up here. I have a project. If it comes off, it'll make me one of the richest people in creation and one of the most powerful. I won't mince words on that. Your shares will be tiny for assuming the risk and doing the labor, but they'll still be enough so that you'll never have to work again and can do pretty much what you want forever. Interested?"

"We're here, aren't we?" Jerry Nagel responded.

"Let me start at the beginning. I'm a collector. Antiques, mostly, but historical stuff, and stuff that inspires or stimulates. I go to a lot of auctions, or send representatives there who know my tastes, and I wind up with a lot of stuff. Some of it is junk, some of it is truly wonderful, and some of it is blind speculation. I went to one where they were auctioning off the personal effects of Dr. Oscar McGraw. Anybody ever hear of him?"

Most had not, but Randi Queson knew the name. "He was a brilliant physicist. Said to be on a par with Einstein, Newton, that league. Is that the one you mean?"

"The very one."

"I thought he held a research professorship on Marchellus."

"He did, but he passed away about six months ago. It was a tragedy to science, maybe, but the guy was like almost two hundred and fifty years old and had every kind of rejuvenation process and youth serum you can name. They say he was sharp to the end. Looked like a prune, confined to a wheelchair, but he taught a class the day he died.

"Anyway," Sanders continued, "the doctor was super-famous, had been since he was a kid. He'd lived a long time, knew or met everybody famous in our end of the universe, and had accumulated every honor and prize there was. I figured the historical stuff alone would be amazing, and it was. He'd been alone for years, after his sixth wife died, and there were no heirs this side of the Great Silence, so he willed his papers to his university and a bunch of stuff to various libraries, and the rest he said to put up on the block and use the proceeds to endow scholarships in physics and mathematics for bright kids who needed them. There was a *ton* of stuff to go up, and lots of interested, well-heeled bidders, but I managed to get a lot, including some trunks and such that turned up in his attic. Lots of personal stuff, so they let it go. I had people go through it and catalog it, and I began to notice some interesting names I would never have associated with him. The one that really got to me was Dr. Karl Woodward."

"The evangelist who disappeared a ways back?" Lucky Cross asked.

He seemed surprised that the knowledge had come from this quarter. "Yes, indeed. How do you know about him?"

"Oh, my mom used to be a real regular with him. Sent him money and stuff almost all the way to the end of her days. He was her kind of preacher. Cussed like a sailor, smoked, hated most other preachers. We used to get videos from him now and then. He was a real stemwinder."

"He was indeed. He was also a doctor of astrophysics, and had been a classmate and university research partner with McGraw until something caused a big change in Woodward and he dropped out of science and got religion. Not sure of the story there, and McGraw never understood it, but they stayed friends, or so it appears from the notes. I have a ton of voice diary reminiscences by McGraw of old Doc Woodward, but it was their last meeting that suddenly got me to sit up and take notice. Woodward, it seems, had come across a stuck pirate band and a derelict old ship that pointed him directly to the Three Kings. How to get there, that is. Woodward wanted McGraw to run the physics and get it exact as possible. McGraw wanted to talk Woodward out of it. He didn't; he did the figures and gave 'em to Woodward, who promptly took off in his tent-meeting spaceship and vanished, apparently forever. I have McGraw's calculations. Everything else is still there, and it checks out. I've had it looked at. We even think we know why Woodward's ship couldn't have survived the trip, at least two ways. I think the problem's solvable, and so do the brains I hired to look at it. I want you to go there and stake it out for me."

There was absolutely no apparent reaction from any of the others there, unless you counted the unsuppressed belch Lucky Cross gave. Finally, Jerry Nagel said, "You have the figures from the smartest guy who's ever lived in our lifetime, the stuff used by Woodward? And it didn't work for Woodward? And you think that, decades later, those same figures that this smart guy with his super-computers and whole university brain machine got not quite right can be made right by lesser brains? Who are you kidding? Things are getting worse every year, breaking down more and more. We're on the skids, not the way up. You're offering us a one-way trip to a sure death."

Sanders shrugged. "I'm offering you a way out, a chance to make a bundle, get free of all debts and clear your reputations, and no strings. I've got money and position, but you can't have too much, and I've always dreamed of owning my own studio, top to bottom, without regard to cost. Risk? Sure. Lots of it. A hundred times more than the usual salvage-type job, but you know that going in, something you didn't last time. Right? Blank check on equipment, whatever you need. And *nobody's* gonna follow you and try and collect one way or the other, I can guarantee that."

An Li looked at her companions and sensed that they weren't nearly as dead set against this as they were making out. You couldn't tell about the Doc, particularly after what she'd been through, but maybe, just maybe, there was real interest there.

"Let me talk to my former crew in private for a few minutes," she suggested to the producer. "Let me see if things can be worked out."

Sanders shrugged. "Take some time. But *my* time is valuable, and there are a lot of other crews here that can be put together. My offer won't be on the table indefinitely."

"We're just gonna step outside for a bit and talk," An Li told him, ignoring the implied threat. "Then we'll give you an answer."

He nodded, and dismissed them with a near-regal nod, getting up from his chair and, with his two too-good-to-be-true companions, vanishing back into that bedroom or whatever it was.

"Li—" Queson began, but she waved her hand and shook her head to indicate that there was to be no talking here. They all got the message, and, as a group, trooped out and went down to the lobby area.

An Li led them to a particularly noisy part of the reception area and then said, "We were almost certainly bugged in there, probably still are, but between the ambient noise here and the small leaky communicator I have in my pocket we should be reasonably secure. If not, it's better than nothing." She looked at each one of them in turn, then asked, "So? What're your thoughts?"

Cross shrugged. "No different than most other jobs, except the getting there. I also don't like this split. Standard in this business is fifty-fifty, financing and crew, after expenses. He thinks he's got us 'cause there's nobody else gonna hire us right now, but that's bullshit. We all know that. There's nobody else better to do this kind of job, and if he plunks down a few million on a throwaway crew he's throwin' money down a hole. We're the best chance he's got and he knows it."

Sark and Nagel nodded. Only Randi Queson seemed a bit hesitant. "You *really* think we can do this?" she asked them all. "I mean, nobody's *ever* come back that went looking with a chance of finding it. Not one. That tells me that either you die on the way there or there's no way back once you get there."

An Li looked at all of them carefully. "Honest opinion? I think we can do it, yes, but there's more to it than meets the eye here. I looked into that damned gem that's supposed to be from the Three Kings and something or somebody looked back."

"Huh? What?" They were all interested now.

"You can *see* things in it. Strange things. Some of it's out of your mind, some of it is no place you've ever been, but I don't think those things are natural. I think they're set up to collect information on us, or maybe anyone or anything. Like alien-type ferrets. Only *we* take them around. *We* wear them like jewelry, and the public and the rich and famous actually stare into them."

"More than ferrets," Queson said, thinking things over. "Baited hooks. I'd love to actually *see* one of those."

"Ask him. I think he loves showing off all the things he has and you don't. It's part of the fun of being rich and powerful," An Li responded. "Still, you won't sleep good when *He* shows up in your mind."

" 'He'?"

Quickly she told him of the sensation.

Queson now had her anthropologist's hat on. "Makes me wonder. We're being baited and hooked by these empty ships with *just enough* treasure to make sure we'll keep coming. You seem to think we're being scouted, but it sounds more to me like we're being *studied*, in small and manageable groups. Hey, rats! Here's some great cheese! Come to our maze! Let's see how clever you are!"

"If that's true, then there's no bankable treasure over there," Jerry Nagel pointed out. "Just bait and a trap. That *really* lowers the odds."

"Maybe. Maybe not. We just outsmarted a creature that had the collective knowledge and wisdom of an entire human colony," An Li reminded him. "And we're no colony or group of Holy Joes. We're salvagers."

"I don't like it," Nagel said firmly. "If they're that technologically ahead, and we're in their own den or trap or maze or whatever it is, then we haven't got a chance in hell of getting out of there."

Randi Queson was deep in thought. Finally she almost breathed, "I wonder . . ."

"Huh? Wonder what?"

"How many ships are on record as having returned from the Three Kings with bait but no people? What kind of ships were they? If they weren't cyberships, then we may have an edge they didn't."

"That first scout who reported the place was a cybership," Cross noted.

"Yeah, that's right. Only I wonder if they got any *more* reports from it on other discoveries after they got the Three Kings report. An, give me a little time this afternoon to research this stuff and see what I can come up with. Set up a late dinner, on Mr. Megabucks, with all of us to settle things once and for all. The later the better. By then I hope I'll know just what kind of chance we might have, however slim, of pulling this thing off."

"Fair enough," An Li replied, and she saw the rest of them nodding. "Tell you what. We'll meet in the courtyard outside the hostel at, oh, twenty-one hundred hours. That give you enough time, Doc?"

"Better than nothing."

"Okay. I'll try and set up dinner for an hour or so later. The one other question is, do we need to replace Achmed if we agree it's a go?"

They looked at one another and shrugged. "I don't think so," Sark replied. "We're still a team, accustomed to each other's signals and timing. Adding somebody on something like this and breaking them in isn't gonna be easy to do. We're not taking apart a colony here. It's almost like prospecting or exploring. I think we can handle it. Anybody think I'm wrong?"

"Well, if we can replace him with that actress pet of his, Suzy what's-her-name, I wouldn't mind," Nagel commented wryly.

"Funny, I thought Jules the Sweet would be more your style. Seriously, replace him or not?"

She looked around and saw nobody contradicting the big man.

"All right, then," she said. "Doc, you go do your research. Jerry, I want a workup and laundry list of just about everything and anything you think you'd need if we do this. The rest of you, well, whatever you can think of. Let's be ready when we go back there tonight!"

✧   ✧   ✧

Norman Sanders almost choked on his claret. "*Half? Half!*"

"It's reasonable considering the odds," An Li pointed out. "You get an expert crew and the only front money required is the list of necessary equipment and supplies and the ship's lease itself. We know pretty much what you're worth, Mr. Sanders, and what this all costs. It will take you almost six months to make back the up-front cost of this expedition on interest alone. We agree on your bills up front, before we leave. We add that to your half. Other than that, it's a split."

"It's outrageous! You're *nothing* without my information!"

"And once we have it you become irrelevant," she noted.

"This is blackmail! You're all a dime a dozen! I can go out and hire a crew for next to nothing on this asshole of a world!"

"Then why don't you and stop wasting all our time?" Randi Queson came back. "It's because half of something is quite a bit, but half of nothing is nothing. You're not buying bodies here, or you wouldn't still be bothering with us at all. You're hiring expertise that nobody else has, and you're hiring the best. The best usually get a premium, but we're offering this to you at standard rates because the profit potential is so high."

"You don't take this, what will you do? You'll all be scrambling for garbage in the backwaters of this hole!"

"Not at all," the doctor responded. "I'll go back to teaching until something else comes up, and Jerry will stop figuring out how to disassemble things and go back to making things work with what's at hand. Lucky will go back to tugs or some other commercial piloting job, Li may need a bit of help but she'll wind up the same, and Sark, there, well, there's always work for someone like him. A real jack of all trades."

"I'm thinking of taking an offer as a contract enforcer with the entertainment guilds," Sark said with a kind of eerie combination of smile and growl.

"You see, Mr. Sanders, we have lives, both real and future," Randi told him, sounding quite confident. "You want the best, you need to pay for the best."

Norman Sanders looked for a moment like he was going to have a stroke, then he calmed down enough so that at least his face no longer appeared to be bright red. He reached out, took the rest of the wineglass, and downed it.

"Thirty percent," he managed.

"Fifty, Mr. Sanders. We're not negotiating here. We're setting a price. If you want to make it negotiations, though, then our share is seventy percent."

"Seventy percent! But you said fifty!"

"That was before you said thirty. Now, we can go back and forth and wind up at fifty or we can just settle at fifty. Or, we can thank you for a good meal and a bad offer, leave, and get on with what we were doing before we met you. Your choice."

Sanders was breathing hard, but the others noted that neither of his attractive assistants seemed the least concerned, so they weren't, either.

"All right, all right. Fifty percent of the net."

"Only if the maximum costs are set as part of our contract," An Li came in. "And no overruns. Anything not listed and priced in the contract is your tough luck."

Sanders sighed. Finally he said, "All right, all right. Let's do it."

"Look on the bright side, sweetie," Lucky Cross put in. "Odds are we're all gonna die over there anyway, so why be such a penny pincher?"

"I guess we *all* are betting on long shots here," he admitted.

"Yeah, but you're not one of the targets," Sark replied.

Still, it was done.

Afterward, well away from their new patron and long into the night, they discussed, hashed, and rehashed both the deal and what was to come.

"He caved too easy. I don't trust him," Randi asserted.

"Nobody trusts him," An Li agreed. "I doubt if his own mother would trust him with her laundry, assuming, that is, that he *has* a mother and that he didn't sell her to finance one of his early deals. Still, he's risking pocket change for a massive payoff. I'm not sure he'd risk *real* money, from his point of view, on something like this, but I wasn't kidding. He really *is* that rich, and our job is to make him richer."

"Our job is to get as much valuables as we can and somehow get them and us back alive," Jerry pointed out. "Anybody really feel comfortable that we can do it?"

"Comfortable, no," Randi said, "but *possible*, yes. There are eight known ships, three in good condition, the other five derelicts, to have somehow made it back from the Three Kings. All had Three Kings–type stuff like that creepy gem or other equally weird things. Some had bodies, some didn't. At least two, though, had a number of bodies who died from the effects of riding a wild hole back to our space after having been damaged getting there in the first place. In other words, they *did* manage to get out, to escape. Their hardware just wasn't up to the stress of the job. Jerry?"

"Doc's right," he agreed. "No matter if this thing is a trap or not, the fact is that people *did* manage to escape, and the only reason they didn't get all the way was that their ships couldn't hack it."

"None of them were cyberships, which is important," Randi put in. "The one cybership, the original discovery scout, that *did* make it there in fact sent back other reports, two others, after its incomplete Three Kings report, so either it was let go or it just went right through the system. Whatever happened to it after that was probably, almost certainly, unrelated to the Three Kings.

Only the scout's report was garbled, in several strate-
gic places, so that everybody in creation couldn't get there
because they didn't know where. The scout probably
never knew his full report didn't get through. And that
first ship, intact but crewless, with all the bait aboard,
that didn't find the Three Kings because of the scout's
report, or at least not because of that report alone. But
it *did* have a highly sophisticated homing logic that
triggered only if it was either told to return by crew codes
or if it had been abandoned for more than two years
in place. While not as sophisticated as a cybership, the
system had many things in common with cybership
systems makeup. No, it's possible. We can do this. I'm
certain of it."

"My problem is Sanders," Lucky Cross put in. "No
matter what, I just can't trust the son of a bitch. He's
got some way to cheat us, I'm sure of it."

"Well, we've let the Guild lawyers do the contract, so
that part is solid," An Li assured her. "And we're gonna
have the valuables under our control, so we'll have
possession. I agree, he's slimy and he'll try to pull stuff,
but, frankly, considering what we're about to agree to
do, handling him is gonna be the least of our problems,
and something I'll happily worry about when we're
back."

"Agreed," Sark said, nodding. "If all else fails, I'll gladly
just shoot the son of a bitch and take my chances. Out
here, your word and your contract are the sacred things.
Who the hell's gonna convict me for popping a crooked
producer?"

"That's important," Queson pointed out.

"What? That I could kill him and get a medal out
here?"

"No, no. That *he* has to come *here* to settle, or at least
we settle here. The contract's signed and sealed here,
we're hired for the round trip from here, so this is where
it ends. We don't play in his yard."

"Agreed. Okay, folks, there's nothing more to do but to do it," An Li told them.

Maybe, Randi Queson thought, *but Norman Sanders isn't the only slimy crook around here. This time you don't get to sit high and dry up in orbit while we put our necks in a noose. This time, your neck's on equal footing with mine. You're not the boss anymore.*

Sanders was all smiles, which made the crew collectively uneasy, but he assured them that he would sign the agreement and that their own attorneys would verify it before they left. He did choke a little at the list of equipment the various members came up with, but he still agreed that he'd provide it all, or at least the closest equivalent he could find on this junkyard planet.

"I've transferred the *Stanley*'s lease to my production company," he told them, "and a crew is already up there making modifications and repairs to outfit it for the trip. Just out of curiosity—any of you ever ridden through a wild hole before?"

"Not too many people have," Cross told him. "At least, not too many have and lived to tell the tale. None of us are looking forward to it, but we're ready to give it a try."

"Yes, well, that's not really your job, is it? Your job starts when you arrive. I've placed the navigational information in encrypted form in the captain's navigational computer, by the way. The captain will have access to it, but nobody else, and even she won't be able to get to it until she needs it, and only during that period. You've been making snide remarks about my honesty, so this is my way of insuring yours."

"That's not fair!" Cross almost shouted at him. "What if something goes wrong? We won't have any data at all to be able to use manually!"

He shrugged. "I suggest that if something that bad goes wrong then manual control will be the least of your problems. Manual control brought back mangled ships and dead bodies. The captain's signed off on this. The rest makes no difference. Oh, and one other thing."

"Yes?" An Li responded, not liking this a bit.

"You're going to take along a robotic camera unit. It's quite intelligent, almost to having a personality of sorts, but it consumes nothing and its sole function is to record this entire expedition. If you get back, this footage alone will be a sensation."

"I don't like it," Sark grumbled. "I don't like to shower in public."

"It's smart enough to know what's appropriate, and to take criticism and suggestions. It absolutely will not get in the way. That's not its job. But refuse to take it, and it's a deal breaker. That's the one and only condition I place. At the very least, I want to see where my money's going."

And whether or not we're trying to put something over on you, An Li thought. Still, it wasn't worth arguing over.

"If it's smart and doesn't interfere and if it can even help if need be, then we'll take it. One problem or funny move, though, and it's history. You understand that?"

"I think we understand each other perfectly."

"When will the supplies be aboard and the ship refitted? In other words, how soon can we go?" An Li asked him.

"Two more days. Some of the weaponry you wanted isn't exactly legal, you know, and many of the sensors and such are also pretty tough to find in good condition. Still, most of it is repairing the damage to the *Stanley*. Oh—the shipfitter wants to know if you want to take the smelter. Even if you *did* use it to good effect last trip, it seems rather excessive here, and the object is to streamline the outer hull as much as is possible in a salvage ship."

"We can send that one back," Jerry Nagel told him. "It didn't really do a whole hell of a lot of good for us, and even less for poor Achmed, and I can't think of anything we'd use it for on this kind of trip. What few of its functions might be useful we can get from the weapons array. A lot of what we asked for isn't for shooting, it's alternative tools, you might say. I suspect if we face off against an alien race that's been running this kind of experiment or scam or whatever all these years, they can probably outgun us anyway. My feeling is they'll keep hidden, let us hang ourselves, as it were. I'm not itching to fight somebody who actually might be able to use stuff that's brand new."

"Fair enough. I'll stick around long enough to see you off, but then I have to get back home. I've put off work far too long now," Sanders said.

"But we meet here to settle up," An Li reminded him.

He smiled sweetly. "Of course! You couldn't *keep* me away. So, that's it now."

"Well, one more thing," An Li told him.

"Oh?"

"Petty cash. We're going to need to pick up some personal things here, and we're gonna have a nice little going-away party as well."

Norman Sanders sighed. "Oh, very well. How much?"

"Two thousand apiece."

"*What!*"

An Li shrugged. "Don't worry, Normie, Baby. It comes out of *our* share. . . ."

He wasn't mollified. "What the hell are you going to do with money like that?"

She smiled sweetly. "That's none of your damned business."

VII:

THOUGHTS AND HISTORY

"Hello. I am Eyegor," said the thing floating just in front of Randi Queson. The voice was pleasant enough, but it had that ring of artificiality, of machine, in a clear undertone, and its emotional range was somewhat limited.

The thing itself was about a meter high, and was mostly a stalk filled with folded-up arms and tools, almost like a gigantic utility knife, with a "head" that was a small translucent globe with a thin, reddish-brown band going completely around its equator. It floated in some fashion, keeping the "head" roughly at a height just below parity with whomever it was addressing.

"Let me guess. You're Sanders's camera, right?"

"One of many, yes. In this case I am his primary documentary unit. My sole function is to record as much raw footage as possible of whatever happens and then get it back to my company. I am used to making myself as unobtrusive as possible."

"Well, you better be *very* unobtrusive when it comes to us," she warned the robot. "We're not actors or film people in any way, and we treasure our privacy. There isn't much on a ship like this, even less on an away team, so whatever privacy we can get we demand. You should understand that."

"I assure you that I am unobtrusive."

"You misunderstand Doc," Jerry Nagel commented, approaching the two of them. "We don't want unobtrusive. We want *nonexistent*. In other words, if you get into our space or photograph and record anything we don't think you should, or if we just *think* you did that, well, then, just remember that you will be alone and unable to get any additional instructions, and *our* primary occupation isn't exploration, it's *salvage*. Now, how smart is that dedicated positronic brain of yours, camera? Do you understand your rules among us, or do I have to spell it out?"

"I believe I get your meaning," Eyegor assured him, sounding a bit uncertain.

"Well, let's just put it up front. You record *anything* having to do with us, you ask permission first. And when we're doing our job, which means any time we're working aboard ship or at any time down on a planet, you will obey our orders instantaneously no matter what. Either do that, or we will demonstrate how quickly and efficiently a salvage engineer can disassemble a robot of any sort and catalog its parts for later sale. That clear enough?"

"I believe you have made yourself as clear as need be," the camera responded a bit nervously.

Queson looked the thing over and frowned. "Does the name have some meaning?"

"A show business joke," the robot told her. "If you do not know it when you hear it, it is not worth explaining, nor is it my choice anyway."

"Okay, suit yourself. At least I assume you don't sleep or eat or need any maintenance?"

"I require no maintenance, that is correct, and my redundant dual power supplies are sufficient for centuries to come. I have a small number of spare parts that I carry, and the ship's own maintenance section can fabricate anything else I might need. As I said, I should not be in your way. You should barely notice my presence unless you wish to."

"Oh, if you're a member of our crew then we'll all want to be aware of your presence," Nagel assured the robot. "You could come in handy for us as well. If we'd had you last time we'd have saved ourselves a lot of grief."

"I shall be happy to assist you if I can do so. I am, however, a robot, not an android or a cybernetic device. My programming is not something I can get around, so please remember this. I was designed for a single function, so my initiative is limited. My primary function comes first."

"Well, so long as we don't have any surprises, that's the main thing," Nagel warned it. "If it appears that your programming requires you to do something against my interest or the interest of my crew, you're salvage, so please remember that. That, too, is something you will find yourself unable to get around."

Nagel was already walking away, going towards Sark, who was checking a bill of lading on a hand tablet. One by one, pictures of everything loaded aboard the *Stanley* came up, along with coding as to which prefabricated cube it was in and just how to get it. A small earpiece told him what each was and any specs he requested. The big man glanced up as Nagel approached.

"Any problems?" the engineer asked.

"Not if that shyster was as good as his word and what's listed here is actually in those things. This is high-quality stuff. Mostly salvage, of course, but still the best, mostly new or lightly used. Makes you wonder where the salvage barons here got a lot of this stuff."

Nagel nodded. "Trust nothing from Sanders. Take a container or two at random and check it physically against the bill. Test anything you want in any of them to make sure it works. Let me know if there's any funny business."

"Already in the works. So far so good."

Nagel nodded and turned away. He still didn't feel good about this. There was too much legend, too much not in control, too much in the way of question marks. He didn't mind going up against some smart-ass humans or aliens or whatever was there, and he sure didn't mind the profit potential when it looked like everything was deep down the toilet, but what he'd told the robot was true. They were a salvage team, not explorers. They didn't go out into the unknown trying to find stuff, they went to places where others had found potential valuables and they took it apart and hauled it back for sale. He hadn't known about that damned worm, but he'd had all the specs on the last planet they'd gone, all the scouting reports, climate, geology, you name it, and even though they hadn't been able to get much information on the dead colony he'd had great three-dimensional photos of the complex from orbital surveys, so he knew pretty much what he was going to find and had plenty of time to research just how to get it out of there.

Not here. An ancient legend, some crushed ships and bodies, and a spook jewel. That was it. He'd researched the legends, of course, and what little was truly known from the stuff those ships had brought back, but there were more blanks than information.

The Three Kings. What did that mean? That ancient scouting report from that cybermonk said three worlds, but much of the information in the physics of that report suggested that they weren't planets at all. Planet-sized ships? Moons? What?

Further research suggested that the only kind of setup that could sustain wild holes over such a period of time was powerful gravitational forces caused by massive bodies in a kind of cosmic conflict that were, nonetheless, stable enough to just sustain the stresses and keep reopening the cracks. The original report had suggested some sun-sized gas giants that might do it, but then how would you keep things like moons or even orbiting stations from being pulled apart in the stresses over time?

He didn't like it. He wanted a picture, he wanted the scout's complete reports, he wanted every expert opinion cranked through the very best brains organic and inorganic and everything in between. This was riding a wild wormhole into a maelstrom.

Well, at least this grand expedition to Hell wasn't for some kind of noble reason like scientific research and exploration or shit like that, and it sure wasn't to keep the repo men off An Li's back. If you were going to be this dumb and this high risk, you'd better be doing it for money.

Either Sanders really was already richer than Midas or he was pretty damned confident this was going to succeed, though. Sark reported that everything seemed to check out, and now, boarding from a tug, Jerry Nagel was impressed with the repairs on the *Stanley*. It didn't even smell anymore.

In fact, it was *so* comfortable and homey looking that he suspected that the refurbishing had been done less for the crew than for Eyegor's benefit. You didn't go to see entertainment, not anymore. You went *into* the entertainment, interacted with it, became part of the whole thing. Who the hell other than a masochist would want to experience a *real* salvage environment?

He sat down in his office just off the wardroom, an office he'd never had before, and began going through the routine as best he could.

"Comm Nav check. Good day, Captain," he said in a conversational voice.

"Hello, Jerry. It's good that we're able to go out

together again," responded a pleasant, melodic woman's voice. It didn't seem to come from any sort of speaker, but seemed centered as if from an invisible person standing in the middle of the room.

"Yes, well, I'm not too pleased with the setup—I think I'd rather have another go-round with that worm, since I know more about it and its world than I do where we're going—but at least we're not all up the creek with no paddle. I guess your share of this, if we pull it off, will pay off your debts and make you fully independent and self-sufficient?"

"We will see. It would require a lot of money. Still, that is what I've been working for. Being leased and sent out on orders is something of a cross between slavery and prostitution. I think I'd rather be well away from that. It is worth the risk."

Talk about a lack of privacy, Nagel thought, but neither he nor the others ever really minded the captain. She was the ship's chief operator, and boss in the getting there and getting back department. Even though her brain and parts of her old nervous system were all that was left of her human days, integrated, preserved, protected in some sort of gelatinous mass deep within the ship, linked to a massive synthetic computer and to every sensor and point within the ship as if it were her natural body, she was still part of the salvage crew, an equal with the others.

"Do you really think you can thread this needle, Cap?"

"It does not seem impossible. I'll be busy, but it's not impossible. When you're inside a wormhole you are outside of many of the rules of space-time, and you must anticipate and adjust thousands of tiny settings to keep centered. I look upon it as a challenge. As for the mission, it is precisely why I chose to become a ship in the first place. I want to know what the Three Kings are. I want to see them, and be among the first to return and tell others."

"I want to bring back millions in exotic but marketable merchandise," he told her. "This is just the means to an end."

"I do not believe that. Not entirely. I believe all of you really want to be out there, to be in exotic places seeing things others never will. What would you do with your money? Retire? Do nothing for the rest of your life? I do not believe you studied all that long and hard and became expert in all that you are in order to become a playboy and wastrel. The Doc even less so. She could have remained teaching and living a decent life until she was ancient, not going through all this. You all have your reasons, but they aren't the ones you even tell yourselves. An Li, for example. Tough, self-centered, cold as ice— but it isn't for money that she is doing this. She is doing this to make a mark. To do something important. To wind up *somebody*."

"Well, maybe you're right about them," Nagel allowed, "but not me. I'm doing this because it's the only damned thing I was ever good at. I don't particularly like it, or enjoy it, but it's the only thing I can do well. There's something to be said, I guess, when you find you're one of the best folks in the known universe to tear things down and blow things up."

"We may see."

"So, why did you decide to stop piloting ships and become one? For real?"

The captain thought a moment, then answered, "It is difficult to explain, and it will sound very egocentric, more than anything An Li ever did. Nonetheless, it is true."

"Yes?"

"It is the closest any living being can get to becoming a god."

He thought about that a lot of times after the captain first said it to him, but he never could quite understand it. Perhaps it was all power and perception,

like most everything else, but what was godlike and
the ultimate to somebody like the captain wasn't *his*
idea of paradise. He was never sure that he ever
knew what his idea of paradise really would be,
anyway; only that without lots of money he couldn't
begin to find out.

Even the captain had that in common with him, and
probably with the others as well. You could even decide
that you hated money and try to live without it, but that
was much easier to do when you knew it was there if
you absolutely needed it.

He'd discussed that with Randi on the last trip, and
she'd brought up some long-dead queen in some long-
forgotten kingdom back on old Earth who'd lived in the
world's greatest palace and had never lacked for one
thing in her whole life, but who really wanted to try
and understand her subjects. So she had a little mock
peasant village built on the palace grounds, and she and
her courtiers would go there now and then and play
peasant and grow flowers and cabbages and whatnot.
Of course, the servants did most of the real work, and
kept it antiseptically clean and nice, and no matter how
realistic they wanted to get they all knew, and could see,
that golden palace up on the hilltop that they could
return to at any moment. It was a sincere attempt, but
it was doomed.

He seemed to remember that the Doc said that the
real peasants finally got so pissed off at actually living
in shit and watching their kids starve from the *other* side
of that big castle they finally stormed it and cut her head
off or something equally drastic. She probably died, totally
confused, unable to comprehend why her "children" had
so turned on her.

He'd known a number of dictatorial types on various
worlds who had wound up with nearly identical fates,
and, to a one, they, too, had had baffled and bewildered
looks on their faces as they were shot down.

One thing the money folks rarely remembered: Give the little people some small share of the pie or else one day they're gonna come after your neck. And if you play peasant, make sure you play with real peasants.

He was sick and tired of being a peasant, but things were too broken to get up a lot of enthusiasm to storm the palace. They *all* were tired. They weren't really peasants, either, in the traditional sense—he was university trained, the Doc was, as the title said, a doctor of philosophy, and even An Li, Lucky Cross, and Sark had knowledge and skills that were the products of a lot of training and hard work. All any of them wanted was a score so they could relax for a little bit, or be comforted that their palace was somewhere up on one of those hills if they needed it.

They were all worse than peasants, really. Peasants continued to grub for food and take it until they boiled over or keeled over. Not them. *This* crew took about an hour to decide to gamble on a tiny chance that maybe they *could* jump off that bridge and live, knowing that it was most likely suicide. And if it stormed any castles, it was to get enough to last out their lives in comfort, not for any vision of a brighter future.

Even that queen had been an optimist. Optimism was in short supply these days, though.

He'd seen the photos of the wrecked ships and wizened bodies. They all had.

"Ever ridden a wild hole?"

Who had? Wasn't there a reason, maybe, why nobody in this well-traveled, highly experienced crew had ever met anybody who did? Couldn't even *think* of somebody who had?

His research showed a ton of ships and crews trying. Sometimes the ships came back, most times they didn't, but when they did their crews were almost always dead, dead, dead. The few who survived were never the same, as broken and battered as their ships.

Suddenly, storming the golden palace with pitchforks seemed like the eminently more sane activity of the two.

So the Captain wants to be a demigod, and all I want is to pay off all my creditors and stay in suites like the one Sanders was in, maybe with at least the female companion he had with him or a reasonable facsimile thereof.

It didn't matter what they wanted or didn't want. They all had to be pretty damned desperate or pretty damned insane to take this job.

Three worlds, or something like that. A small, pretty one, a cold, ugly one and a big messy one. That was all that had ever really come through.

Gold, frankincense, and myrrh. Which one had the gold and which had the spices?

Gold was pretty common out here, so common it wasn't even worth the salvage in most cases. The other two had reasonable imitations of equal or greater value. He didn't know what frankincense and myrrh were anyway *except* that they were some kind of ancient precious spices and perfumes. Gifts for a king, or a King of Kings?

He wished that somebody other than a religious fanatic had discovered these places. Then the data might make sense without having to go to a court astrologer.

Well, he'd go over and over what data was there all the way to the Three Kings. *If,* that is, Sanders's information was correct and not a bunch of junk, and *if* the theory that a cybership could ride the wild hole and emerge both ways in decent shape was correct, and *if* there was really anything there of value.

And it wasn't just the wild hole, either. Whatever forces created and sustained it as a near permanent fixture had to be massive. The ship might well have a smooth ride there and then be torn apart as it emerged. Certainly the captain knew that, but that was all she really knew, and it was the unspoken biggest question mark about her part of the journey.

What happens if, at the end of a tricky but successful journey, you are suddenly rushing into a massive stone wall?

Oh, he was going to get a *lot* of sleep *this* trip! Sheesh. . . .

Norman Sanders and his bookends looked absolutely resplendent in their finery as they came to see the *Stanley* off. He was all smarmy smiles and platitudes and shaking hands all around with that dead fish handshake of his, and sounding so confident of success that you almost believed he really thought so himself.

Like the others, An Li was only impressed that he bothered to get up early enough to show up at all.

"Well, it was the least I could do for you brave explorers," he said effusively.

"Yes, the very least you could do," An Li agreed a bit cynically. "All right, we've got your pet robot, we've got the supplies, the Captain says she's got your data, so the only thing left to do is to do it. We've got clearance in less than an hour, so I'd suggest you get off now unless you've reconsidered and want to come along."

Sanders sighed. "I'm afraid that I lack some essential skills and attributes for such a mission," he admitted, sounding genuinely contrite. "Courage, for one thing. Skills to do more than get in the way, for another. I think it's best that each and every person do what they do best. On the other hand, deep down, I honestly *do* wish I could just ride along, somehow, seeing what you're going to see, things that nobody else knows or has ever seen and lived to tell about it. With communication through a wild hole impossible, though, I guess I'm just going to have to make do here and watch the raw footage when you get back. Good luck and godspeed to you all, and I *do* very much mean that."

She almost believed him on that last one, although whether he meant it because of his own potential for risk-free profit or because, deep down, there really was something inside him that wanted to know—well, who could fathom that Machiavellian mind and darkness of soul to ever know for sure? She wasn't even certain Sanders himself could tell sincerity from the act anymore.

She watched them go, heard the hissing of the airlock, and waited until she felt the vibration of the service tug pulling away before she turned and headed for her own quarters.

The ship looked and smelled almost brand new; it was hard to even grasp that this was the same tub they'd been on when they went for salvage and found a great worm.

Randi Queson hadn't even bothered to see Sanders off, and was sitting in the renovated wardroom hunched over her portaterminal. She barely glanced up when An Li came into the room.

"What are you doing so intently?" An asked her.

"Just going over all the data again and again. Jerry's an engineer and the closest to a physicist we have on the crew, but engineers don't see things the way scientists do. I'm more a scientific mind, but my background's not in the physical sciences. Still, a different point of view, a different emphasis, and just as he might see something I'd miss completely in the same data, I might see something he wouldn't. Still, what bothers me most is that time and again I see an intelligence that we know nothing about behind this Three Kings stuff. It's kept very hidden, except maybe for that gemstone gimmick—unless that's just an interactive property that triggers paranoia within our own minds. I mostly believe it's the latter, since we get such personalized visions until the perceived That Behind All That shows up."

"I still kind of wish he'd let us bring it along," An Li said. "If that last sense *is* real it might be a way to

pinpoint where they're hiding. That's what I like least—
they get to hide and maybe play games with us, while
we've got to go in blind."

"It's always that way, or so it seems. Still, I'm glad
old status symbol Sanders *wouldn't* let us have it. If there
is some kind of communication within it, then the *last*
thing I want is *two* Eyegors wandering around the ship,
one Normie's and one God Knows What. Still, I think
we have to separate the suggestion of an intelligent
behavior pattern from things like the Magi's Stones. As
a social scientist, I can sense the logic pattern at least
enough to form theories about it, but until I have proof
that the stones aren't just giving off some perfectly
explainable phenomena, such as radiating something that
interacts with the electrochemical patterns in the brain,
I can't accept the things as spies of the mind. Still, I'm
going to keep an open mind. If we find them scattered
in some geologically similar areas, they're natural. If we
find them in little sacks or stacked up like coins, maybe
not. Either way, I'm wondering what the effect would
be of a large number of them aboard ship. Drive us all
psychotic, maybe."

"That's a cheery thought. How would we tell?"

There was a sudden sounding of a klaxon-like horn
and then the captain's voice came on all speakers.

"Attention. We are now powering up to leave orbit.
Time to first genhole two hours twenty-one minutes."

"Never mind the first one," Lucky Cross called into
thin air. "How long until we get to the wild one?"

"I have not been able to access that information. I must
relinquish navigational functions to the subroutine and
thus cannot access anything not on my standard charts.
I will certainly let you know when we arrive and before
we enter. At that point I will have complete control
restored, as only I can take us through."

"Normie the Weasel strikes again," An Li grumped.
"Like we can broadcast this information?"

Lucky Cross came into the ward room and settled down in a large padded chair. "But we could," she said simply.

"Huh?"

"If the cap had full access to that data, we could sell it, trade it, do whatever we wanted with it. And pirates, military, you name it, could pry it out of us. As it stands, what we don't know we can't divulge, voluntarily or not. No, I think you underestimate the little bastard just because he's a little bastard."

Randi Queson still felt uneasy about it. "So what happens if we get there and there's no 'there' there? I mean, what if the thing's screwed up?"

"There's either a wild hole exactly where it says or there ain't," Cross pointed out. "If there ain't, then we turn around and go find Normie." She sighed. "I'd almost like that better than there *bein'* one there."

"Huh? What do you mean?"

"Look, the only way we get from Point A to Point B is through wormholes. They was all wild holes of one sort or another once upon a time, but we tamed 'em, shaped 'em, made 'em bigger or smaller to suit us, and made sure they opened at the same place and went to the predictable place on the chart. That's the genhole— generated hole. A tunnel through space-time. You get where you need to go faster than light 'cause you don't pass through no space in between. What you *do* pass through, nobody's still sure. Like a lot of things. You listen to all the so-called brains give a zillion different explanations, you say 'So what?,' then you use it—not 'cause they can explain it, but because it works. It works the same way every time. But a *wild* one, now, that's a different story. No genhole generators, no shaping, no stability, no nothin'. Hell, there ain't even supposed to *be* any wild holes, at least not that you can use. Worm-holes wink in and out all the time, but they last from a few millionths of a second to a few seconds, period, then they wink out and wink in someplace a thousand light-years away."

"But not this one," An Li noted.

"Nope. Oh, there are fields where wild holes wink in and out all the time. Somethin' causes 'em, some kind of forces of nature, who knows? But they still wink in, wink out, wink in, wink out, and who knows where the hell they go to? *This* one, and this one alone, supposedly always goes the same place, and it's been doin' it for at least the couple of centuries or so since it was found, maybe a lot longer. It's a natural hole that's also consistent and predictable. And that ain't possible. Even *I* know *that* much physics. Like some kind of predictable lightning bolt. Nope, this sucker may *look* natural and *feel* natural, but if you can go there and it shows up, *it ain't natural.* And that to me spells 'trap.' "

Queson shook her head slowly from side to side, almost in disbelief. "Everybody's suddenly so *gloomy* about this, even me. Is it the new paneling or something in the coffee? I mean, didn't we all just *volunteer* for this? And didn't we all know we were probably going into some kind of trap? I mean, why else all the weapons and sensor equipment? We're about as well-armed with weaponry and probes as a naval destroyer! If everybody thinks this is a one-way trip into an alien dissection lab, why did we all volunteer?"

Cross looked at An Li, who stared back at Cross. Finally, they both shrugged, and it was An Li who answered, "Maybe because we had nothing better to do?"

It took eleven days to reach the entry region. From the command center aboard the *Stanley,* they could see that this was in fact one of the places you'd expect to find the entry point, but picking the right wild hole was something else entirely.

It was one of hundreds of such places in the galaxy which, for unknown reasons, had from dozens to hundreds or even thousands of natural holes winking in and out. It was not a region that ships stayed in for long, but almost all trips had to go through such a region, since the genholes themselves tended to anchor at these spots.

Normally, a ship would emerge from a genhole and then immediately head into another in a preprogrammed sequence; in this case, they emerged into a kind of space that looked as ordinary and as empty as the rest but which set off every sort of alarm a ship might have— and caused even one the size of the *Stanley* to shudder, shake, and apply some real power just to stay in one spot for long. Things were happening out there, things well outside the visible spectrum.

There were no windows in the *Stanley*, nor any space-based visible cameras. They weren't needed and wouldn't show much in any event. The master board, though, in the C&C could show things the way the captain, with all sorts of sensors, could see things. The main difference was that they could see each method of viewing serially, while the captain saw them all at once.

They were looking at energy surges and hot spots, and the only things that came to Randi Queson's mind were a Christmas display and some sort of ancient artillery battle.

"*We're* supposed to go in *there?*" she asked, incredulous. It didn't appear that there was enough room to do it without getting potted by one or another of those flares.

"Oh, it's not as bad as it looks," Cross assured her. "I've been on ships that went all through this area, and hundreds of ships come through the genholes here all the time. Things are a *lot* farther apart than they look. We're looking at several parsecs of space here. No, getting in the way of one of those isn't the problem. It's the fact that the next thing we have to do is fly into one."

"You can sure see why nobody's found this thing,"

Sark noted. "I don't think you'd get far with trial and error."

"Maybe not," An Li responded. "One of them keeps winking on and off in the same space for generations."

"It is not as easy as all that," the captain's voice came in. "No wild hole is all that consistent in where it emerges. It could emerge almost anywhere in this field, and the only thing you'd notice was that it lasted a bit longer than most—several seconds, in fact. But once I get the pattern, it becomes predictable. When we get one flash that holds for precisely the same length of time and repeats a location or a series of locations according to the pattern fed into my memory banks, *then* we will be able to go right through. I will have to match speed, trajectory, and a lot more, but the figures I have will allow me, with the observations, to know which one is the one and only gateway to the Three Kings."

"Um, out of curiosity, what would happen if you picked the wrong one?" Queson asked anybody else in the C&C.

"Simple. You either go the wrong place if you make it through," Cross responded, "or, more likely, you wind up in an uncontrolled vortex that sucks you in and instantly compresses you to the size of a pinhead. Gives you a whole new respect for the ones who set up the first genholes, don't it?"

"They were mostly robots," Jerry Nagel told her. "Very few lives were risked in that kind of operation. Robots made the tries, drew the energy needed to keep the things open and stable long enough to get the genhole anchor on one end, then—if the robot inside made it through— it retained enough of a linkage to allow another anchor to go through the hole and shore up the other end. Even when they had it down cold, they ran robotic ship after robotic ship through until they were sure it was safe."

"That isn't correct, Jerry," the captain commented. *"First* a scout went through, a cybership like me, only designed specifically for the job of threading the wormhole needle.

It was the scout that provided the anchor on the other end and used it to transmit data back. The Three Kings, of course, are an exception. Somehow most of the report got back, but there was no anchor, and, thus, nobody knew which of these was the right one."

"*Somebody* knew," Randi Queson pointed out.

"What? What do you mean?" the captain asked.

"We have the information. We got it from somebody else who had it, and they got it from somebody else who had it and so on. No, that information got back here, somehow. It just never got into the public record. I bet if you really worked on the problem enough you'd discover that somebody got greedy, that that somebody truncated or erased part of that report after they'd copied it. They went for the Kings themselves, and vanished just like everybody else, and now they're pretty well lost to history. But they knew. This doesn't have to be an alien plot. Just some good old-fashioned greed and corruption, I'd wager."

"Interesting idea," Nagel said. "If not, that description sure covers people like Sanders and us, doesn't it? I guess all us greedy, corrupt skunks get attracted to things like that."

"Kind of ironic, though," Randi noted.

"Huh? Why?" Nagel responded.

"Discovered by a monk who named them for the three rich and powerful men who brought gifts to the Christ child, then turned almost immediately into an object of greed and a source of death."

"Well, that's what people have always done to religion. Why stop with this?" An Li said cynically. "Cap, when do we go through? You found it yet?"

"I have it, yes," she replied. "But it will be a very difficult maneuver to enter it at just the right time and angle so that I can avoid damaging the ship. You do seem exceptionally eager to get on with this, though, which could very easily be the last thing any of us does."

"Beats being bored, Cap," Sark commented. "Nobody lives forever."

"I dunno," Jerry Nagel said. "I always thought an exception would be made for me."

"Very well," the captain replied. "I think you all should strap in for this one. It will make things much easier for me. Once you do that, I think we might be able to do this in another twenty minutes."

Randi Queson exhaled loudly. "Well, here goes nothing," she said.

VIII:

THE THREE KINGS

"Get out of here and hang on, you little creep!"

Eyegor didn't seem to have real feelings but it was apologetic. "I am sorry, but I have nothing else to photograph at the moment."

"Well, go photograph the C&C board or something!" Randi Queson snapped. "Just not me, not here, not now! Understand?"

"Yes, I believe I understand. You are—"

"Get the hell out of here before I smash you! Now!"

"Oh, well, if it's *that* way . . ." Eyegor responded, but it floated away and outside the room.

Go piss off An Li, she thought with a wicked smile on her face.

They were all in their cabins, lying down and strapped into their bunks, waiting for the big bang that would tell them they were in a wild hole. It might well be instant death, or at least a quick death, or it might be nothing at all, but if they were to live through it, nobody

165

wanted to be the one with the broken arm or gashed forehead because they didn't heed the captain's cautions.

No human pilot could do what the captain was doing now. It could only be done by a pure machine or a hybrid like the captain and the *Stanley*. At velocities approaching a third of light speed for short bursts, with no real margin for error, and with a target that had to be hit dead center even though it wasn't there yet, this was one hell of a tricky maneuver. Any mistake, whether in calculations on where and when the wild hole they wanted would appear, or in just when to start for it or precisely how much thrust was sufficient, meant they were either doomed to fail or they were burnt toast.

This was what the captain was designed for, what she gained from her sacrifice of her humanity.

The calculations came through as simply as a grade school addition, and she didn't even consciously think of doing them and putting them into action. She had done three trial runs and had completed full diagnostics on the hardware involved, and now she was ready.

It was almost certainly best that none of the people within the ship could see what was really going on, for nobody without the captain's massive calculating abilities and tremendous database of information would believe that this was anything more than idiocy.

The ship came around, sighted on a trajectory so precise that the margin of error was under one millimeter over the vibration of the ship at full thrust. The engines roared into life, shuddering as they did so and causing a massive series of subsonic vibrations that went through the entire ship and all within it, and then it was off at increasing speed, on that precise line to a point in space where there was most assuredly nothing at all.

Although cushioned in artificial gravity and a stable internal environment, they could all slightly feel what was going on, and for the longest time nobody breathed.

At just the precise vanishing point of the original trajectory, and just as the ship reached the mathematical point it had represented, a hole opened up, a hole in space and time. It had no elegant look, no sense of symmetry, nor did it give off the sensation of brute force, although it certainly had that. It looked in fact like a ghostly, twisting plasma of something indefinable, some sort of plasma that was unlike anything in the known universe, and which throbbed and swirled.

The captain took her best data and punched right into the center of the throbbing mass, which slowly enveloped the ship. At that moment the ship seemed to sway in all directions at once, and it took some fast experimenting to keep it solid, as it now appeared to be riding dead center through a ghostly translucent tube.

Most instrumentation was now useless, but enough was known about the energy properties of a wormhole to allow at least a calculation of the amount of subjective time they would be inside and during which the captain would have to be constantly in control.

There was no need to add power now, beyond positioning; the hole simply ignored things like thrust and mass and did its own things according to its own dimly understood extra-universe rules.

The main engines cut off and the internal buffered living environment stabilized. Everything was suddenly unnaturally quiet and even more disconcertingly still.

An Li unbuckled herself from her bed, sat up, opened a small box on a nightstand near it and removed a Styngan cigarette and an elegant lighter with a stylized rat embossed on its side. She pressed the stud, and the top element glowed. She brought it up to the cigarette.

For some reason, it took her several tries before her hand would obey enough to get the heat where she wanted it to go.

She finally got the thing lit, but just sat there, staring

at the blank bulkhead, barely puffing on it, allowing her nerve to come back and her heart to slow down.

Everybody, she thought, needed at least one bad habit, if only for moments like these.

And there would be several days more to go with things probably getting worse for everybody. Days and days with nothing to do, but also nothing more to learn. They didn't have anything new, no data on what was at the other end. But it was going to be bedlam and constant tension and work once they broke out, from the very moment they broke out, assuming all went well.

And she was right. By the time they got the warning that it was only a matter of hours left, they were through all the diversions and all the drugs and cyber entertainment aboard and were starting at each other's throats. That, though, would change the moment things started to happen. It was already happening as they began to think of the job ahead.

The captain, though, was quite pleased. "We managed to get in, we've had no incidents, and we're in excellent condition," she assured them. "I was afraid that others would try following us in; that's a good way to destabilize the interior of a wild hole and cause all sorts of nastiness. We had a few followers, early on, but if anyone was present to tell our course, speed, and match us going in, it wasn't clear on any of my sensors."

"Do they really need that?" Randi Queson asked her. "I mean, if they have a surveyor unit in the area and just register us—course, speed, which hole—they don't *have* to risk any destabilization or detection, do they?"

"Perhaps not, but it's not that easy. Without the data Sanders had downloaded into me, I do not see how they could determine the pattern and pick the correct hole and appearance with sufficient time to get through. And if we get back, we're going to *own* the destination."

"Do you think you can hold us together on the way out?" Lucky Cross asked her. "I always suspected that it was that that tore ships apart. Got to be a fuckin' *monster* to keep a hole like that re-forming over and over. Those forces and the inevitable debris field have got to be Hell itself."

"Who can answer that sort of hypothetical?" the captain mused. "I don't know. I *think* so. The ships that returned as beaten-up wrecks appeared to be victims of the wormhole itself, and the one that didn't showed no apparent outward damage, although its data banks were fried. If that happens to me, then you will have to take it through. I am confident that this ship can do it, with or without me, if need be. In the meantime, I'm going to ask that you be strapped into the emergency bridge in the C&C while we emerge, just in case, and that everyone else be firmly fixed in their bunks. I will transfer holograms of the C&C board to every cabin so that you can see what we see and are facing. If we get clear, I will unlock and extend the visual camera, which has so far been useless to us. Fair enough."

Cross sighed. "I guess." She didn't see how the hell she was going to fly this thing if the captain couldn't, though.

"All hands," the captain announced throughout the ship. "If you have not eaten, I suggest you do it now, then secure everything loose throughout the ship. At the fifteen-minute mark I will sound an alarm indicating that you are to go to your assigned places and strap in. I will then cue you up until we emerge. At that point, deduction suggests that there may be some periods of brief power fluctuations, weightlessness, and/or severe movement of the ship beyond the abilities of the inner core to compensate. Just hang on until Lucky or I tell you it's safe to move about."

"Aye, aye, ma'am," Sark grumbled. "Me, I don't care *what* happens by this point, just so long as it's *something.*"

Nobody ate a meal, although a couple of them drank

a little bit and nibbled on some energy bars, mostly to settle nerves. There was a lot of loose stuff to pick up and store, but they all knew they'd miss some of it anyway. Nobody was really thinking of anything but the end of the trip that everyone else had spun stories and legends about, and many had died trying to get to and from. And there wasn't one damned thing they could do except wait for it.

At fifteen minutes, the emergency alarm sounded and the captain said, "All hands to rough-condition stations and strap in."

Everybody except Cross went for their quarters with one last look around to make sure they weren't forgetting the obvious. Lucky headed down and aft to C&C, only to find Eyegor waiting for her there.

"You better find a way to hold on or you're going to get smashed against this equipment," she told the robot.

"I will use internal energy beams to secure myself to the bulkhead," Eyegor told her. "I have determined that nothing critical runs through it, so I should not disrupt anything. I must be here and active to record this historic event."

Lucky Cross sat in the command chair and belted herself in, then reclined, triggering two command panels next to her right and left hands and activating voice control. It would have no effect unless the captain were cut off from the controls, but if that happened she would have complete command of the ship in nanoseconds. It was the last thing she wanted, nor was she trained for it, but she was the best qualified of the group if it came to that.

"Comm check," she said in as cool a voice as she could manage.

"Comm check aye," responded a more mechanical-sounding version of the captain's voice from the panel in front of her.

"Emergency backup power."

"Backup power at one hundred three percent of nominal," the board assured her. "Connection time three nanoseconds."

"Very well. Display on, forward, wide."

The big display board came on and showed . . . nothing. There was as yet nothing really to see that any of the instruments could pick up other than constantly fluctuating energy surges.

And then there was the clock. The simplest, most primitive device on the board, it was the one that interested Cross the most. It read "00:00:05:35:16," and it was counting down.

Five and a half minutes.

She felt a curious detachment now, as if she were cut off, watching from some safe and far-off place and time Eyegor's recording of the moment rather than experiencing it. It was often like that, when push came to shove. It also somehow caused five and a half minutes to go by in a kind of agonizing slowness that physics would never explain.

"Five minutes," the captain's voice said throughout the ship. "I will call each minute now until one, then count from ten seconds."

Lucky Cross wanted a cigar, but she knew it would be some time before she could have one. She sat there now, watching the timer crawl down, and she found some personal satisfaction in the situation as tense as it was.

Big, fat, foul-mouthed, coarse lowlife Gail Cross, she thought. *They'd laugh and tease me, they'd call me names and make me the butt of their jokes, and they'd go off to their fine places while I went home to a ramshackle junk house built from yesterday's disasters. Nobody ever gave me nothin', but I didn't take like An Li. I learned and I earned, and look who's sittin' in the C&C chair now ready to set eyes on the Three Kings!*

"Thirty seconds."

C'mon, c'mon! If we're gonna die, then let's do it. Either that, or a share of the biggest pie in creation!

"Ten . . . nine . . . eight . . . seven . . . six . . . five . . . four . . . three . . . two . . . one . . . *egress!*"

The board came alive with so many things it was impossible to make them all out, but that wasn't the thing that Cross and the others thought of just then. The vibrations, the crashing sounds, the objects they'd missed shooting lethally around them as they lay strapped in, the ship's lurching, nearly out of control movement in all directions for what seemed like several minutes, all combined to give them a carnival ride and a sea of sensations, mostly unpleasant.

The captain's warning hadn't been the half of it, and even the lights, the blowers, everything except the flying and clanking junk around flickered on and off and they felt themselves growing sick and disoriented.

But the captain definitely had control of all engines and energy controls and stabilizers, and although it took some time the ride eventually smoothed out and the noises, smells, and spinning sensations ceased.

Cross hit the intercom. "Everybody check in! An Li?"

"Here! I've got strap bruises and a small cut, otherwise okay."

"Doc?"

"Bad bruise on my right arm above the elbow. At least I *hope* it's just a bruise. Something hit it with tremendous force. Still, I'll live."

"Jerry?"

"Yeah, I'm okay. Something put one hell of a dent in the bulkhead here, though."

"Sark?"

"Broke one of the straps and got tossed a little, but I'm okay. Just feel like I've had a few back-alley brawls with some ghosts from my growing up years."

"Well, I seem to be no worse for wear, but I had more

protection. Cap? I don't have to fly the damned ship, do I?"

"Not yet," the captain responded. "Damage control reports a great deal of minor damage but nothing that can not be attended to by self-maintenance systems. I believe we made it in very good shape, although it will take a little bit of skill and a *lot* of power to navigate in *this* system."

They all immediately forgot their bruises and turned to the hologram of the primary C&C screen in front of Lucky Cross. Cross gave a low whistle.

The G-class star was slightly larger than average but not outside the range of such suns in the database of known systems; what was spectacular was the fact that there was a series of debris rings where solid planets might be expected, and, beyond, well out from its star, was a single gas giant so massive that had it ignited there would probably be nothing else around at all. At a diameter of almost three hundred thousand kilometers, it dominated *everything*, and it had not one spectacular ring but two, eerily paralleling one another above and below its equator. But the oddest thing about it was that, even beyond its terminator, on the half turned away from its sun, it had an eerie but bright luminescence that transferred a good deal of light and even some heat from internal forces to the moons. It was what made at least three of those moons capable of life support in spite of long periods when the moons hid from the primary source of their energy.

There were three more gas giants farther out, none nearly the size or complexity of the massive inner one, and a number of very thick asteroid belts that might well have been other planets if the gravitational forces of the monster planet and its interaction with the others had permitted them to form.

"There's little use even looking at the other gas bags, they are too far out," the captain noted. "And while the asteroid belts contain some of extraordinary size, I cannot at this point sense any with any sort of atmosphere that might be stable and life supporting, let alone old enough to develop anything. That leaves that inner monster. Of its many moons, two currently visible are planet sized with atmospheres, and indications are that they are within tolerances for sustaining life as we know it. A third might be on the other side at the moment."

"So the Three Kings are moons. Curious that the monk who discovered them wouldn't nail that down," Nagel commented.

"Not necessarily. The survey was considerably garbled, and much of the information we *did* have was reconstructed and some of it interpreted," Queson put in. "There certainly were suggestions of it in the report, but who would have thought that they would be three among many around some monster that size?"

"I'd like to know what stabilizes the temperatures on those worlds," Nagel replied. "I mean, running the two visibles we can see, I get fairly reasonable surface and low atmospheric temps even on the night side. There's some heat from the giant, which, like most of that type, is virtually a failed sun, but why don't they broil when they get into real sunlight? There's no way they can do both. It's almost like they have thermostats."

"Perhaps they do, in a way," the captain said. "The combination of inert atmospheric gases might well interact with the sunlight on the other side to filter out some of the solar heat and disperse it. That is certainly true of the pretty blue and white one. I just ran a simulation, and the addition of sunlight to that mixture would almost create both a heat and light shield. You could almost think of it as a planet with a natural sunscreen. It's still going to be *very* hot on the other side, but if you limited your activities to 'night,' when it was turned towards the planet and away from the sun, and took shelter during the day, you could live through it. It's also got quite a lot of water, so think of it as a tropical steam bath."

"That other one isn't any steam bath," Nagel pointed out.

"No, it's mostly desert, and a cold desert at that, at least on this side of the planet, away from the sun. Still, there is considerable water, much as ice, on the surface, and a good atmospheric mix. It probably gets just cold enough to be nearly unbearable when it rounds the big one and gets hit by sunlight. I think it might well be a whole different world on the solar side. Warmer, liquid water, who knows what else? Heated up just enough to sustain it and anything on it that knows how to compensate during the cold outsystem time. Roughly thirty standard days on this side, about the same on the other. Our jungle world is faster, under fifteen days each side. Wonder what the third is like?"

"Well, it's a long way from here, but I haven't anything better to do," Cross noted. "Let's go see."

"Moving in-system. I'm going to take a little extra time to leapfrog that nasty inner asteroid belt as much as possible. In the meantime, we've all got lots of new information to work with."

"Any scan of radio or other broadcast signals from in-system?" An Li asked. "Or the remnants of other ships?"

"Hard to say on the ships. There's nothing recognizable as a ship's power signature, if that's what you mean, not in orbit around any of them or in the visible system, but we've only seen half of it and haven't begun to map things yet. There are life signs on both worlds, even the frozen one, but it's much too far to tell what sort of life we're talking about. The pretty blue and white one has a few surface energy signatures that *could* be ships of some kind, but, if they are, they aren't big suckers. More like the shuttle we use to go from planet to orbit—only there are no evident ships in orbit, if you see what I mean. That says that they could be anything.

The cold little desert one has a vast number of really odd energy signatures, no fixed locations, but there is simply nothing in my data that matches any of them. Could be your alien masterminds, but more likely it's some kind of energy signatures from minerals or deep down interactions below the crust. I have no records of any readings like this before, but, then again, I've got hundreds of cases of readings just as bizarre and all turned out to be natural phenomena."

We've all got aliens on the brain, Randi Queson thought to herself. *Still, we had no such thoughts the last trip and look what we met up with. That cold little world there, for example, reminds me a little* too *much of where we've already been.*

An Li's "cut" caused by a flying something turned out to be a pretty nasty slash right across her forehead in a jagged and bloody shape. It was easily attended to, and they even had skin repair in the medical unit that would, over time, make it vanish completely. For the moment, she refused the full repairs, much to everyone's surprise, and accepted only the treatment pack that would seal and heal it in a day or two. It would also leave a pretty nasty scar that would mar her delicate beauty, and if An Li was anything she was quite vain about that.

Randi's "bruise" turned out to be a fracture, but, again, it was easily set within the medical unit. She would have very limited movement there and have to wear a healing splint for a few days, but, again, there would be no permanent damage. The fracture was clean and rather slight, not a full break but more a chip. As she was left-handed anyway, it wouldn't crimp her style very much, and it was likely that both would be fine by the time they got close in on the big planet.

At least the monk scout's information as far as it went was borne out. The pretty little moon was almost certainly what he'd called Balshazzar; the cold and inhospitable but still livable moon was Kaspar; and still among the missing was Melchior, supposedly much larger than the other two and far more active and violent a world. Kaspar was almost two thirds of the way through its cold side transverse, and Balshazzar about midway. It was likely that all three were within sight for at least a good part of their short "years," so either Melchior had set just before they'd gotten there or it was due to show up any time now.

And show up it did.

Balshazzar was about 30,000 kilometers around, and the smaller Kaspar was a shade over 22,500 kilometers, but Melchior now was impressive in its own right.

Over 50,000 kilometers at the equator, it was certainly the king of moons even in this system. It was also a nearly impossible mixture of nasty and nice. Mostly ocean, it had one huge continent straddling the equator almost three quarters of the way around, but it didn't look like anyplace you'd want to go for a vacation. The land was riddled with volcanoes, some huge, most active to some degree, and the entire continental mass was slightly on the move, shuddering here and there with volcanic earthquakes and causing huge fissures, some of which ran for hundreds of kilometers, opening up to reveal bright hot lava. It reminded Randi Queson of a giant jigsaw puzzle in which lava seemed to run at every junction of pieces, but there was sufficient motion that sometimes the pieces were so tightly fitted the meeting edges could not be seen.

It was also smoky, with a permanent cloud layer over a good share of the planet. Still, there were enough forces at work both below and in the gravitational effects of the big planet and other passing moons that the atmosphere was constantly in motion and there were often virtually clear spots. In most areas, though, and particularly in the highest volcanic ranges of the continent, it seemed to be raining all the time, often torrentially. There was certainly vegetation, though; the atmospheric mix, minerals in the volcanic soil, and warmth both from the planet and sun and from the near-surface volcanic activities fed a nearly perfect organic stew.

More comfortable but by no means pleasant were the islands of the mid latitudes, some of enormous size. Like the continent, they were primarily volcanic, but whole areas appeared to be either ages dormant, with often only one, or even no, active ones. There were still active volcanic regions in other respects, but their mountain-building days seemed to have slowed to a crawl or stopped.

Still, the place seemed to teem with life. Vast areas of foliage, low broad-leafed trees and enormous vines, and possibly a lot more, and not just on the islands, either. Life always found a way if there was one, and even on the most active areas of the continent there were large areas of vegetation. White steam rising said that hot magma might not be too far below the ground even there.

Sark looked at the pictures of the three on the big screen and commented in his low, perpetually sour voice, "Well, if I got stuck out here I know which one *I'd* head for and move to."

"Huh? Oh, you mean Balshazzar?"

"The pretty one. Sure."

An Li wasn't as convinced. "I wonder if it isn't supposed to be that way. Everybody who likes our kind of climate would be naturally attracted to that one, but if there's any kind of rhyme or reason to this then that's the one I'd stay away from. You draw the bugs with sugar and then you trap 'em."

Nagel chuckled. "Ah, the secret hidden alien master-minds again, huh? Why would they want to lay a trap for such as us? And keep such an elaborate and expensive trap open to little bits of us over such a long time? No, I can't buy it."

"Three worlds that all could support human life? That's not suspicious?"

"I don't think so. Unprecedented, sure, but it's a big universe. One, two, three, a dozen, what's the difference? And if not here, then somewhere else."

"But they *are* here," she persisted. "And linked to human regions via a self-renewing wormhole."

Randi Queson thought a moment, then said, "You might both be right for all that it matters. The point is, Li's got a point. Look, from the point of view of sheer pragmatism and a knowledge of human nature, let's look at the three. Want to find remnants of anybody who came before and might still be around? Go for the pretty one. But don't expect to find much of value there other than refugees. You'd have to have mines and other heavy-duty works to find much of value on it, particularly with that necessary level of erosion and deposition. Now, if you want to hunt for those mysterious artifacts of some long-gone alien civilization, I'd take Kaspar, the little cold one. Anything left there in the sands or probably in the cliffs would eventually be exposed by the wind and such, and the cold would be a good preservative. But if you want your gemstones, I'd take Melchior. It's far too dynamic for much else, but those kind of internal forces are just the kind that create unique mineral recipes from whatever compounds are beneath the earth. So, what do we want to go hunting for first? Refugees and aliens, maybe, or even alien refugees, or artifacts, or gems?"

"Gems," An Li, Lucky Cross, and Sark all responded as one.

"Then we go to Melchior and we hold our noses. I bet you that world is gonna stink something awful. And considering those rains, everybody better know how to swim, too."

"I think we ought to do a systematic survey before committing to any planetfall," Jerry Nagel said to them.

"Why? What's the difference?" An Li shot back.

"Because we don't see any derelicts here, that's why. Lots of forces, lots of history, but no clear-cut signs we aren't the first ones here. I think I want to know what I'm getting into before I go down, particularly this time. It may not be as easy as it looks to park and go down and scoop up treasure, even if we can find it. Let's look at them all. There aren't enough of us to do any kind of real exploration, and none of us are gonna live *that* long to completely cover one, let alone all three, of these things. It makes it all the more important that we decide right off which one we want to commit to this first trip, make sure we're landing where there's something worth taking, and, if possible, spot what we can of ugly surprises. Why not? You got something better to do?"

His logic wasn't what they wanted to hear, but it made too much sense to be argued with. Gold and frankincense and myrrh were not lying all over the ground down there waiting to be picked up and stuffed in their pockets. The Three Kings weren't quite the easy El Dorado of spacefarer legends, but just three new and very odd worlds. They needed more information, and getting it wasn't something you could argue yourself out of.

Lucky Cross sighed, a little disappointed. "All right. Agreed." And, one by one, the others echoed her sentiments.

"I'll plot a systematic route," the captain told them, sounding very satisfied with their decision. "Kaspar, Balshazzar, then Melchior. Then you'll have to decide."

"Fair enough," Nagel replied. "When we go down and come back up, and when we go back, I want to already have enough stuff so that no matter what Normie pulls or tries to pull on us—and he'll definitely try and pull *something*, bet on it—our share will still be enough so we don't have to worry or ever come back again unless we want to."

They settled back and headed for Kaspar.

IX:

FOLLOWING YONDER STAR . . .

"I found something interesting in the database," Randi Queson told them as the *Stanley* approached the ghostly and frozen moon of Kaspar. "An old Christian melody. I wonder if that monk was tweaking our future collective noses a bit?"

Nagel's bushy eyebrows rose. "A melody? You mean a religious song?"

"One of many about them, although hardly a religious song in the usual sense. There wasn't any real agreement ever on whether or not they really were kings or more likely astrologers or some sort of magicians high up in royal courts. I looked through the bunch—there are even some operas—but this one is kind of interesting. I half suspect that if anything was running through that cybernetic brain when those reports were sent, it was this one."

"Not my background, but let's hear it."

A sonic hologram just above her desk began a chorale singing,

*We three kings of Orient are, bearing gifts we
   traverse afar,*
*Field and fountain, moor and mountain, follow-
   ing yonder star.*
*O star of wonder, star of might, star with royal
   beauty bright,*
*Westward leading, still proceeding, guide us to the
   perfect light.*

Nagel shrugged. "Sounds pretty innocuous to me, the parts that make sense."

"Christian tradition, mostly, The Christian Bible really says little about them except that they were so naive they inadvertently made the local king so paranoid he tried to kill all the babies. But the traditions would be in the mind of this monastic scout, that's for sure. He would have been raised with them. It might just be a kind of perverse sense of humor—monk humor, maybe. In *this* case our kings don't follow a star but a failed star, but it's sure a star of wonder and beauty as these things go. But in the song *all* the kings bear gifts to give to the Christ child. They come, they do it, but in the process cause infanticide. A warning, perhaps, to those who know the story?"

Nagel wasn't impressed. "Maybe, maybe not. I remember an old legend once about the oracle that always gave infallible predictions, but in riddles. Trouble was, you could never figure out what the oracle meant until the thing came true, so it was useless. If that old boy had any kind of message in mind, other than being creative in his names, I doubt if we could figure it out until after it's too late, so what's the point? Maybe we should have brought along a priest, huh?"

"Not with the percentage Vaticanus would demand. And I don't think Normie was the religious type, and *definitely* not that kind of religious. Interesting, though, if even that was a part of the old monk's description. They're a strange lot, those people. I mean, which star is he talking about if he's referring to here? The conventional one, or the almost-star that traps the Kings? That planet gives me the creeps anyway. For all its awesome beauty, the fact that it's active enough to send out light and heat on its own, and that kind of throbbing luminescence on what should be the dark side . . . I don't know."

The captain's voice interrupted them. "I am placing us in a medium orbit above Kaspar as we speak. On the way out, I will launch a mapping satellite that should be able to produce an excellent and detailed surface study over time. Do you want to just look over the place with the screens now, or send down a surface probe?"

"We just want an overview for now," Nagel told her. "We'll launch a probe if we see anything we really want to look at."

At 180 kilometers above the planet-sized moon, the instrumentation and cameras could do an excellent job. If somebody had stopped off there and left graffiti on a rock, they could read it. The trick was noticing the rock in the first place.

It was a forbidding-looking place. The residual heat from the big and still officially unnamed mother planet, plus pressure deep under its oceans, freezing around the coasts but still liquid for most of their expanse, allowed it to maintain a barely habitable temperature during its long semi-night, but just gave an even more eerie look to the place.

"Not any signs of glaciation," Nagel noted. "It must melt pretty good on the sunward leg. Lots of erosion in the regions against the mountains, but the main land masses have been so chewed up they're just cold, powdery desert. Those dunes and that wind would make it even nastier. And we thought that overrun colony's choice of worlds was bad!"

"Could you breathe down there? Without aid?" An Li asked him.

He checked the figures. "Yes, looks like it. Pretty damned cold at the moment and dry as a bone, but the oxygen and nitrogen mix is within our limits. I wouldn't like to do it without some sort of facemask to keep the grit from choking you, but the air would be okay. I don't know what you'd eat, though, and any fresh water in those big lakes would take a fission reactor to properly melt for use. It's probably as ugly but very different on the solar traverse. No way to tell until we can see it, and that's still almost fifteen standard days, I think."

A subsurface scan showed even more similarities to the old world they'd grown to hate.

"We've found a good second home for that worm, though," Randi noted. Lots of caverns, vast openings beneath the surface. You could get lost in there fast."

"Yeah, but not much water in them, interestingly enough," Nagel pointed out. "Most of the interior caverns, some of which seem to go *way* down, appear to be relatively dry, and those figures there just *might* indicate some running water even at this point. That's how you survive the cold cycle. Ten to one the caves maintain an above-freezing temperature that's either constant or nearly so. The surface is only comfortable half the year. Odd, though."

"Huh? What?" Queson responded.

"Well, caverns of that signature tend to be sedimentary rock, easily eroded away over time by the underground rivers and streams, and certainly all the makings are there for a classic setup. Note, though, that there are *no* such caverns within a hundred or more kilometers of the coastlines. They're away from the oceans and in the highlands no matter where you look. There doesn't seem to be a major change in bedrock composition in most of those cases that would explain it. The planet's got a heavy but mostly solid core that's maintained the gravity and kept the atmosphere, but a lot of the underground water doesn't seem to obey the laws all that well. It's probably scrambled data from all this interference, but on the face of it it seems like as many of those deep rivers are flowing upward as down slope."

"Water does not run uphill. Even *I* know *that*," An Li commented.

"Precisely my point. Either these readings are wrong, or the signals are being distorted before sending back, or we have here a good example of the repeal of the law of gravity."

"Water in pipes or under pressure can flow up, down, or anywhere at all," An Li pointed out.

"Plumbing for a race driven from the surface? Interesting idea, but we're getting heavy organics but nothing that would suggest a civilization or even a big colony that would justify building works like that. If your aliens are down there, then they're probably long dead or reduced to a primitive existence. This is a planet you can *survive* on, it's not one you ever want to try and live and work on if you don't have to."

An Li settled back in her chair and looked at the passing parade of the dismal, cold world below. Suddenly she sat bolt upright. "What the hell was *that*?" she almost shouted. "Go back! Go back!"

"What? What did you see?" Nagel and Queson both prompted her.

"A structure! I'd *swear* it wasn't natural! Cap, can you back up the video ten seconds at a time?"

"Will do," the captain's voice responded, and the visual segment began the backing up. An Li was almost ready to admit that she'd been hallucinating when, suddenly, it showed up again, and this time they all saw it.

"There! Freeze that!"

It *did* look very much like an artificial structure, but not for humans. It also gave off virtually no power signatures, meaning either that it used a power system unknown to them and therefore unmeasurable or, more likely, that it was a derelict from times long past, covered and then uncovered by the shifting sands.

It was a huge ball shape, perhaps 300 meters across, sticking out of the sand. It was light gray in color, and all over its surface it had short probelike protrusions. A closeup didn't reveal much more about it, but it *did* reveal at least one clear breach of the hull or exterior or whatever it was. A jagged hole, half in the sand and possibly anchoring it there.

"It's nothing natural, that's for sure," Nagel agreed. "And I doubt that it's much of anything from any kind of ancient Kasparian civilization. That leaves the obvious, boys and girls. We've just discovered our first-in-history, honest-to-goodness alien spacecraft."

"Yeah. Too bad we ain't in the salvage business any more," Sark growled, tongue a bit in cheek.

"He's right," Queson noted, not echoing the humor. "There's a lot of potential down there, but it's not what we're here for. If you look at the size of that thing, even the *Stanley* isn't big enough to handle it whole, and we don't have aboard all the equipment to break it up even if we knew how to do it properly and save what's valuable. If, that is, we could figure out what was valuable. No, we have to plot it, mark it, and go on, I think. When we can stabilize that wild hole and turn it into a genhole, *if* that's possible, *then* it's possibly the most valuable thing here. Until then, it's more valuable if others come to it."

"Man! Goes against all my instincts, though!" Nagel sighed. "Damn! Even *I* would love to go down there and look through that ship."

Queson wasn't so enthusiastic. "Yeah, that's right. None of you have ever talked to an alien close up, have you? Still, you got to wonder."

"Huh? What?" Nagel asked.

"That's been down there a while, You can *smell* it as a long-term derelict, an ancient shipwreck. Sure, you

wonder if any of 'em survived, and, if so, did they
manage to set up something permanent down there, but
it's a long shot. More telling is that it's there at all, and
that there's good evidence it's been buried by the sands
and winds several times, and maybe baked and thawed
as well on the sunward side. How many more might be
down there, I wonder?"

"What? You think they were a colony or a military
squadron or something?" Lucky Cross asked. "Don't see
that. Not out here."

"No, no, I don't mean *that*. I suspect they were scouts,
explorers, maybe even some commercial vessel or a lone
military one. I don't mean how many other ships like
that one might be down there someplace, hidden for now.
Just the idea that we've seen the wreck of even one on
the surface of the first world we looked at makes me
wonder just how many ships from how many different
races have come through here and not left. Remember
how Li kept thinking of this region as some kind of trap?
Maybe it is, either planned or just naturally one. Either
way, it's not a trap set for *us*, I don't think. If the former,
it's set long ago for somebody or something very different than us; if the latter, it's effective against just about
anyone that comes here regardless of shape, size, or racial
origins."

"You want to go down there and have a look around?"
Lucky Cross asked them.

"Not me," Nagel replied, and, one by one, Sark, An
Li, and most emphatically Doctor Queson also shook their
heads "No." With that weather and those caverns, their
experience with the unexpected worm kept coming up
as well.

"We could send Eyegor down," An Li suggested. "That
would solve a *lot* of problems at once."

"Not a bad idea," Nagel replied, only to see the
hovering robot in the back area of the command and
control center.

"I am not programmed to become an explorer," it said, sounding no more enthused about going down there than the humans had.

"Ah, but what about your primary mission?" An Li pressed. "Look at the pictures down there! The first close-ups of the exterior and perhaps the interior of a truly advanced alien spacecraft. And who knows what else might be valuable?"

"Sand is not good for my workings, and I do not know if my mobility might be impaired. I believe the ship's cameras will suffice for this one for now."

"Then why are you *really* here?" Nagel put in. "If it's not your job to get those kind of pictures, then the only conceivable mission you could really be on is to spy on us. That *is* what you're really doing, isn't it? Spying on us?"

"I am *documenting* you, not spying on you," the robot responded. "If you go down there, I go down there. But without you, the potential for fulfilling my mission is greatly diminished."

"Sounds fishy to me," Sark growled. "I say we take it apart now, file it under spare parts, and forget about it. It can do us no good."

The robot said nothing, but even the others weren't sure whether or not Sark was joking and, worse, none of them cared if he wasn't.

"We could send down a probe," Cross suggested.

"Too limited," Nagel responded. "It wouldn't be able to do much if it could get inside the thing, and we've got a finite number. Best to use them when we have questions that *have* to be answered. This is just something we'd like to know, not something we can easily turn into money."

After a long silence, An Li asked, matter of factly, "So, what do we do about poor little Kaspar here? Go down or go on?"

"We need stuff that can be picked up and hauled back

and turned into money," Lucky Cross pointed out. "I can't
see it down there with what we got. As you said, we
couldn't haul that thing back on a bet."

"Any of the life that might exist down there, native
or survivors and survivor descendants, will be underground at this point, or maybe underwater," Queson
pointed out. "This isn't the right time to go looking for
them, nor is there a lot of profit in it. I say we note
this as potentially valuable but go on. I've had enough
freezing cold and blowing sand."

An Li nodded. "Anybody else? Then we're agreed.
Captain, launch your probe and survey satellite and let's
move on. We can always come back if nothing more
promising turns up."

"Very well," the captain's voice responded. "Let the
log show we are in unanimous agreement. I think per-
sonally we should examine all three before doing much
in the way of landing anyway. That goes even if the next
one has streets paved with gold and the Fountain of
Youth in the center."

"I might stop on that," Nagel commented. "Still, we
all agree with the general sentiment."

"Setting course for Balshazzar," the captain told them.
"At least it's very pretty as worlds go. Were I still human,
that would be the one that I think I'd go down and look
over first anyway."

"How long?" Nagel asked her.

"Two and a half days. We have to go slow and careful in this miniature solar system without charts and nav
beacons. Planets this size don't just accumulate moons
and rings, they pick up a ton of junk."

And now, from the bleakness of Limbo, they turned
towards the spectre of Eden.

Even going the slow and careful route, though, they
were well within instrument and sensitive optical range
of the second livable moon long before they reached it.

"There's altogether *too* much life on that moon," Randi Queson grumbled. "Can't pick *anything* valuable out of it. In fact, the only interesting parts are these energy signatures against some very small but measurably dead points. At least two could be the remains of routine solar-system lander power supplies, and a third could even be the remnants of an interstellar worm drive. There are several more such signatures elsewhere on the planet, but they don't give off anything familiar or recognizable to the database. If we assume that at least one is ours, from some prior expedition, and maybe two, and we make the reasonable assumption that even a very alien civilization would probably wind up doing it for sheer practical reasons pretty much like we do, then we're looking at the signatures of at least a dozen shipwrecks down there, at least a few of which are not ancient history. I keep thinking about Dr. Woodward and his evangelical space colony. We're following in his footsteps and we got here with the same data, so why should we assume that he didn't?"

"Yeah, but the old records say he had a humongous ship, a real artificial world moving through the universe," An Linoted. "If that's so, where is it?"

"It wasn't cybernetic," Queson pointed out. "And, as you say, it was *huge*. Put both of those in our wild hole and you might not be in any condition to get back once you get through, if you do. So let's assume they did. Lucky, you've looked at the old records with the lay-outs of Woodward's interstellar holy land. Am I off base here?"

"Nope, right on. In fact, Woodward was a physicist. He *had* to know, as did his pilots and crew, that it was gonna be damned near impossible to bring something that huge through, and, even if they did, to stabilize it in this environment when it emerged."

"Faith," the doctor responded. "Faith moves moun-tains. He would have no choice but to act on his faith, particularly if he thought God was directing them here."

"Yeah, faith moves mountains. Faith Explosives, Queenspark, Marchellus," Nagel said with a chuckle.

They ignored him. "So be speculative based on what you know. What might happen if Woodward got this far but with a banged-up ship?"

"He'd never fully control it if it were really banged up," Cross noted. "And that thing was a fuckin' nightmare. All patchwork, the drives of different shapes and sizes and manufacture . . . Wouldn't take much to really screw 'em up, and this system's got everything you need. If he had no real control, then he's gone, either into the void, into the big gasbag there, or into the sun, and so are all his followers. But if he could get it stabilized to any degree, long enough to cram his people into his planetary lander, then he'd be able to do something if he and they got away from the big mother fast enough. That far out, you'd spend most of your fuel fighting gravity for control, and even then you'd be pulled right into Mama's orbit here. That many people, that big a craft, that antique equipment and long struggle to get in-system . . . He'd have to make a quick decision. Pick one and head for there. And which one would *you* pick under those circumstances, assuming he could see and get some details of all three?"

There was an easy answer to that. "So you'd say the big part probably went into the planet or the sun, but my largest residual power supply is probably his lander?"

"That'd be my guess. Unless they were really creamed, there's no reason they shouldn't have gotten down all right, but they would stay there."

"You think the moon would prevent a takeoff?"

"Nope. But takeoff to *where*? You ain't got power to get back *to* the hole, let alone get through it. And you'd be in a ship with no instrumentation or drives capable of wormhole travel. That's certain death even if they did the impossible and made it that far back, and I'm damned sure they couldn't. The best they could do would be to risk that topheavy, probably damaged and over-large antique to go to one of the other moons. So where do you go? Volcano City or Sandstorm Hell? Even if you *could* even make it *that* far."

"Point taken. But that was only . . . what? Under a century, certainly. There could very well be survivors of Woodward's original crew still living down there, assuming it's not a blind and that some of this life we're reading is edible. And they'd have a pretty solid colony there by now."

An Li looked at the optical view of Balshazzar in the C&C main board view window. "Yeah, and I *bet* there's edible stuff there. The thing is, those other signatures. Put that together with our alien ship from Kaspar and we got a more interesting question on this one."

"Yeah? What?"

"If those are *alien* survivors and groups down there— the other signatures, I mean— then did they wipe out the humans as they prayed, or are they commingling, or is there war in Paradise?"

Randi Queson shrugged. "I think we'll know in under a day, assuming *we* can keep off the damned surface of the place."

It *was* a pretty world, whether a moon or a planet. The explorers and scouts would classify it as a Class One Terran, not only a world capable of sustaining human life unaided but one that might even evolve such life. If An Li's aliens existed and were in any sense of the word life as they knew and understood it, then this was the world they would have come from.

"Sixty-three percent ocean, another three percent internal lakes, and thirty-three percent land masses," Jerry Nagel noted. "Axial tilt's under eight degrees, so there's probably little in the way of seasons from that source. Rotation on axis twenty-two point six standard hours, pretty close to nominal. Two northern continents with several huge islands, and a matching two southern continents, different in shape and size, plus more islands big and small. The majority of land is in the mid-latitudes, which is all to the good, since the periods when this sucker is getting hit from the sun have got to fry almost anything within those eight-degree tropics. Otherwise, we're talking a high when facing the mother planet of roughly thirty-one degrees centigrade, a low about eighteen, those at sea level, of course. Ocean water is saline, temperatures from the tropic lines to the continental borders roughly twenty-seven to thirty degrees, polar side temps about twenty-one degrees down to maybe thirteen at the surface. Within the tropics the temps are bearable now, but even if they cool down at the current rate while on this side they'll be within tropical norms for this type of planet. Sunward, I'd put those tropical regions at crisp, extra crisp, well done, and deep fried."

"So the life's on the continents, mostly, and the islands?" An Li asked, looking at the pictorials.

"Well, that's the thing. It's *everywhere*. The oceans are teeming with it, the continents have their sparse spots but dense concentrations in the best overall geographic areas. Still, I would suspect as much from the wide variations produced by this system. Since there's no evidence of roads or major structures to accompany the areas of dense population, I'd say that unless some of them have wings, they walk everywhere, and that probably means they stick fairly close to home. Territorial. When your 'year' is only fifteen or sixteen standard days, your 'seasons' basically last for maybe three or four days each. Not much time for real variation, but it sure keeps the weather systems stirred up. Most storms are produced by cold air meeting warm air. I bet the transition from sun to planet source only is pretty violent in the weather department, and you can see a lot of nasty-looking local stuff swirling around in the tropics right now. Give them solar heat and they'll become monsters."

"You're making it sound a lot less appealing all of a sudden," Randi Queson commented. "Stuck in your local garden, killer storms and tropical rains, and no machines worth a damn. That's a recipe for taking humanity back hundreds of thousands of years or more."

Nagel shrugged. "Maybe. They probably don't have to do much hunting, though, or wander too far to eat. That looks damned rich down there, and if there are human heat signatures then a lot of it is edible for folks like us. And, of course, it's a life of essentially leisure, fresh air, all natural foods and drink, and no natural enemies. If the nonhuman elements either don't mix or are friendly, then everybody's in the same boat, as it were. It's probably pretty damned dull."

Queson sighed. "Poor Dr. Woodward."

"Huh? Why do you say that?"

"A man of his great intellect and great faith, down on an alien world, meeting up with aliens as smart or smarter than we are who also are probably the survivors or descendants of survivors of expeditions past. Imagine the meeting. Imagine how it might shake him when he discovers they haven't discovered Jesus, or perhaps have a totally different concept of God and the universe, perhaps even no religious beliefs or concepts at all."

"Wouldn't bother guys like him a bit," Nagel assured her. "I seem to remember that those types went looking for civilizations that hadn't heard the Word as they themselves saw it and then converted them, by force, hook, or crook if necessary. Vaticanus still has an Office for the Propagation of the Faith, or whatever they called it, better known as the Inquisition. Torture them until they either convert or die. Either way, God's will is done. Bring Bibles to the heathen, but make sure you also bring booze to trade for the slaves. Or God tells the faithful to join an army and conquer the world for Him. So they do, and destroy the other religions as heathen, desecrate or destroy the old churches, temples, and monuments, and if you can't convert 'em, well, their *children* will convert, or be slaves. Naw . . . He wouldn't see it as a break in his faith. He'd see it as being handed by God the opportunity to be the first one to convert non-humans."

"My, you *are* cynical," she responded.

"You're the social scientist. My world is hard science. Numbers, experiments, repeatable data searches. We hard science types never were great at grasping how human behavior works on the grand scale, but I think I have my history pretty much right, don't I?"

"More or less, I guess. But not everybody is like that, even within a religious faith."

"Well, much of human history's misery has been caused by religion. As far as I'm concerned, it's all bunk."

"Well, we'll all go our own way on that. Coming up on Balshazzar now. Cap, you have an energy signature that might in any way match a downed shuttle of the type Woodward's group used?"

"I've got a possibility," the captain responded. "I am trying to hail it on all standard frequencies in use at that time. Nothing so far."

"Yeah, well, I think if I were down there and spent eighty years calling with nobody picking up the other end I'd probably stop hanging out near the phone myself," Nagel said. "Still, there's enough power for them to keep things going assuming the ship's intact?"

"Oh yes, although one would expect it to be half buried and overgrown in that area by now. There has definitely been flooding in the area, although the floodplain may not have been in that area when they landed. These do shift."

"What's the population in that floodplain area right now?" Queson asked her. "Roughly speaking, of course."

"Difficult to say. Rough estimate would be between one thousand and one thousand five hundred. They are camped just off the plain, in a very large area of groves and springs, but it may well be that we have had some luck if we want to contact them. I am not at all certain you are correct that they remain in one place. This looks like a migration of sorts, or perhaps a pilgrimage. They are just now gathering. It is impossible to know how many there will ultimately be, but it could be a *lot*."

"All human?"

"*Mostly* human. There are readings that indicate some lateral traffic from some sort of life giving off nonhuman signatures."

"Does it appear like a hostile movement?"

"Who can say? Logic tells me that if you are thinking of being hostile to a group of one to two thousand you'd best bring more than a few dozen of your own."

"Good point. Okay, so either they don't go into the old ship anymore because they can't, they think it's holy ground, or they already have everything they can get from it, or they just haven't gotten enough of a crowd yet. In any event, we're in no position to wait for them to do it, and we have no idea whether they can or will pick up the communications. It's pretty clear we need some way to talk to them, after first letting them know we're here at all. Any suggestions? Anybody?"

"I could just take the shuttle down and say hello," Lucky Cross suggested. "That seems the simplest and easiest."

"On the surface, yes," An Li responded. "But if that's Woodward's ship and people and it's got power, they might be expected to have checked the rest of the system out. They didn't. Neither did the aliens, if that's what they are, and we have signatures from *their* ships as well. How many ship-to-ground shuttles have we got on this run, Lucky?"

"You know damn well we only got the same one. Otherwise it's just the escape pods."

"I say we need a unanimous vote, then, to take that shuttle down *anywhere*, since we have no evidence it can get back up again from down there and some evidence maybe it can't. Without that shuttle, we may as well go home."

Jerry Nagel looked over at Eyegor. "There's always the robot. Hell, this is a *much* better place to send the thing than the other one. At least it won't be alone down there."

"You seem bent on getting rid of me," the robot responded. "In response this time I ask a variation of the same question just asked on the shuttle. Is it plausible that at least one, perhaps *most* of those stuck down there brought with them AI devices of some sort? If so, where are they? They should also show up on our scans."

"The thing's got a point," Nagel said, nodding. "Not much in the way of mechanized anything down there, unless it's levers and ropes and pulleys. There are several known combinations of radiation and energy fields known to damage or destroy AI synapses while being harmless to humans. There are more the other way around, I admit, but the former's not that unusual."

"So what does that leave?" Queson asked nobody in particular.

"A probe," the captain responded. "It is simple and has minimal AI circuitry and maximum shielding. It is used for low-level measurements."

"Yeah, but that's just a remote-controlled camera ball like old Eyegor's head there," Sark pointed out. "What good does that do us?"

"It can be rigged to carry a few things," the captain reminded them. "Its cargo is limited, but we could put a couple of ferrets in there, or perhaps simply use it not as a recorder but as a playback device. If they can call us, it'll tell them to do so. If they can't, we'll work out a way to send something down that can."

"Too much AI in the ferrets to take a chance until we know for sure they'll work," An Li said firmly. "But the idea of using a probe as basically a speaker works well, and since a probe is designed to be disposable we don't have to worry if it can't get back. Stick a handheld ship-to-ship intercom in the storage compartment just in case. I'm not thrilled about losing one, but we *have* to talk to them."

Once decided, it was easier to rig up and execute than it was to discuss it.

The probes were very small devices shielded for entry and designed to send up close-in data across any spectrum, do soil and atmospheric analysis, and give the basics they or anyone else would need before planning a manned landing on an alien world. In essence they were simply small, remote-controlled data collectors made cheaply and designed for simple tasks. Analysis was always aboard ship; they only sent a data stream of what they were told to examine.

It was something of a microphone, and all a speaker is is a microphone in reverse, creating the opposite pattern on a surface capable of receiving it. These were strictly single use, send or receive—but they included the ground-to-air handheld transceiver in case they didn't have a better way.

"Last chance," the captain warned. "Everyone still all right with this?"

"Send it," Nagel told her. The probe was quickly away.

To keep it intact and from burning up as it entered the atmosphere, they took about an hour and a quarter to get the thing into the atmosphere. After that, it was a simple matter to fly it towards the supposed human colony while the *Stanley* took up geosynchronous orbit.

"Jeez! I just thought of something," Randi Queson said worriedly.

"Yeah? What?" Nagel was just hoping to hear about all those weird jewels for the taking, or maybe alien technology, and other stuff like that.

"I was just thinking—if they've gone this long without anything mechanical, and if life is hard enough down there so the elders are basically dead, then what kind of reaction are we gonna get when this—this *voice* suddenly comes out of this little ball? They might think God is talking to them!"

"All the better," Nagel replied cynically. "Then God can just command them to go gather all their valuables. *Much* easier than telling them, 'This is a stickup.'"

X:

WEST OF EDEN . . .

"You don't live on a floodplain if you don't have to," Randi Queson noted, talking as much to herself as to the others. "I wonder why they leave better pickings up north and come down here? It certainly must be something they do at broader intervals; it wouldn't make any sense to do this except once in a great while, maybe as a ritual, maybe as simply a gathering of a clan that's otherwise spread out."

"Well, you're the anthropologist," Nagel said. "Me, I have a hard time spelling it. But if that's the old preacher's ship, and it's sure looking big enough to be a whole damned cathedral, then maybe it's Christmas or something."

"Well, maybe they can tell *us*," An Li commented. "We're in heavy air and going in close. Cap, can you turn the live shot on from the probe?"

"A few more seconds," the captain responded. "Nothing

to see yet. Ah! *There!* Well, at least they're human and they're not *quite* Adam and Eve."

"Sure they are," Queson breathed. "Just after the Fall."

It was quite an assembly of bodies they saw, all weathered and darkened by exposure. There seemed to be a mixture of philosophies on how to deal with the primitive conditions as well; men and women either tended to have very long hair, the men beards as well, or they shaved their heads. There didn't seem to be anybody obvious with a middle-ground point of view.

None of them, save the youngest children, were naked, although the women tended to be bare-breasted, with a few exceptions for some sort of halter top, and just about all had their private parts concealed at least in a basic fashion, primarily by vines worn tightly at the hips with some kind of leaves or short woven grasses draped over the front and sometimes back and held there in some way. All were barefoot.

They were roughly equally divided by sex, although there might have been a few more women than men per plot of ground, and they seemed to represent all ages. None appeared particularly chubby, but likewise none looked to be starving, either. The thin ones were naturally thin, the more full-figured types seemed to be, well, filled out a bit more, that was all.

But they *did* have possessions. Clearly somebody had figured out how to make cloth by hand out of a cottonlike plant, and others had found dyes, for there were blankets, even homemade tent shelters made with the blankets and gathered and trimmed sticks so the little ones, and anybody else who felt he or she needed some shelter, could get it. There were also gourds that clearly carried water or other drinks.

"I doubt if they go back long enough to have evolved to this social and technological level," Randi commented. "From what I can see, these are people who are forced to primitivism and know it, not people who are necessarily primitives."

"Could be," An Li agreed. "Catch the Elders there."

What she referred to were a number of men, perhaps a few dozen within the range of the camera, who seemed markedly different from the others. They had manes of gray or even snow-white hair, flowing beards, and carried long walking sticks, possibly staves of office. They were also the only ones who wore full-body clothing, a robe made of what seemed a lighter-grade cloth than the blanket material that hung on their bodies, with a hole cut in the center for the head and two other holes for the arms. They were all dyed a kind of pink-orange color, which made them very easy to spot in the mobs.

"Buddhist monks who fell off the wagon?" Sark asked cynically.

"The Kingdom of Prester John," Randi Queson said, ignoring the snide jokes. "An ancient legend of a European-style kingdom far off in the Himalayan Mountains, the source of Buddhism, but yet Christians. It's just what I'd expect a Karl Woodward to come up with."

"We'll take your word for it," Lucky Cross responded dryly. In point of fact, Queson was probably the only one there who knew what the term "European" meant, let alone the details and legends, but she was right about one thing.

Karl Woodward would have known, and it was very much the sort of thing he might come up with.

"We've been noticed," the captain pointed out.

The probe wasn't very large, designed more for carrying information and perhaps a soil sample than anything else, but it was certainly larger than anything native to Balshazzar, and very, very odd looking.

The kids had seen it first, then started shouting and pointing at it, and this caused the adults and ultimately the pink-robed elders to pay attention as well.

"It's showtime," An Li said. "Enable probe speaker mode."

"Enabled," the captain reported.

An Li took a deep breath, then said, in a calm, measured tone, "Hello, people of Balshazzar. We are the exploration ship *Stanley* in orbit around your world. If you still have any functioning communications devices on your ship, please have someone who knows how to use them do so. We will wait. If you do not, please indicate this when I say the word 'over' and we will drop one to you. *Over!*"

There was a hushed silence as the probe again became a receiver. Even the kids had suddenly fallen silent, and save for the cries of some of the infants there was a nearly dead silence.

"You think maybe they don't understand us?" An Li asked.

Queson shook her head "no." "It's just shock. They didn't expect this. Wait a little bit."

Finally, one of the elders with flowing white hair and beard, looking, save for the saffron-colored robe like some Biblical patriarch, came forward and clearly meant to address them.

"We must wait for the Doctor before we can enter the Cathedral," he said in the kind of tones you might expect from some ancient epic. "Only he may enter, then we follow."

"Jesus! You don't suppose old Doc Woodward's still *alive* down there, do you?" Lucky Cross exclaimed. "He'd be like three hundred years old or something!"

An Li shrugged. "Enable speaker."

"Enabled."

"Can you tell me when your leader will be here? Are we talking days, weeks, or whenever? Over," she asked the old man. Then, to the captain, "Receive mode."

" . . . will come when the faithful have all gathered here," the elder said, the first couple of words being cut off before the mode could be reversed. "It is his decision alone when after that to come."

"Speaker. Sorry, sir, but we can not wait on another calendar. I realize that your people aren't used to clocks and schedules anymore, but we are. We need information, and we will provide what we can to tend to your people's needs, but we can not wait around indefinitely. Can't you or someone already in the gathering speak to these issues? Over."

" . . . is not a democracy but an assemblage of God under the loving but firm discipline of the teacher," the old man came back. "It is not for us to decide what only he can decide."

Suddenly, from within a grove a few hundred meters from the hovering probe and the old elder, came a figure much like the elders in the flowing white hair and beard—but this one was clearly different. *His* staff was also thicker, almost machined, and topped with some kind of design, and his robe was not saffron pink but a dirty gray. People made way for him deferentially as he approached the other, and even the elder, turning and seeing the approaching figure, bowed slightly and moved away.

"Could that be Doc Woodward?" Cross wondered.

"Somehow I don't think so. That man doesn't walk like a preacher, he walks like a cop or a naval officer," An Li noted.

The figure was really imposing; the gray man radiated a power, confidence, and strength that even came through the viewing screen. This was somebody to be feared, but who said by his very posture and look that he himself feared nothing.

"I am the Chief of Security for the Congregation of the Faithful," he said in a voice that fit the image perfectly: strong, sharp, cutting right through you. "Drop me your communicator. I can get inside, but getting that old junk up and operating would take a while after all this time."

An Li saw no reason to doubt him. She positioned the probe just above the gray man and opened the small, iris-like hatch and tilted the ball slightly. The communicator fell out, and the man caught it and examined it.

"Still surplus," he commented, as much to himself as to them. "I gather the Great Silence is still—silent?" He punched the controls like a man who knew the equipment perfectly. "This better?"

"For us, yes," An Li told him.

"You are here but your ship is still functional?"

"Yes. We used a cybernetic pilot. It seems to be the only way to do it right."

"Damn! We should have thought of that! The Doctor, however, doesn't feel comfortable with cyberships. He tends to think that one of the things that doesn't get moved is a soul."

"Could be," An Li told him. "I've never seen anybody's soul so I can't comment on whether the captain has one or not—or me, either, for that matter. But I sure didn't sell it, so if I had one it's still here someplace."

"Most people do not sell their souls," the gray man told her, taking the comment seriously. "Most people give theirs away, and far too cheaply. And you are . . . ?"

"An Li, Exec of the *Stanley*. Other than the captain, I have a ship-to-surface and surface-craft pilot, Gail Cross; a chief engineer, Jerry Nagel; a technician, Olon Sark; and a cultural anthropologist and sometimes geologist and lots of other things as well, Dr. Randi Queson."

"My name is Cromwell. How did you find the route to this place, if I may ask?"

"You are Dr. Woodward's colony?"

"You might call it that, yes."

"Well, that's how. The Doctor consulted with an old colleague and gave him the key to finding the Kings, knowing the man would never violate the trust nor come himself. Well, that colleague died, and someone with too much money bought the effects, including that, and then went looking for people dumb enough to see if it was real. Here we are."

"You are an exploration ship?"

"No, actually, we're all salvagers. Just not this trip. Salvagers were the only ones crazy enough to take this job. And desperate enough."

Cromwell thought about it. "I see. Well, first and foremost, you must not land here."

"Is there a problem? Or aren't we welcome?"

"You are as welcome as anyone, but if you come down you will not get back off. This is not a natural place. It looks like Heaven, but it is not. Cain went to the lands east of Eden and began human civilization. This is more or less *west* of Eden. All our basic needs are here, but there are no heavy metals nor other major components that would allow us industry. In other words, we're pretty well stuck like this, and so is everybody else who lands. Limbo, we sometimes call it, or Eden with the snake already in charge. I have your communicator. Try and retrieve your probe. Go ahead, try it."

An Li looked at the others, who pretty much shrugged, so she said, "Cap, bring the probe back."

"Retrieving," the captain responded. The probe lifted off rather normally, quickly reducing the people below to dots and then to nothing as it got high and encountered a cloud layer.

"That must be a hell of a cloud layer," Cross commented.

But it wasn't. "The probe ascent has slowed to almost stationary," the captain told them. "I have it at full power and I appear to have full control, but it simply will not rise any more."

She took a horizontal approach, but every time she tried to increase altitude above the six-thousand-meter mark, it stuck.

"Dump your samples, see if that will work," Cross suggested.

"Did that already. Something is exerting a specific gravitational or magnetic or whatever kind of force on the probe. It kicks on at six thousand, it kicks off at any point below it. I believe we have experienced the man's demonstration. I am returning the probe to its old position so we can see them again easily."

An Li didn't wait. "All right, we're impressed."

"So were we," the gray man responded. "And so was everyone else who landed on this world. You can come here, you can live here, within its limits, you can do what you like, but nothing, once down, rises again. We tried to track it, assuming it was some sort of beam or directional ray, but our instruments showed nothing. Perhaps yours . . . ?"

"Nothing here either," the captain told them. "I have no idea how or from where it's being applied."

"I take it, then, we should attempt no landing here considering this situation?"

"I would not advise it, although there *are* advantages to living here. For example, I not only should be dead of old age here, I in fact *was* killed here when we first landed. And yet, here I am."

"Are you saying that you're immortal? That you rose from the dead?" Randi Queson was more of a believer than Jerry Nagel, but not to *this* degree.

"Oh, not really. You just don't age at the same rate here as you do off this planet. I have no idea if it is a natural phenomenon or something connected to the same force or forces that prevent anything from leaving— if, indeed, they *are* artificial forces and not just some other natural phenomenon we haven't any way to measure as yet. Your guess is as good as mine. At least it appears that we have no problems communicating outside the atmosphere, although we've been unable to communicate with any of the other moons."

"You've tried?"

"Yes, we did everything you'd think of all those years ago when we finally wound up here. And, before us, several nonhuman groups as stuck as we are tried as well. We have only limited contact to this day with most of them—I don't believe anyone ever really realizes what the term 'alien' really means until you face it—but one set, the Meskok, we've had excellent relations with from the beginning. I am by no means convinced that they are any less alien than the others, and physiologically they are bizarre, but they are also directional telepaths, meaning they don't read minds in the mass but can convey thoughts and receive directed thoughts when speaking to specific people. They are very good at it. They seem, mentally, just like us, and they are quite sly and yet knowledgeable about us because they can get things from our minds. Whether they are simply adapted to being great interspecies communicators or are truly good poker players can't be known, since we, obviously, can't read *their* thoughts beyond what they use for conversation. They are also excellent at adapting to even the most alien biology. It was one of them who brought me back to life within minutes of my being shot and killed so long ago, not far from this spot. They've been essential to us as basic medical resources, since, like most people in our age, even our doctors don't know how to fix a hangnail without a computer surgery."

"And what do they get from you?"

"Diversions. A new group for study. They are fascinated by how different races of beings come to be, and how they come up both in invention and cultures. We were the first humans of sufficient numbers for their study. They know it probably won't mean much, considering they're trapped here as much as we, but it gives them something to do. I suspect your anthropologist could sympathize. This group is more or less in the same business."

"Are any there?" Randi asked him. "I should like to speak to one."

"Not possible. I could bring one over, but you'd need a translator, and it would be awkward considering how they communicate. There is no way for them to broadcast over any of our communicators, nor for you to receive and comprehend any of theirs."

"What did you say your name was?" the anthropologist asked, disappointed but realizing the impracticality of using audio channels to speak to a telepath.

"Thomas Cromwell," he responded crisply, some of the old military snap suddenly back in his voice and stance.

"Got him on the list of Woodward's people from the archives," the captain said to them, but not for broadcast. "That's not his real name. Said to have been a spit-and-polish naval admiral with a totally ruthless outlook on orders and duty. He is said to have been responsible for the death of whole inhabited planets during that period. Then, something happened. Nobody knew what, but it was profound. He resigned, joined Woodward as security chief, and became dedicated to Woodward and Woodward's view of the Christian godhead. A very mysterious character and still considered very dangerous when he served Woodward's flying mission."

"So what was his real name? Is it somebody so infamous we'd have heard of it?" Queson asked.

"Possibly. Probably. But we don't know it. This material is gathered anecdotally and indirectly. I'm sure intelligence and military groups know it, but it's as if he were wiped out of the public and general private records. A man powerful enough to get that kind of official cover is somebody who can unbury every secret body of everyone in power this side of the Silence. A man they're so scared of they didn't even dare kill him."

"Maybe they were right," Sark noted. "I mean, according to him, he was shot dead and even *that* didn't stop him."

Nagel turned and looked at the big man. "You really believe that story?"

"Cromwell's got a dozen or so aliens within a couple of hundred meters of him right now," An Li noted, pointing to the signatures. "We haven't even picked them up on camera; he's been living with them for decades. How many aliens have *you* ever met, Jerry? *Spacefaring* aliens. *Technological* aliens. Who knows what they can do? Hell, *we* could probably have brought him back if the shot was just so."

"Yeah, provided he was shot in the hospital, right in the casualty ward," Cross noted. "Still, there's no reason not to believe him. Funny, too. Haven't heard a goddamn religious term yet!"

Queson thought about that, and opened the channel. "Mr. Cromwell, what about your and Doctor Woodward's theology? Has encountering all these other races and points of view changed things?"

"Only in amplification," the gray man responded. "Nothing changes. Most people never read or gave any thought to religion; it's the one complex field where everybody is a self-styled expert even though they've done not the most basic study of it, not any more than the twisted and vile traditions they grew up with or the wrong-headed visions they were taught by those same ones. And when God throws a fast one at them, or kills their innocent loved one, something like that, they lose what little faith they had and curse God or ignore Him. The Doctor was one of the few who studied religion the way he studied physics, and drew his own conclusions."

"Yeah? And what does he say to somebody when their kid dies even though that person prayed to God to let the kid live?" Nagel asked.

An Li rolled her eyes and hoped she could head off any theological arguments here.

"The question to ask isn't why God didn't cure the child, but why God *should* cure the child," Cromwell responded. "You see, God's our boss. We work for Him, and we're stuck with whatever He demands of us. What did *we* do that makes us deserve special attention? He's not a magic genie granting wishes, He's not Daddy in the Deep Universe, He's God. It's not a popular vision, but that's why our Bible says that so few people will ever make it to Heaven. God knows *this* isn't it. We didn't have much choice or time to explore, you see. We were in bad trouble and had to land, knowing we almost certainly would be stuck, unable to take off on our own. The Doctor picked this one for the same reason any of us would, and he was fooled. He has never forgiven himself for it."

"Well, it still looks a lot nicer than the other two," An Li put in, thankful to be able to steer the talk away from theology, even though she could see Nagel just primed to go off on some angry rant.

"Yes, it does, but it's the *easy* way. You don't have to work here. There is food everywhere, and water, and fruit for juices, and you can even ferment things. There are no natural predators, virtually no biting things, and the climate runs from extremely hot to very warm. The other races who crashed here are not hostile, just stuck like us. It's quite *boring*, you see. Kind of a sweet Hell, which is why we think of it as Limbo. You can't build much, you can't do much for posterity, you can't look to the future because the future's most likely to be the same as the present. And, as I demonstrated, even using someone else's ship, we aren't going anywhere. Here, at the crash site, is the only repository of human knowledge, the only source of human and theological writings, the only place where you can learn anything and at least keep some things alive. We can't stay here, though—the place floods every couple of years and we have to come and dig the old ship out—yet the seals are good enough to protect the knowledge inside and the energy cells, with some solar help, can go for a very long time. So we gather at set times, and we learn from the Doctor and from those he's trained, and we pray together and keep our faith and our identity. But we can't do much else."

"And your ship's unmovable? Even short distances?" Cross asked him.

Cromwell nodded. "It suffered major damage to the drives. Only God's will got us down in one piece, but we're stuck here."

"And you and the Doctor still think you'd have been better off on either of the other moons?" Queson asked him, fascinated.

"The Doctor certainly does, although we can't know if we'd be as stuck there as here. Do you?"

"We only surveyed Kaspar, the cold one, and we attempted no landing. Crashed alien craft on the surface, though, so it doesn't bode well," Cross told him.

"Yes, perhaps. Perhaps not. You are the first ship to seem to manage a safe passage, at least so far, so you may learn and return. If and when you do, please contact us before leaving. We have a list. I don't know how we'd pay you, but perhaps someone would."

"A list? Of amenities?"

"Not exactly. Recordings, books, plays, all sorts of things like that. Learning and study machines. This is a noncelibate monastery of sorts. We need material."

"Our boss was born without a heart, so we can't promise anything, but we'll certainly take the list," Randi assured him. "In the meantime, there is *nothing* down there that is of any value in the Three Kings legendary traditions?"

"No. Not that we've ever seen. A wealth of aliens, with their own technology and such, but nothing native."

"What about Melchior?" Nagel asked, having calmed down and getting back to business. "Any of your aliens know anything about it?"

"I suspect you may be able to get down and back,"

Cromwell told him. "At least one of the races here stopped there first and managed it. That was why they were so easily suckered into landing here. I know through exchanges of information that the legendary Magi gems come from there, but where and how I can't say. That's certainly worth your trip, though, if you can get them and get back."

This was interesting. "Any sign of any habitation there, like here?"

"There is habitation on all three worlds," Cromwell told them. "We have seen the evidence from here when the other two rise in the night sky. Moving lights, huge but regular vegetation areas, that kind of thing. Melchior is often hidden by its smoky atmosphere and volcanic activity, but you can definitely see evidence of what seems to be artificial things using simple optical scopes from here. Be cautious, though. It's got to be a greenhouse down there, hotter than you can imagine with all that volcanism, and we've seen huge patches through those clouds where the very continents seemed to break into irregular jagged islands floating on bright lava cracks. You don't see much, but we've had a lot of time and, as I've said, nothing much else to do."

An Li sighed. "Okay. Well, look, that's our next stop. We'll try and locate you via the communicator when we leave and drop by if at all possible. Maybe we'll meet your Doctor then."

"Maybe you will. I think you certainly should. He'd like you, and I think you'd like him."

"With all your gathering, I'm surprised he isn't already there to greet all of you," Queson put in.

Cromwell laughed, something he clearly didn't do much of. "No, he *would* be here, but he has something to finish first, and that always comes first."

"A religious period? Some kind of solitary wilderness preparation of prayer and fasting?"

"Oh, my, no! He went to a small Meskok village to

negotiate for some superb sparkling wine they get from one of the other less approachable races, and I believe he got sucked into a poker tournament there. Texas hold 'em, I believe it is. For a full cask, of course . . ."

"He was putting us on, you know," Jerry Nagel commented as they prepared to leave orbit. In the back of all their minds was whether or not they'd be *able* to break orbit, but it wasn't something any of them wanted to dwell on until or unless it happened.

"What do you mean, putting us on?" Randi Queson asked him. "According to the records, if that indeed *was* Thomas Cromwell of the Woodward expedition he was not known for having *any* sense of humor whatsoever."

"Nevertheless, he made his joke. Think about it. These—what'cha callit— *Meskoks* were telepaths, right?"

"So he said."

"And poker is based on cards and on your ability to convince opponents that your hidden hand can beat theirs, whether or not it could."

"Yes, I—*oh*! I *see*! How could you play cards with telepaths? Fascinating. Either Woodward's discovered a solution to that problem or, you are correct, Cromwell was pulling our leg. The odds are he was doing the latter, but if a man who's not known for his sense of humor does *that*, he's got an ulterior motive. He also was a lot gabbier than the files say he should have been."

"I wouldn't put too much stake in that last thing," An Li commented. "I mean, he's been a very long time between conversations with folks from the outside."

"True. Funny, though, that aside from commenting on how our technology wasn't any better than he remembered from way in the past, he asked no questions at all about things back in his home region. Not even whether or not they'd been missed," Nagel noted. "Yeah, they're hiding something, that's for sure."

"You think they were doing that bit with the probe

to keep us from coming down and finding out their secrets?" An Li asked him.

"Could be. Probably not them, but maybe their alien friends. We didn't see any of them, but we *do* know they're there because of the energy signatures, and we had indications of their downed ships as well. I don't know. That's Woodward's survivors, though. I'm pretty sure of that. And I really do think they got stuck there. What they're hiding, what they found, and what they might be working on under those pink dresses and white beards, well, you got me, at least for now. As to whether or not they or the aliens or some mysterious force was doing it with the probe, who knows? The solution there is a lot more pragmatic. *Something* was doing it. It was for real. It means that if we did choose to find out what's below there, what they're hiding, then we'd probably be stuck there anyway. We can still take some more looks later on, though. Let's see how many probes we have left when we finish up here. If it's any at all, I'd like to take a real close look at some of the other parts of that planet."

The captain broke into the conversation. "You will all be relieved to know that we have just pulled out of orbit around Balshazzar and are now heading for Melchior. Unless, of course, you have second thoughts on that."

"Huh? Why should we?" Nagel asked her.

"Because that's where your Cromwell sent us, the man you just decided was lying through his teeth. Magi gems all over, he said. That's a good lure for saying to us all, 'Don't look here any further, go over to Melchior. The riches are all over the place there.' "

"Well, they invited us back before we left," Sark pointed out.

"Yeah. To pick up their grocery list. Please send milk, bread, and toilet paper. And maybe some dyes that aren't a shade of pink," Lucky Cross said. "That also gives them time to get together and decide what the hell they want to do about us when we *do* come back. I don't like it."

Randi Queson sighed. "Maybe we *should* drop Eyegor off on the way out. It could get great footage of alien civilizations and technologies to beam up to us or other ships when we return."

"That is not my primary mission," the robot said, repeating its favorite phrase. "If I cannot leave once down, I cannot fulfill my entire mission, as I will not be able to be on this ship when it leaves. My footage means nothing if it does not get back."

"Yeah, well, I'm not sure whoever runs things around here *wants* detailed directions, pictures, and a road map to get back," An Li pointed out. "The record isn't very good on that score."

"We got to keep that in mind at all times," Lucky Cross said firmly. "Nobody's ever gotten back, and no ship's even gotten back with all its data. We're not even halfway yet—we don't have nothin' to cash in to pay the bills and make us rich and famous. And that last third, getting back whole, could be the roughest part of the deal."

XI:

FIRE AND SMOKE AND MIRRORS

"I don't know what frankincense or myrrh smell like, but I bet neither of 'em smells like Melchior does now," Lucky Cross commented, looking at the planet coming into full-screen view.

If Kaspar had been cold and forbidding, and Balshazzar warm and sweet, then Melchior could only be described as someone's vision of Hell.

Clouds shrouded the planet, which was much larger than the other two combined yet seemed to have a gravitational pull only fifteen percent or so above "average," or one gee. There were oceans down there—in one way it might be called a water world, as it had countless enormous islands but, for its size, no great continents—but the oceans weren't the warm and pleasant blue-green of Balshazzar nor the icy but crisp ones of Kaspar, but rather oceans dark and deep. Measurements using subsurface scanning often could not find their bottoms.

It was, however, simply a matter of time, for Melchior seemed hellbent on spewing its guts out. Every one of the islands, great and small—and they were so numerous that definitions had to be changed in order to properly count them—seemed to have a volcano or two or three or several dozen that, if not active, was certainly not dead. And so active were the forces coming up from below the ocean floor that some of the larger islands could be seen coming apart, with that rippling jigsaw magma creating a patchwork quilt. Just as suddenly the magma would vanish, leaving black border scars and smoking black lava marks across even the regions that had no active belching mountains.

"Now *that* is not a land to cross in your bare feet," Lucky Cross said with a shaking of her head. "I'm not sure I want to cross that place at all."

"What I want to know is whether or not the damned moon's coming apart or coming together," Jerry Nagel said. "This place almost redefines the term 'geologically active.' Doc? You're our part-time geologist. What do you think?"

"I think it's another example of when you believe you've seen every combination in the universe you come up against something strange. This place is totally volcanic; I can't see any signs of massive erosion except on the very oldest and largest islands, and they're most likely to come apart in that nasty fragmentation effect. Plenty of flowing water, but I doubt if it stays the course long enough to create great canyons, and the eruptions and fragmentations tend to break down attempts at walling it up as lakes. Still, with the combination of sudden heating and cooling and the large amount of dust up there, it appears that what saves it from becoming a total oven is that it's only facing the sun one quarter of the time. It loses that heat pretty fast, but convection causes massive storms. Look at it now. It's raining over probably half that world down there, and it's a big one."

"It's closer than it should be to its mother planet," Cross noted. "That's what keeps it right in line to be victimized by all the forces tugging at it. Still, I see an awful lot of what looks to be vegetation down there. Just like Balshazzar, that soil's got to be absolutely wonderful for growing things, as long as it lasts, that is."

"Some green," Queson agreed, "but also a lot of purples, yellows, reds, oranges, even patches of vegetative white. I wonder how edible it is?"

"For us? Who knows?" Nagel responded. "Same problem as every new world. Which is poison and which isn't? Mineral content's mineral content, but who knows what vitamins it might have, or other nastier chemicals?"

"One thing's for sure," An Li put in. "You ain't gonna build any cities down there. Your roads would be washed away or crumbled away or dissolved by that lava, and the shakes and the rain would make permanent building a mess."

"Floaters," Jerry Nagel said.

"Huh?"

"The best place to live down there would be on a boat. A ship, maybe."

"Ship? You mean like on *water*?"

"I mean exactly that. You avoid that uncertainty, tie up and go ashore to harvest what you can there and bring it back, have an area where you make salt to pack things, and maybe you also have things in the sea you can catch or fetch and eat. If I were going to try to survive down there, that's what I'd have. A big boat."

"And what about those storms?" An Li argued. "There's lightning down there, you can see that, and ashfalls, and who knows what else. Out on that ocean in a monster storm, you'd be at the mercy of the elements more sudden and dangerous than the lava."

"Well, maybe. But there are so many islands there you're just about never out of sight of land, and if you chart the area there are, I'll bet, a ton of sheltered harbors. And for anything other than a direct hit, you might get seasick and damaged, but being out at sea during a severe storm is, believe it or not, the best place to be if your boat's built to take it," Nagel pointed out. "I was a sailor once, for fun, on an associate's boat."

"Anybody remember where we packed the yacht?" Sark asked in his usual cynical tone.

Randi looked over at Nagel. "He has a point, Jerry. Boat or ship or whatever or not, could you build one now, with just us, by hand?"

"With the salvage robots, maybe. That and a lot of design and some useful programs. That would presuppose that some of those trees down there are tough enough to take it and waterproof enough to build with. And, if we had access to ship's stores here, I suspect I could knock out a pretty good set of plastic plugs and bolts to hold it all together, and strong, unbreakable ropes for rigging and control. Yeah, with a little help from what's down there I might just be able to do a decent one."

"You mean people-type help?"

"No, I mean wood and such. We have a lot of stuff here that can disassemble a prefabricated unit, but I don't have a fabricator for large structures like a hull, keel, full decking, that kind of thing."

The captain interrupted. "Have all of you stopped discussing your dream sailboat long enough to look at the night side right now? If not, you should."

They all immediately looked at the screen and saw what the captain meant.

Melchior was a large planet with a low axial tilt; it revolved on its axis once every forty standard hours, giving it an average twenty-hour night.

They might all have expected some spectacular views, clouds or not, from the dark side, since it would produce full illumination of volcanic activities on the surface, lava flows, magma beds, and the like, and it certainly did that. The place was lit up like a festive holiday ornament, and from pole to pole. Factoring out the clouds, it was spectacular.

But there were other kinds of lights as well, much less pretty to look at but much more difficult to explain. On the larger islands and the smaller ones, and even in areas that should be ocean, there were definitely patterns that looked very much like the lights of small towns seen from a height. Most seemed to be on volcanic plains between large, dormant but threatening monster mountains, but some were up almost against the big volcanoes where the latter met the seacoast. Beyond the land areas, small but unnaturally regular shaped fields of lights could be seen in the waters, often rectangular or square, and in some cases triangular in shape.

"Is it just me, or do a lot of folks manage to live there somehow?" Sark asked.

"It appears that they do indeed, although none inland. Nobody's that crazy," Nagel pointed out.

"Who or what are they?" Randi Queson asked. "Can't we get detail?"

"We are stuck with infrared and off-spectrum measures down there," the captain informed them. "*Lots* of lifesigns, very little in the way of recognizable signatures. I'm going to put us back on the planet side and we'll see what we can see. I hope you *did* notice that there was considerable light but not heat from the forests, jungles, or whatever they are? And along the volcanic spillways? It appears that there is a great deal of natural phosphorescence down there. Not practical if you require a fire, but very handy if you protect it when you are suffering heavy clouds, ashfalls, major storms or a twenty-hour night."

"You said there weren't many recognizable signatures. I gather you mean that the people or whatever it is we're seeing aren't human?"

"That would be a good inference," the captain agreed. "Coming into daylight. I'm going to scan and see if we can find one of those towns or floating whatevers and enlarge it. The problem here is that there's a fair amount of stuff in the upper atmosphere that's distorting good visuals. I can't get more than a rough picture. Let's see if close-in IR helps at all."

The infrared pictures suffered equally because of the volcanism and the apparent inner heat that close to the surface. There were *some* pictures, both visual and IR, that showed vague shapes and strange-looking creatures, but they weren't detailed nor could much be inferred about them.

"Natives?" Queson asked.

"Don't bet on it," the captain replied. "A half dozen distinct signatures with larger numbers, more with very small numbers, and some definite power sources that are not natural. No shipwrecks, if that's what you mean, but the way the sources show up almost implies that they are from disassembled or salvaged interplanetary or orbital craft. Nothing big enough to go interstellar. Still, what would happen if you came down here? If you land in the water, you are vulnerable to those storms, and if you hit one of them or are otherwise breached, then your next stop is nineteen or twenty kilometers to the sea bottom. If you come in on land, better hit solid crust or you'll punch right through into liquid magma. If you *do* make it down, watch out for flows, torrential runoff on the clear downward plains from the first real rains, and so on. I suspect on a world this dynamic that landing and taking off again are going to be your biggest challenges."

An Li sighed. "I guess the next thing to do is to prep a probe and then send it down to see if we *can* get down and then get back up again. If we can, then some of us, at least, are going to have to go exploring. Any idea what the temperature is like down there?"

"Hot at sea level," Nagel reported. "Thirty-six, thirty-seven on the planet side, no lower than thirty even on the night side. Estimates are you can expect as high as forty-eight to maybe even fifty on the full-sun exposed day side, going down to a chilly forty-two or so when that side's towards the planet. The only reason it's even within *that* range is because of the heavy rains that seem to happen at some point every day for ninety percent of the whole damned planet. We'll need the probe to find out what kind of particulates are in the air. Bet on a lot, which isn't going to be great for the lungs, so protective masks might be in order. The humidity's going to be very high at any point where there's vegetation or other life, so anybody without air conditioning is going to broil pretty good."

"We could go down with full environment suits," Randi suggested hopefully.

"No dice. With a fifteen percent average gain in weight on the surface, those suits will weigh a ton. The gravimetric ground shuttles aren't going to be much good, either; they weren't designed for it. There's a surprising magnetic field, though, for being a moon. We might be able to use the maglev scooters Li got us over Normie's yowls. We'll see. Let's get a probe down and back first."

Within minutes, the probe was programmed and sent on its way by the captain.

"Jeez! I'm not sure I ever was anyplace that hot," Lucky Cross noted.

"You have the second easiest job here, after the captain's, at this stage," Jerry reminded her. "I don't think we want to keep our shuttle on the ground any longer than we need to get out and drop equipment. You'll be our cover, shuttling between the ship and us and staying on station in case we need the navy to come to the rescue. Our greedy selves have left us with not nearly enough people for this job, so we'll just have to suffer for money. First things first. Let's pick our spots and then we'll create a prospecting plan, as it were."

"Be nice if we knew even a little of what we were looking for," Randi Queson sighed. "In salvage, you're just looking for the inconsistent, the artificial in a natural environment, like the colony on that wormball. Even in the old days, you prospected for gold, silver, uranium, even copper and lead. Here we're just looking for 'valuable things' we can haul back. Some guidance."

"We'll know it when we see it," An Li said confidently.

"Yeah? Alien changeling gems just lying in heaps all over the place, right? Yeah, sure. I don't think it's gonna be that easy."

"You worry too much."

You will, too, Randi Queson thought looking over at the small woman. *You'll worry a lot when it's you who are down there, not safe up here, and it's your dainty little ass on the line.*

The probe did its job and quite well.

"Very low particulate readings," Nagel reported. "Interesting. The rains must wash most of the junk out, although the winds bring some of it in and, of course, there's always a little of it aloft and falling. Most of it is staying up there, at least in *this* region. That's good. Oxygen and nitrogen content is very good, more esoteric inerts than I'm used, to but being inert they shouldn't have any real effect. You want to get cool, climb one of those big volcanos. They've got *snow* on them, although it tends to melt when they heat up. Surface ocean water temperature is between thirty and thirty-five, almost like a warm bath. Probably as much sea life, animal and vegetable, as land life, if not more. Looks like there's enough force for the mag bikes, like I thought, so at least we'll be able to ride, and since their engines are encased in solid core blocks they won't tend to get fouled, either. Too bad we couldn't have used them back on the worm world. Not much magnetic field there."

"And no mag lev bikes on the *Stanley*, either," An Li reminded him. "This is Normie's money."

"You ever ridden one?" Sark asked Nagel.

"Me? Yeah, a few times, years ago. They had some in the labs where I did my training. You?"

"Never. Ladies?"

None of the three woman had ever used them.

Nagel nodded. "I see what you mean. Well, they're not hard to learn if you don't get overconfident," he told them. "We'll do a little practice before we go anywhere anyway." He turned back to the view screen. "Take it towards the ocean, Cap. Let's see if we can see some real live aliens close up. Keep unobtrusive, though. If we can get around them without them noticing us, all the better."

"I'll see what I can do," the captain responded. "However, this is much the same sort of position as you were discussing with treasure hunting. I have no idea who or what I am looking for, might not when I find it, and certainly I do not know how they even perceive things, let alone how close is too close, how high is too high, and so on."

"Understood. The watch phrase here is 'Do your best.' That goes for all of us."

The probe rose up, then headed for the ocean near the largest volcano on the island it had been examining.

The vegetation looked to be very junglelike, although it was difficult to tell the shape or relative sizes of the plants, let alone their composition and other qualities, from the top. One thing was certain, though: the jungle was thick enough in areas not refractured or overrun by lava flows that it formed a multicolored but effective canopy over the forest floor.

"That's where you go during the twenty hours of the sun side season when that sun's out and beating down during the day," Randi pointed out. "That's shade down there. Probably makes things habitable and keeps them wet. Note, too, that the oldest growth is established on high, rolling hills. Evolution in action. The lowlands get flood surges from the storms that hit up against the mountains, and they run quickly down the lowest and sharpest slopes to the sea, taking a lot with them. Some growth survives, of course, but it's a rough area. The old stuff that grows big and strong watches the floods go by."

"Yesss," Nagel muttered. "I was thinking of evolution myself. Lots of life, even if it isn't any of the smart stuff, in a situation as dynamic as this is probably running at one hell of a pace. Say! Look at those!"

The probe was showing a grouping of what seemed to be flying creatures coming up from the ocean and diving into the jungle and back again. They were very fast, and it was tough to get a really good view that could be resolved to a decent level. They weren't all that big, half a meter tops, most much smaller, but they did have a number of obvious curiosities about themselves. They didn't seem to have any wings at all, for example, appearing like pear-shaped artillery shells. How they maneuvered so well, and how they flew at all, wasn't clear.

"Well, we have flying critters here that seem natural," Cross pointed out. "I hope they don't drill easy into our hulls, though."

"I hope they're vegetarians," Randi Queson said uneasily.

"Uh—yeah. Hadn't thought of *that*."

"I got us energy body armor," An Li said confidently. "Those belts have enough power in their power packs to generate a protective energy barrier for over thirty standard days."

"*If* they work against the creatures here, and *if* we don't need them longer than thirty days," Randi responded.

"You worry too much, Doc."

Then you don't worry enough.

"Funny," Nagel commented, still half in his deep thought mode.

"Yes? What?"

"I mean funny odd, not funny ha ha. I was just thinking of all these damned aliens we seem to be running into. Not the worm—if they'd run into *that* in the old days they wouldn't have told anybody because of the possible paranoia it would cause. Here. Alien races on Balshazzar, alien races up to the armpits here, probably alien races somewhere on or under Kaspar, and what is our past? The old Earth System Combine sent out hundreds of cybernetic scouts, hundreds more robotic ones, found and settled a *ton* of worlds so we could all breed like cockroaches, and not once, *not once*, did it run into another thinking race. Not even remnants of that race. Oh, alien animals, alien plants, all that, but not a thinking race. Not a creator, a builder race. All that time, all that effort, and never once did we meet anybody. The Holy Joes took that as proof that God of the gods created us as unique. Now here we are and we're up to our fuckin' *armpits* in other races. Not that we've actually seen one yet in the flesh, but, still . . ."

"Well, you can see one now," the captain told him.

She had taken the probe out over the ocean and made a slow turn up the coast, and now there was sure and certain sign that humanity not only wasn't alone in the universe, it never had been.

The very design of the town was alien. No human being would ever have carved out of rock the twisted cones and bizarre geometrical forms that now filled their view. These creatures were certainly air-breathers, though, and had emerged under a biochemistry not alien at all, and so there were certain things that they had in common with people in this kind of environment.

They made and sailed boats, for example.

The boats themselves were exotic looking, and the complex setting of a lot of small sails would never be done by humans the way they were done below, but the hull was still practically shaped for reasons of pure physics; masts and sails were still the best way to work under these conditions, and it didn't take Nagel more than a couple of minutes to realize that, with a few modifications, he could probably sail those boats providing he had a crew who could carry out commands.

The boats were not, however, designed for your average weekend sail on quiet waters near your university.

"Good *God!* Are they *ugly!*" Lucky Cross exclaimed.

Randi had an instinctive and instant fearful dislike of them because they looked somewhat like worms or at least snakes, with long, slender black legless bodies, but they were more than that. They had slender forearms with long, spidery fingers and they appeared to be able to slither and stick to just about anything anywhere, and even a small area would suffice. But the most repulsive thing about them as they oozed and swarmed over the boats and rigging was that they all looked like they'd had their heads chopped off.

Where the head would be expected to start there was a flat area, and a series of concentric, oscillating rings of pulpy flesh surrounding a central hole that appeared to be ringed with more sharp pointed teeth than could be counted. When idle, they appeared to put this flat top section face into a bulkhead or even the side of the ship itself and stick there.

"Good lord! How do they *see?*" Jerry Nagel exclaimed, open mouthed.

"How do they do much of anything, let alone build ships and towns like that?" Randi Queson added.

"I'll bet they're the universe's greatest kissers, though," An Li put in.

They ignored her. "I'm not sure I want to try contact

with them, at least by anything other than radio," Lucky Cross said, echoing their sentiments. She sighed. "Well, now that I've seen these guys, I think maybe I was happier the other way."

"Take the probe out and down the coast a ways," Nagel instructed. "I think we want to find out if these characters are typical or if there's a better group somewhere further on."

"I agree, at least at this point," the captain told him. "I certainly would classify them as probable carnivores."

Nagel nodded. "Still, the ship was kind of outfitted like a trawler of some sort. I didn't see any catch on the deck, but it's probably below being butchered and processed or already stored for unloading. There's something in the seas, maybe not anything we'd like or could use, maybe or maybe not anything even remotely fish or reptilelike, but *something* in their ecological niche that those characters have discovered can feed them. I've got to admit, though, I never would have thought of creatures like that as town builders or sailors, let alone intelligences capable of interstellar flight."

"None of us would," Randi Queson agreed. "And that's the problem, I suspect. I always used to wonder if it wasn't that *we* never discovered other civilizations but maybe that other civilizations discovered *us* and decided not to let us know. You saw those things! We'd have been in some kind of war with them almost instantly, just because of their looks."

"Could be," Nagel responded. "First time I saw *those* things, I'd figure some race got overrun and eaten by those carnivorous worms and started blasting away. Still, they had hands, fingers, arms. They're builders, all right. I wonder what they'd think if they met us?"

"Let's not find out," Randi suggested. "Let's let the next group here do that. On the other hand, I'd pay money to see old Normie show up down there and demand they all sign contracts or be evicted."

"Well, I'd love to see the deal-making handshake," An Li agreed.

"Here's the next settlement. Definitely *not* the same family," the captain told them.

"On the other hand, I'm not sure I want to walk in and say 'Hello' just yet there, either," Nagel responded.

The best word you could use to describe *this* group was that they were bugs. Not insects—they seemed to have only four limbs, like humans—but they also had chitinous exoskeletons that gleamed with a sort of reddish-brown metallic reflection in the light, and their oversize heads were a mess of proboscises, eyelike pads, mandibles, and cilia put together in the same, but not to the onlookers any rational order. Three fingers and a sort of oversized opposing thumb appeared tipped with large yellow suckers, and the exoskeletal armor on their arms and legs looked as sharp as sword edges. The feet were oversized versions of the hands, with the even larger suckers being far more prominent.

While the average one was probably a meter or more tall, they certainly had no problem getting around, walking straight up cliffs and having no apparent stairs or climbing aids on their gumdrop-shaped houses, all of which appeared to be made out of some kind of secretion and then hardened, possibly by heat.

"Well, they're not dumb," Randi noted. "They're distilling salt from seawater in a big way in that squared-off area over there, with a kind of roof of tree fronds or something of the sort that's retractable. When you get the sun bearing down on that, I bet it dries up nicely. They've got fire, and they've got it contained. Those poles look to be permanent torches, and there are several smoldering fire pits around with good protective drainage and covers on the pits that can be used if they get a downpour."

The captain saw something else, being able to see all ranges at once. "Back up on that hilly area about a kilometer back and raised a bit over the village appears to be the remnants of an interplanetary ship," she pointed out. "There is sufficient power from a single engine source for it, and the signature is surprisingly close to what ours gives off."

"Interesting," Jerry Nagel said. "So they could take off from here if they wanted to?"

"Maybe. You are assuming that the ship is actually spaceworthy without maintenance, without seals checks, and for who knows how long? Even if it could, though, where would it go? It's clearly interplanetary. There's nothing there that could attain the speed, power, and stability to keep from being crushed in a wormhole, and if they have another way of traveling, then why are they still here living a basic life? And if it *did* work in-system, where here? Kaspar? I wonder what *their* temperature range for survival is? And if they go to Balshazzar, they get trapped on the surface there. No, I think they have kept it primarily as a resource and perhaps as a way to contact home if somebody from home ever shows up, just like Woodward's ship on Balshazzar."

"Well, let's go before somebody notices," An Li prompted nervously. "We've seen our creepy-crawly aliens, now we have to decide where *we* are going to set down and, when we do, determine that we can get back up."

"Head towards more recent volcanic activity," Queson told her. "I think that anything that's valuable and near the surface is going to be in new areas not yet flooded clean. Head for that gigantic island to the northwest. It's pretty well out of the clouds but it has a lot of recent volcanoes from the looks of it."

The probe left the heavily populated area and headed towards the one their part-time geologist suggested. It didn't seem inhabited, probably due to the more recent activity and the amount of dust all over half the island, but it looked pretty mean.

"You don't think we can turn up anything in a place like *that*, do you, Doc?" Lucky Cross asked skeptically.

At almost that moment the probe came over a rise and looked at a huge volcano with a massive and impressive caldera smoking and grumbling away. Flows came from all points on its sides, but were a combination of old and new.

Randi almost jumped from her chair. "*There!* Look at *that!*"

An area of the volcano had apparently broken away in a recent eruption, and part of the side had collapsed down into rubble, revealing a great expanse of reflective wall, very light brown in color and translucent but glassy smooth. It was the largest obsidian wall she ever remembered seeing, even in pictures.

"If we're going to find anything unusual and valuable created by these, it'll be near or around a formation like that," she told them.

Precious metals weren't exactly in great demand; there was a lot of almost everything on otherwise dark and useless rocks within range of most ships back home, but jewel-quality gems of unique types were something else, depending as much on the very different combinations possible on other worlds and unique conditions for getting them out onto the surface.

"How hard can it be to find Magi's Stones?" An Li mused. "I mean, almost every ship that got back, no matter how wrecked, had a couple at least, and even if they're extremely rare back home they have to be kinda obvious to pick up here, right? I don't see things like that forming easily on Kaspar, they couldn't'a gotten 'em off Balshazzar, so they've *got* to be here."

"They're here," Randi assured her. "They just might need to be examined close up by hand. This is a tremendously dynamic place, changing constantly, and it's not likely to keep things obvious and on the surface for any length of time. Look at the volcanic dust alone here."

"Well, all the same—hey! What's *that?*"

An Li's cry drew all their attention to a small but obviously artificial structure, vehicle, or whatever it was, sitting there atop the rubble near that vast obsidian cliff.

It looked to be about twelve meters long by six meters around, a cylindrical body pierced on the bottom by big, oversized wheels on a covered but obvious axle assembly that allowed the wheels near-total independence. The wheels themselves were grooved, almost like tank treads, but these were no tires or treads but single integrated structures, each rising almost to the top of the central cylinder.

"It's an exploration vehicle of some sort," Nagel commented, staring at the image. "I'll be damned. How old do you think it is, Doc? Cap?"

"Impossible to say," Randi told him. "It's clearly not one of ours, so who or what made it is unknown, and so's its composition. There's ash piled up on the top and on the top of the wheels, so it's been there awhile, but it definitely is newer than the rockfall that began exposing the obsidian. Captain, any signs of life or energy?"

"Negative, but that just may be because what I have can't penetrate the cylinder. Still, educated guess would say that it's abandoned in place."

"That's where we start, then," Randi Queson told them. "If this area attracts me, and it attracted others, then I can't see how we can find a better place to start. Any objections?"

"Let's see if we can get the probe back, first," An Li suggested.

That was easy to find out, and within a half an hour the captain reported that the probe was safely back and in containment and analysis aboard ship. This area was strictly automated; no probe could be permitted to bring back any nasty little things that might not be anticipated and loose them aboard ship. The whole lab, in fact, could be ejected into space and destroyed by remote command should something show up in the probe that they could not otherwise contain or analyze.

"Analysis looks okay from this end," the captain told them. "You are right—take a simple breath mask to keep out the big volcanic dust particulates and you should be okay. How much equipment do you want to break out for this?"

"Four sets," Randi Queson told her. "I think we need as much cover as we can for each other on our first trip down. Lucky can cover from the shuttle. And bring up Eyegor. This time the little bastard is going documenting with us, like it or not!"

XII:

FINDING WHAT YE SEEK

"They're really not that tough, and they have one big advantage," Jerry Nagel said as they stood around the maglev scooters dropped off with the packs, before Lucky Cross took the shuttle back up to a low orbit to sit and be ready just in case a quick extraction was needed.

All four below were in excellent physical shape, and all looked like they were ready to pass out even as it was, although Nagel and Sark were trying to keep up a brave front.

First, it was *hot*. Hotter than the worm planet had been cold, if not quite as windy, at least at the moment. The handhelds made the surface temperature where they stood at an almost exact thirty-seven degrees centigrade; not enough to cause physical problems for the healthy, only to make them feel like it would, particularly with a humidity level hovering in the eighty percent range. The light was also a bit strange and caused some disorientation. It was reflected light from the gigantic gas ball in the sky rather than direct sunlight, and, while it was bright enough, it was still less than optimum for eyes designed to see best in full daylight.

When the additional fifteen percent in weight was added, they all felt tired from the moment they hit the ground, and found it hard to move and difficult to do even routine things quickly. This world would take some getting used to.

Eyegor hovered a bit above the ground and griped, as usual. "I should not be exposed to this dust and these potentially harmful radiations," it complained. "I am not designed for this sort of thing."

"We don't know what you *are* designed for," An Li snapped, "but if it isn't for this, then what good are you? Keep quiet and keep up or you can just stay here!"

In front of them sat the four maglevs. They didn't look like much; nice, padded seats behind rather standard-looking handlebars with grip controls, and a readout panel with touchscreen centered between them. There were clips for packs to be attached, but Jerry wanted them to get the feel of the things first without complications.

"The trick is balance," he told them. "The units will power up if you press these two control symbols at the same time," he went on, pointing to the touchscreen. "As you can see, you can't really push the two acciden-tally; you have to contort a little to do it, which is the idea. Power down the same way. The power cells inside are good for several years at standard gravity and shouldn't be a problem, and they can be recharged with a power source, so you're not likely to run out of juice."

The body of the scooter was, under the saddle, basically a long and smooth rectangular block with no particular features; stirrups came down from under the saddle to provide foot and leg support. There were no wheels or runners, and the four units sat there quite simply resting balanced on their flat undersides.

The four of them had all chosen light face masks to

filter out the dust and ash that blew around, but otherwise each was very individually dressed. Jerry was wearing an off-white pullover robe tied with a belt at the waist, with a hood hanging back off the neck, and a pair of calf-length boots. He was also wearing not much else, judging from what was revealed when he got on the scooter nearest him, although that didn't bother any of them. They'd all been together too long to be titillated by the sight of anybody's skin.

Sark wore a light khaki-colored tunic and shorts, also bound with a belt at the waist, a broad-brimmed hat tied under the chin with a strap, and ship's utility boots, which were light and comfortable but might not be as insulating as Jerry's.

An Li wore basically bikini style briefs and a halter, revealing a better figure than she usually showed, but also a more problematic one on a heavier gravity world. She did, however, wear a head scarf, mostly to control her hair, and high leather boots that might or might not be good for a hike but would certainly do if she could master the scooter. Randi kept her ship's uniform, basically a light pullover shirt, jeans, and ship's boots, and a baseball cap.

Jerry sat on the saddle, turned on the power, and then gripped the handlebars as the scooter rose about fifteen centimeters above the rocky ground and hovered there. If it made a sound, it was masked by the sound of the wind and far-off volcanic noises.

"The right control is your accelerator," he told them. "Go easy on it, build to speed and then hold it comfortably. You can lock it in if you need to scratch or reach for something, but it's not a good idea to use that much. The left is your levitator. Pull the two calipers together and you'll rise from the default fifteen centimeters up to about five meters. Leave it in default for now; five meters is pretty high up to fall off a moving scooter onto hard rocks. You can switch them in function by simply flipping this lever on each to give the hands a rest or to reach for something with the right while still going. Pulling the levitator all the way in will cause it to lock and leave the scooter in a stationary position at whatever height you happen to be at; just remember that it'll also override your accelerator. Whatever height you set, the scooter's sensors will keep you at that height relative to the ground until told to do otherwise. You steer with your body. It'll go where you lean or want it to go. Turning radius isn't all that great, so practice a little with that. That said, a little steer goes a long way."

"How come no safety harness?" An Li asked him.

"If you lose control, you'll find that, on these, you're better off jumping off, even at five meters and thirty kilometers an hour, than sticking with one. Remember that. Now, I'm going to take this one for a little demo around the area here. Watch me and see what I do. Then we'll have each of you try it in turn, with me monitoring nearby, and then it's everybody for themselves. Deal?"

He rose about five meters into the air and started forward. The fact was, it looked easy and fun, and by that point they were all grimy, dripping with sweat, and feeling all their muscles ache. Any way to let a machine do the heavy stuff was all right with them.

An Li volunteered to be next. She found the saddle hot against her choice of mostly bare skin, but she said she'd get used to it. Smaller than the others, she needed Jerry to adjust the handlebars and the stirrups, and now he showed them, with An Li aboard hers, the other functions of the panel—intercom, various sensors, things that were useful but not essential to the basic task.

An Li proved something of a natural once she got going, although she did have some problems adjusting to the speed control, and she almost fell off when she reached for her canteen with her right hand, thereby releasing the calipers and bringing her to a more abrupt stop two meters up than she expected.

Sark's big body had some trouble with the subtleties of steering, and it took him a good half hour or more to get even the basics to where Jerry felt confident Sark wasn't going to kill himself or, more importantly, them.

Randi Queson was somewhere in between, riding comfortably and well from the start but occasionally forgetting to do something critical and causing potentially dangerous problems. Still, Jerry was satisfied she could keep up if she didn't do anything fancy.

Now it was time to attach the packs and instrumentation, practice going a little with those unbalanced loads, practice a little more going together at a consistent speed and altitude, and then decide they could do it.

Randi found that the worst problem was judging distances at any kind of speed at all. The light was just so strange and soft that it was disorienting.

The last thing to do before heading out was to hand out the guns. These were settable energy pistols for the two women, and precision needling guns, riflelike devices with long ranges held by holders on the saddles themselves, for the men. Neither needed a lot of skill; if you could see what you wanted to shoot, the logic in the guns would pick it up and you *would* hit it.

Salvagers with guns and maglev scooters, Randi Queson thought to herself with discomfort and amazement. *My god! Where have we taken ourselves?* She felt uncomfortable with the pistol in its holster on her belt, but she also couldn't help but think that she'd have given her right arm for one of these back on the worm's world.

Jerry put them in a kind of diamond formation, with himself bringing up the rear. "This way I can see all three of you and know if there's any trouble," he explained. "And you three can keep eyes on each other. Just remember that if you hear a beep from the pad then turn around, because it's *me* that's in trouble!"

Eyegor did not prove to have a lot of speed in this environment. Even though the scooters went at a maximum speed of under forty kilometers per hour, it *seemed* much faster when you were on one, and it also was considerably faster than the tiny levitator in the robot was designed to do, no matter how close in principle was the design of Eyegor's propulsion unit and the maglevs. Jerry did find that if the thing was partly fastened to the saddlebags, it didn't add much if any weight, and so he put it on An Li's scooter to her right. If anybody could keep the little sniveler of a robot in its place, she could.

Jerry put Queson in the lead. He was more than confident that not only was she the smartest one in the group but also that she had real guts. That stuff with the worm and the absorbed colony had proven that. He punched the intercom. "Where to, Doc? You're the lead."

"The obsidian cliff," she told him. "Let's take a look at that transport, whatever it was, and the area at the base of the cliff. Whoever they were or are, *they* thought there was something worthwhile over there, too!"

"Besides, I really would like to get a look at that contraption," Jerry Nagel added.

Queson was still not all that confident on the scooter and tended to keep it just two meters above the ground and at a leisurely clip. The ones behind weren't thrilled, but they matched pace, and in about fifteen minutes they sighted the strange alien vehicle and pulled up to it and stopped. One by one, they lowered their scooters to the ground, throwing up some ash when the vehicles settled.

Nagel pulled a small pistol out of his pack and just stuck it in his belt. He didn't think he was going to need it, but it was a precaution. The memory of running across those roofs being paced by detached units of the worm had never really left him.

Close up, the alien vehicle didn't look as shiny and nice as it had in the probe pictures. In fact, it looked heavily pitted, although nothing seemed to have penetrated it, and one wheel was slightly off its axle due to a rockslide they hadn't noticed.

"There's why it's stuck here," Nagel pointed to the bum wheel. "They were heading along, either caused the slide themselves or got caught in a mild afterquake from the eruption, and they couldn't go any farther. Anybody got any ideas about how long this thing's sat here? I mean, are we looking at days, weeks, years, or centuries here?"

"Months, certainly, from the lack of any tracks and the buildup of dust on the leeward side," An Li said, looking. "Maybe longer when you look at that pitting."

"I agree," Randi Queson added. "Months, maybe a few years, although not a horrendously long time. The pitting shows it's been stationary a fairly long time, since the particles blowing against it now bounce off, but this slide's not that old, and the eruption on the opposite side of the mountain is very recent. No renewed growth was visible, although it's all over elsewhere, and there were no buildups to naturally channel the rain runoff. I'd say a year or two."

The usually taciturn Sark looked over the tankerlike vehicle. "Where'd they get in and out, and where were they going?" he asked nobody in particular. "No door or window at all that I can see."

Nagel looked under the tank, between the wheels. In spite of low clearance, he was pretty sure that there was some sort of exit there. "See? In the center. Rounded shape with a beveled edge. Most likely some kind of hatch. Either they were small or low to the ground, but that's the way in and out for sure. As to how they see, well, maybe they don't need a window. Maybe viewers are built into the hull of the thing, or it's transparent when you're inside and maybe flip a switch or something. Eyegor's head's a globe, but he sees."

"Be funny if this thing wasn't a transport but a water

wagon or something," An Li commented. "I mean, it looks like a tanker, and in here there are pools of standing fresh water."

Nagel shook his head. "No, if they built this or had it to carry things, it wasn't water. No need on *this* world. No, I think it was their version of our scooters and it just had some real bad luck right here."

"You want to try and get inside it?" An Li asked.

"I'd love to, but with the dust buildup underneath narrowing the clearance even worse, and with that hatch looking shut, I'm not at all sure it wouldn't be a long and heavy lifting kind of job. Maybe if we bring the whole C&C down and set up a base camp here, yeah, it'll be worth doing with the equipment we have. Sark?"

"Dunno what the material is, but if it can be dented by rocks I can pull it apart," the big man assured him. "Most of our equipment's still salvage stuff, after all."

"Then we'll let it wait. I'm less curious about it and its owners than I am what it was doing here. Doc, any clues on that?"

"Not really, but assuming from the angle here that it was heading towards that notch in the obsidian wall about a half a kilometer on, we might as well see."

An Li frowned. "Wouldn't the rockfall have turned it around? Or maybe it was going *that* way instead of *this* way."

The Doc shrugged. "Doesn't make much difference if it was coming or going from there, that's the interesting place. The other direction's going into an older lava plain and then through towards the sea. And if it had been turned much it would have become unbalanced and tipped over on this uneven ground. No, I'm pretty certain that if it was a treasure hunt then the treasure, if it exists, is over there."

"We've only got a few hours until dark," Nagel pointed out, "and without the C&C and all our equipment and a ground defense perimeter I'm not sure I want to spend twenty hours in the dark here. Let's follow the Doc's nose and see if anything smells at the other end."

"Oh, Jerry, you're so romantic," An Li responded sourly, but they all got back on the scooters and headed off in the direction the Doc was sure was the right one.

It was just beyond that notch, in a small rift, that they came upon a glittering fall of shattered but sparkling stones spread in a kind of rock field. They all assumed that they were simply shattered remnants of a dislodged obsidian boulder, but Queson decided to stop anyway and get down and take a look.

An Li sniffed. "Maybe you were right after all, Jerry," she said. "Through the smell of rotten eggs that's all over this place I swear I'm getting a strong directional scent of, well, it smells like lemon, or maybe lemon and orange. That's crazy."

It might have been crazy, but they all smelled it as they walked up to the field of shattered and glittering stones that lay, fan-shaped, in front of them.

"Whoa!" An Li said suddenly, and seemed to stagger a bit.

"Heat and gravity getting to you?" Nagel asked.

"No, it was, well, something very odd. I'm getting a whole series of sensations. Disorienting, creepy, I don't know what. It's getting worse as we come to the stones."

"I'm feeling it, too, Jerry," Randi told him. "Not as bad, but it's there."

In truth, Nagel had been dismissing some dizziness and occasional blurred vision as just heat and exhaustion and now he knew differently. "Li, stay here. Sit down, or lie down, and just breathe regularly in and out and try and get things back. Everybody else, let's see what we got here."

Randi Queson felt increasing effort just to get to the rock field, but she made it, then bent down and picked up several smaller pieces of whatever it was in her hand

and examined them. "These pieces are definitely standard ordinary obsidian glass, common to all volcanoes," she told them. "But *these*—I don't know *what* these are. They seem to be embedded in shards of obsidian, or in one or two cases here entirely encased in it." She took one, pulled down her mask, and sniffed, then replaced the mask over her nose and nodded. "Uh huh. Very much like lemon."

"This one's more orange, and there were a couple here that seemed more like flower scents," Nagel told her. "What the hell is giving the scents off? Trapped gas that's now being released?"

"I doubt it. If that were so, it would dissipate as the wind picks up like now, and it's not dissipating. No, I think something in there, some compound, is actually giving off the odors. Be careful, both of you, about close smells. I got a real weird set of sensations when I sniffed that one."

"Yeah, me, too," Nagel agreed. "Li! You feeling better?"

"A little, since the wind shifted a bit away from me," she told him. "Bring me one of those things. I want to take a look at it. Only one! I seem to have a worse reaction than the rest of you!"

Nagel gestured to Sark, who went back and handed An Li a fairly large one. She examined it, frowned, then said, "I think I know what these are! That swirl pattern around the single large facet in the center gives it away. It's an unpolished, unfinished Magi Stone. I don't remember any smells coming from the one Sanders had, but otherwise I can see the finished, set product in this one!"

"Maybe it loses its scent over a period of time," Randi suggested, "or maybe it's sealed when they cut and shape the gems. I hadn't realized they were cut and shaped at all. Hell, maybe these smell and the others found before don't. Most of them were found on derelicts anyway. Who knows what they went through or where they came from? Melchior, it looks like, but not here, not this place. This one's too new."

"That implies that this kind of stuff is fairly common here," Nagel pointed out. "It means you're gonna have to be very careful in the number of these introduced into the interplanetary economy. Too common and their value's gonna drop like a stone. Still, if we can get a few bags of these, of various sizes, back with odors intact, we're looking at more than enough to amortize the trip right here and now! And if Normie's dumb enough to flood the market later, ours will already have been sold."

"Good point," Doc responded. "Still, while most of these will be put in vacuum storage, I'd like to keep a couple out just for tests and examination. I'd *love* to know what the hell causes these weird effects when you get close to these stones. The odor? Or is their makeup such that they're receiving something, something weird, from someplace else? Who knows? With this many, I'd sure like to find out."

"Interesting those aliens thought these were important, too," Sark noted. "I mean, it can't have the same effect on them, can it? And them ant things wasn't wearin' no jewels."

"I think it's a good point," An Li noted, studying the small one in her hand. "Still, this is almost definitely what they were either going to or coming from, and they sure looked like they was gonna load up. Not much to eat around here, but it seems stable enough to bring in *our* equipment and pick up a fair load. As you say, we can control the output until, at least, ours are sold."

Jerry looked around at the high walls of volcanic rock and dust and the big planet above. "Night's falling, and pretty fast," he said. "Everybody put a handful of these things in their packs and let's get back to where Lucky can pick us up. We got twenty hours to shit, shave, eat, sleep, and analyze. After that, I think we bring the C&C module down."

There was no argument on that.

The captain's own labs isolated the compounds that gave off the odor in the stones, but neither those labs nor the Doc's could do much more. The Magi's Stones lived up to their reputation and shattered when you tried any sort of analysis on them. What jewelers could do was to shape the stones to a very small degree, mostly by shaving away the obsidian. Only in a few cases could the lightest of robotic hands split them along a single outer crystal boundary. Anything more, and you had dust that the analytical labs found little different in general composition from the obsidian plus a few odd and by no means consistent trace minerals.

Every crystal, though, appeared filled with microscopic bubbles of the gas that gave the sense of flavor. Not, it seemed, because it really did smell like lemon, or orange, or lilacs, or whatever, but because it was a mild hallucinogen that stimulated that sensation in the brain.

The hallucinogen might have explained An Li's paranoia about the alien lurker, stimulated by Norman Sanders's theatrical setup, and the sense of looking into the past, but it wasn't all that clear if that was all there was to it.

An Li, using a sealed lab unit in which she was not physically sharing any space with the stone, nor breathing any air nor touching it except in a virtual manner by manipulating robotic probes through a head unit, nonetheless received visions staring at the stone Sark had given her, visions that also now came with odd physical sensations that ran from dizziness to tingling in all extremities and even to mild orgasm. And, after a half dozen minutes or so, she felt the sensation once more of Him and backed out fast.

Randi Queson tried the same tack, and got results that

in some cases were similar, some different. *Her* visions were of darkness and something like spirits moving across the face of a frozen sea, suddenly bursting into a riot of colors and shapes that were beyond figuring out but nonetheless were beautiful and fascinating and, most of all, mathematical to a large degree.

Eventually she, too, felt the sensation of others becoming aware of her, of being able in some way to interact with her, but, unlike An Li, the presences were plural and carried with them no sense of menace, no voyeuristic violation. She had the distinct impression that they were trying to tell her something, or at least convey some sort of message or warning to her, but they were too unfamiliar, too alien, and if in fact they were sending and she was receiving she had no way to decode and thereby comprehend whatever it was they were saying.

Jerry Nagel had something in between, with a sensation of going through space, of light and dark, fire and ice, joy and sadness, but on a level he more sensed than could comprehend from the wash of visions. His overall sensation, though, was clear.

There was a war, he thought. Or, possibly, *is* a war. He couldn't be sure. At times he had the sensation of time covering eons and distances beyond any human ability to comprehend, yet just as quickly he had a sense of seeing things now, or perhaps no older than yesterday. At no time did he sense anyone aware of him, but eventually the lightning-fast visions and sounds and smells and shapes overwhelmed him and translated into running a gamut of physical and psychological sensations in rapid-fire succession until he couldn't take it anymore. When he bailed out, he found that he was soaked in perspiration, his muscles tensed into knots, and yet he was as turned on as he'd ever been in his life.

Sark seemed particularly troubled by the effect of the

stones and would not take them on one on one, even though there was never any question of his courage.

Still, when they compared notes, little really made sense.

"Clearly the gems are broadcasting *something*, and that means it's coming from *somewhere*," Randi Queson insisted. "The question is, what is the source of it and why does it have this series of similar if unique effects on us?"

"Well, we've all wound up really turned on," Nagel pointed out, "but we also have other things in common here. Fleeting but deep senses of hunger, thirst, fear, laughter, all the range of emotions and urges, right down to the bowels. That says to me that something's messing with our minds. And if it's random, as it seems to be, that something isn't necessarily directing them. I've seen similar stuff in drug reactions."

"But we factored out the gas," An Li pointed out.

"Sure, we factored out the gas, but we didn't factor out other things. This is something we've not seen before, and have experienced only in a few of these that survived and got back home," the Doc said thoughtfully. "Now we know the brain is an electrical device, so to speak. It works by being able to store, filter, and then bring together in one central command area what's needed for thoughts and ideas or to compel actions. Even the least of us is smarter than our ancestors because they were genetically bred or enhanced, so our brains are pretty damned fast, although never as fast as the fastest quasi-organic computers. Still, it's fetch data and assemble, then act if A but not B is true. All that's done by electrical signals. Drugs often interfere with those signals to get their effects, or drop blockers or substitutes into receptors to get others. I think something inside these Magi's Stones is some kind of natural electrical transmitter, very small power but somehow on a wavelength our brains can receive. We get that effect, and inside our heads our brains try to make sense of the random signals coming in. There's stimulation while it rumbles around in there trying to find a place to put it, and there's hallucination as it tries to make sense of things. That sound logical?"

"You mean it really is all in our heads?" An Li asked, sounding skeptical.

"I think so. It's this very effect, though, that makes many drugs so attractive to some people, and it's what makes these things unique and valuable to others. I think after we sleep but before we go down again and start setting up we ought to swap stones and see what happens. If we get the exact same sensations from different stones, then it's proof that the signals are random and our brains are doing it from the Magi's Stone's stimulation. If it's wildly different, or if we get each other's sensations, *then* there might be something external that they're picking up. An Li's seeing much the same thing in her stone as she saw in Sanders's gem, though, makes me suspect it's us."

"Regardless, how the hell are we going to mask the effect so we can harvest the pile?" Nagel wanted to know. "And how far away can we stow them here so they won't have any effect on us, or maybe even the captain?"

"I get nothing from the samples you brought up," the captain assured them.

"Yeah, maybe, but we're not talking about a kilo or so. We're talking a ton of the stuff that went right through and along the labs' neural nets," Nagel pointed out. "I keep wondering if some of those derelicts from the Kings weren't because of the shielding or wormholes at all, but maybe were because people went nuts."

"Well, we'll just have to try and be smarter than they were," An Li put in. "I don't like the damned things one bit, but if we pick up a ton of them and get out of here and back home, I *do* know we'll have one hell of a nest egg for all our futures. We sure haven't found anything else we can carry."

"Maybe we did," Jerry replied thoughtfully. "Hell, our primary job is salvage, and we've got a ship designed for it. If we can pick up that alien whatever, bring it up, and stick it in the hold, then we've got an extra-value cargo that might *really* make us all rich, particularly if there's some remains of dead aliens left inside it."

"Great," Randi sighed. "Going back, which nobody's ever done before in any case, with a ship stuffed with hallucinogenic gemstones and rotting alien corpses. What fun!"

"Nevertheless, at sun—er, at *planetrise*, Lucky and we take the C&C down to the surface and we get to work," An Li declared. "Let's get this over and *out* of here before one of those multiple ugly mountains down there decides it doesn't like *us*, either!"

XIII:

HOT CROSSED PILGRIMS

The experiment with swapping stones was inconclusive. None of the trio had the same complete set of hallucinations as before, but each had visions more in tune with their original experiences than with the others', and Queson felt confident that her theory was correct.

Sark seemed convinced that it was a natural sort of thing as well, but he wanted no part in playing with them. They didn't ask why; everybody's past was their own in this sort of business. Still, it was clear that he'd had some kind of run-in with drugs or other stimulations, and the experience had been bad.

Now that it was suddenly more of a familiar operation for them, they felt more confident in spite of the effects that the stones induced. Lucky detached the modular C&C from the *Stanley* with the shuttle docked in it and then brought the whole thing down through the atmosphere of the big moon and onto the huge plateau of lava about a kilometer from the rockfall, where it could be easily docked and lifted off in a hurry but would be away from any sudden avalanches and could be settled fairly level, its support legs doing the rest to make it not just solid as a rock, but considering the area, much more solid than *these* rocks had ever been.

Conditions, however, were much poorer than they'd been when they'd landed the first time. Clouds had rolled in, covering the sky and descending even below the high volcanic peaks all around them, and they rushed to scoop up and dump inside the containers within the C&C complex what they could of the slide and its strange but valuable cargo before it became impossible to do so. They managed to accumulate quite a lot, perhaps a third of their capacity, before the lightning started all around them, striking with increasing rapidity and force and causing thunderous explosive sounds to echo off the mountainsides and cliffs, finally accompanied by rain that seemed to come from under vast waterfalls rather than to precipitate from clouds.

They rushed fearfully back on their scooters to the C&C in the distance, thinking that at any moment the magnetic drives would pull down some of the fierce lightning and electrocute them as they fled for cover. The air already smelled of ozone, but they made it back, soaked and exhausted.

"I wouldn't even want to take off in this stuff if I didn't have to," Lucky Cross told them. "The only good thing is it's not bloody likely that any of those alien thingies are gonna venture out this way, either."

"So we lose a little time," Nagel told them. "And, yeah, we'd probably have been happier losing it up top, but we're better off down here, acclimating to the gravity. I don't know about you, but I'm feeling like I just had to fight my way out of the toughest bar on Sepuchus just from yesterday's action, and we *rode* almost the whole way!"

"Well, take a little painkiller and relax," An Li told him. "Any idea how long this shit will last?"

"Observations say it could be days, but probably won't be," Cross assured her. "Man! You think it's bad now, try it with *my* weight! I feel like I'm in a permanent squat!"

"You weren't out in that stuff!" Jerry Nagel replied, then sighed. "Well, let's spend some time setting up as much in the way of an automated security perimeter as we can. We did that when we thought we were alone, and we *know* that there are other races, many races, with colonies on this dirtball, and that at least one of them knows where this place is, and who knows with this little crew and no mother hen whether or not we'll all doze off. I wouldn't want one of those headless snakes showing up with boundless curiosity during that time."

As they set up the scanners and established both automatic warnings and weapons thresholds, Randi Queson couldn't help thinking of that funny-looking vehicle they were going to try and salvage at the end of this. "I wonder why they left it?" she mused, aloud.

"Huh? What do you mean? Who's 'they' and what did 'they' leave?" Jerry responded.

"Oh—just thinking aloud. But this isn't exactly on the known trade routes, and anything as sophisticated as that alien vehicle had to be brought here as part of their exploration and maybe prospecting, salvage, or whatever operation. One, maybe a lot more, were put into it just like we're here in the C&C module and sent out to look things over, maybe even discover and pick up Magi's Stones. There's no sign of any settlement of *anything*, least of all something that could build and drive that, anywhere on this side of the island, so it was brought here—flown here, floated here, who knows?—to do what it did. And then it got tripped up, stuck, and had to be abandoned or whatever. So why hasn't anybody come for it to fix it? It's got to be very valuable to them, even as salvage. Why did they leave it abandoned?"

"Maybe everybody inside made it back on foot or whatever they travel on and they didn't have what it took to fix the thing," Nagel suggested. "What's the big deal? It's not going anywhere."

"But it is! Don't you see? If it doesn't eventually get rolled over and possibly washed away by storms like these over time, or by a new slide caused by one, then one of these mountains is going to rumble and maybe spew in this direction, or at least cause some major and minor volcanic quakes. That's why we put this unit where we did, and the best we could get was a seventy-six percent probability that we'd be okay here for the duration of our job. No, I would love to know why they abandoned it."

"Maybe they didn't. Maybe the slide was worse than you think and they're all dead in there from shock or something," Cross suggested. "That'd make Jerry happy. He could sell the first alien DNA."

"Then why, if they went to so much trouble to get it here, didn't anybody come looking for them? No, it doesn't make sense."

"Well, maybe someday somebody can come here with all the right diplomatic and translation moves and ask them," An Li said, reclining on a bunk and yawning. "Me, I don't give a damn unless it's worth money to know or it's something that might impact me."

Randi just hoped that the answer *didn't* impact them. They were, after all, now stuck down here surrounded by barely dormant volcanoes on a lava plain of uncertain thickness for the duration of a howling storm.

Had they been able to see through the storm all the way to the cliff face, and particularly whenever the cliff face was struck by lightning, they would have worried a bit more, for then they'd have seen the entire obsidian cliff throb like some living thing, some beating heart, with a glow that pulsed like a beacon in a swirl of terrorizing winds and rain.

One by one, each of the five in the C&C began to feel tired and dizzy, and almost without thinking more about it they either reclined in chairs or went to their bunks to let things pass. Randi Queson did have a fleeting thought that this might be some effect of the electrical storm and the stored Magi's Stones, but before she could grab hold, announce it, and perhaps act to do something about it she, too, passed into a kind of nether sleep.

Randi Queson tried to mentally hold on, to at least keep steady against the onrushing hallucinations, but she could not. None of them could.

She was flying, flying through some strange, alien greenish sky with pink and yellow clouds.

Although it was clearly a point in some kind of atmosphere, she could see through it to the stars beyond, the whole starfield laid out before her, but not in the usual visual spectrum but through some other means. It was almost as if she were viewing some kind of photographic negative of the sky, an alien sky she'd never seen before filled with all the stars and formations of a globular cluster, but where light was dark and black was a kind of bright, soft pink.

Looking below, she saw a vast world that was heavily developed but long past its prime. Great domed cities stretched in uncounted number to the horizon, encapsulating ancient and dying masses whose shape and other details could not be determined from this height.

It would have been awesome if she hadn't felt permeated with a sense of awful hopelessness, a feeling that all those billions plus billions down there were in total despair, creating so much unhappiness that it collected and beamed from every individual and every dome and perhaps every centimeter of the planet, and beyond, going to and right through Randi Queson. She felt tremendous sorrow for them, all the more because she knew that she could not help them in any way, only watch their decline into despair and death.

The others were all with her. She could feel them, sense them in a hundred inexpressible ways, yet she could not see her companions. They were wraiths, flying over a planet of the dead, but they were still wraiths, as help- less as any specter.

And now they were off the world, and into the strangely inverted and bizarrely colored void.

There were others out here as well. Many others, but wraiths just like themselves, able to witness but only to witness, as they went from world to world, system to system, in a flash of darkness, instantly going from world to world and finding only the feelings of horror, despair, and death.

There were Others, as well, on some of those worlds, and going between them. It was no more possible to tell anything else about them than it had been to tell details of the first and subsequent civilizations, but this was a different realm, a different sort of sensory perception, and they were clear as could be.

These were the Bringers of Despair, hatching from the dark, hidden places and wrapping themselves around the worlds they found and helplessly sucking the life out of them. The ones the Others attacked wanted to fight back, wanted to push back this horror, but they could not. Once attacked, they progressively lacked the energy to push against this overwhelming darkness, a darkness that seemed both infinitely collective and yet of one mind and attitude.

An Li had finally met Him.

They veered off, swallowing pride, running for their lives, flying through holes and folds in space one after the other, throwing off the pursuer or pursuers. All thought was gone; there was suddenly only panic, only fear, and a sense that they must return together.

And then it was all emotions, rising up like a giant

wave and crashing down, washing over them, bathing them in a range so intense they could not bear it.

Inside the C&C module, as the storm still raged, only Eyegor was unaffected. The robot watched what the humans were doing with total confusion in its logical mind, but unable to determine anything about the cause except that it had to have something to do with the storm outside.

It nonetheless was watching and even recording scenes of sudden and complete human madness.

When they woke up, they were as confused and as physically and emotionally drained as they had ever been.

There were groans, and then attempts at rising, and finally one, then another, managed to sit up and look around.

The place stank. The smell of sweat and bodily fluids mixed with the acid smell of urine and the overwhelming scent of human excrement. One by one, awareness returned, and with it shock.

"My god! I'm *bleeding!*" Randi Queson exclaimed, looking down at herself. There were several wounds and quite a large number of ugly-looking bruises, but none of the wounds looked deep or in dangerous territory unless the surroundings infected them.

What was more startling was that she was mostly naked except for her boots and one part of her work shirt on her left arm. The material, tough synthetics that looked like denim but was much, much tougher, appeared to have been ripped off.

Jerry Nagel was further forward, but he neither looked nor sounded much better. He had his pullover shirt on, soaked with perspiration and stained here and there with blood but otherwise intact, but no pants. His body had a number of clawlike scratch marks that stung like hell, some still bleeding slightly, and he felt like he'd bitten his tongue half through. His balls ached as well, as if they were one big massive bruise.

He looked around, shook his head in bewilderment, and then caught sight of the nearly nude body of Lucky Cross lying draped, head down, over one of the chairs. There were more bloody wounds and the start of some nasty bruises on her backside, but none looked more than superficial. Still, she didn't move at all, and he rushed over, worried that Cross was dead. He turned her over and almost did more damage as the heavy woman fell limply from the chair onto the floor, the heavy gravity making it even harder to cushion her fall. She looked worse in front than in back, and there were a number of wounds that would need attention—good god! Were those *teeth* marks? More like bites that had drawn blood, but he could see some movement and could tell that she at least was still alive.

Leaving her for the moment, he looked around the interior of the C&C module for the others. He found Queson rather quickly, but she was just sitting there, vacantly staring, shaking a little off and on. She looked up at him with a mixture of surprise and shock, but did and said nothing else.

That's it! he thought, trying to get hold of the situation. *We get back up to the ship, we go to medlab, and we get the hell out of this horror!*

He was already formulating a theory of what had happened in the back of his mind, the sensory overload of close proximity to all the stones here and a mountainful not far off, electrically charged particles flying all over from the storm adding up to sheer insanity. He could remember almost nothing of it save the early visions, but you could deduce the rest from just looking around at the ones who'd also gone through it.

An Li was stark naked, lying on the floor, her legs in a spread Nagel wouldn't have thought possible. She actually looked a bit better than the others, no bleeding body wounds, but there were lots of bruises and contusions present and suggested, and lots and lots of deep scratches. Around her mouth was a large amount of congealed blood. She looked like a vampire after a feast, or some kind of weird blood rite priestess of some ancient religion, but a check showed that most of it didn't seem to be hers. She did, however, have a missing front tooth, and he felt a couple of his own, just on his right side, were at least loose. An wasn't going to like the body and facial scars—nor would any of them. Well, at least those could be looked after if they had the money to get them fixed.

And then he found Sark, lying in a pool of more blood than Jerry Nagel had ever seen.

The big man must have torn at his own clothing and ripped much of it off. Still, that wasn't what was so tough to look at.

He was certainly dead; no human being could suffer that loss, and the number of wounds he had, and where he had them, in addition to the one that had not so much slit his throat but more properly torn it out, was ghastly.

And yet Nagel could only stare for a moment and think, over and over again, *No treasure is worth this. Nothing is worth something like* this!

Appearances aside, he and the Doc seemed to be in the best physical condition, so he made his way back to her. She once more gave him that semivacant stare.

"You must snap out of it," he said as firmly as possible, aware of all sorts of pain in his mouth and hoping he wasn't mauling his words too much to be heard because of it. "Li and Lucky are alive but unconscious, and both are in pretty bad shape. Worse than us. We need to get them out of this charnel house here. We need to get them cleaned up. I can't do it by myself. You will have to help me."

"Wha . . . ?" she managed, still in shock but partly responding to his words.

"We forgot about those damned stones. Half a ton in

our cargo, who knows how much just over the rise, and a massive electrical storm to boot. It made us insane. Now we have to pick ourselves up and get out of here or we'll die."

She looked at him, trying to filter the information, but everything seemed so distant, so remote.

"Don't you see?" he almost yelled at her, painful as it was. "That's what happened to that alien scout car out there! And if we don't get a move on, we'll wind up going through it again and again until we're *all* dead! C'mon! Stand up! Get a grip! I need the Randi Queson who had the nerve to talk to an alien worm! I need your strength! *Come back to me, damn it!* I just can't do this alone!"

She seemed to come out of it, at least a little bit. "I— I can't feel anything. It's like I'm dead inside."

"It'll come back. Before it does, we need to be out of here and where we can all just cry it out."

For the first time, she saw Lucky lying there. "What— is she dead?"

"No, I think she's just out cold. Probably a concussion. If you can get me a bucket or something with a lot of warm or cool water in it and maybe a rag, then we can start. The fact that she's not dead doesn't mean that she can't die."

Queson nodded. "You want the medkit?"

"Bring it, but we don't have enough stuff to treat all of us at once. You and I are gonna have to bleed a little longer while we see if we can bring Lucky and Li around. Let me start with Lucky, since I don't think both of us together in our condition are gonna be able to manage a hundred fifty plus kilos, as well as the added weight down here, and move her anyplace. Li I can probably carry on my own once I make sure there aren't broken bones."

The Doc seemed to snap out of it, or at least to put it behind her until the current need was met. She was suddenly aware of the horrible smells.

"Us," he told her. "It played every bit of us like a small child at a control center. No sense in washing ourselves off, not now. We couldn't sterilize if we tried. Once we get 'em to where we can get out of here, then all of us can be cleaned up."

While Nagel was tending as best he could to Cross, Randi asked, "You want me to see to Li?"

"It's—well, don't let any of your imagination run too wild when you see her. Over there. If you can check her for breaks and, if you think it's okay, move her into the cabin area, any low bunk, then try what you can."

"I told you. At the moment I can't feel anything. Not shock, surprise, nothing. And I have seen my share of blood and death."

She got up and went back to An Li.

She saw the blood all over the small woman's mouth, saw Sark farther back lying in a still-spreading lake of blood, and guessed at least the basics. Sark had been almost a meter taller and probably two and a half times her weight, but, deep down, instinctively or by reflex, coming from the background she had, An Li knew how to kill a larger man like that. Poor Sark, she thought. He wasn't much except muscle, but he was a loyal comrade and he didn't deserve to die like that. At least, she thought, he probably wasn't even consciously aware that he was done in, nor, most likely, was An Li conscious that she'd done him in. There would be some small comfort in that.

There was a real goose egg rising on the back of Li's head, which was certainly the source of her coma or whatever it was, and some congealed blood in her hair, but there didn't seem to be any breaks in the neck or spinal column. Her right arm showed a potential fracture, but if she came out of this then that would be bearable.

It would be nearly impossible for Queson to lift even the small woman, but she managed to get a grip under each arm and drag An Li out of the battle zone and back to cleaner and better lit circumstances.

She cleaned off Li as much as possible, used a soaked towel as a sort of compress for the head wound, and treated the other wounds with emergency spray. If there wasn't a lot of internal damage and if the head wound caused no more problems, there was nothing that couldn't be fixed when they got back to the *Stanley*'s excellent medical unit.

She went back into the smell and filth of the torn-up wardroom, wondering if there was some sort of curse attached to it at this point, and saw that Cross appeared to be coming slowly around.

"Li's in her bunk. Bad concussion, maybe a broken arm, too. I cleaned out her mouth, and that whole area, too. Do you really think she bit off his penis?"

Nagel sighed. "I was afraid it might be something like that. Lucky? Gail? C'mon! Snap out of it! It's Randi and Jerry!"

Gail "Lucky" Cross moaned but with the help of both of them managed to sit up on the floor and shake her head slowly from side to side, more because of the disorientation than in response to any questions.

"What the fuck happened?" she managed. "I don't remember nothin'. I was sittin' here and then, all of a sudden— *Ouch! That* hurts*!*"

"You got a bad and still-bleeding wound on the right side of your head," Nagel told her. "Looks like you were hit with something rather than fell, but I can't tell."

"Jesus! What's that *stink*? And where are my pants?"

"We're all a little torn up," Randi told her. "If you can make your way out of here, get cleaned up, sit in the shower, then lie down. We'll be back to do the same."

Cross looked around. "What about the others?"

"Sark's dead, Li's in a coma but I think she'll make it. Her head's as hard as yours," Nagel told her. "C'mon!

Don't slip on this shit!" With Cross steadying on Nagel and being pulled up by Queson, she managed to get unsteadily to her feet, where the two of them were able to help her back into the quarters area.

It wasn't until they were all back there and reasonably cleaned up, with their wounds, if not repaired, at least treated, that any of them thought about what went next.

"We can call the *Stanley* from the shuttle," Cross suggested. "Get pulled up by the Cap on auto—I'm not sure how long it's gonna be before I can fly that thing. My eye's swelling and I can see out of it about as good as it looks, just for one thing. No sweat, though. And at least we can call it in and get the hell back to low gee and good food and proper medical treatment. I don't like it that Li ain't woke up yet."

"I don't, either, but I think you better stay where you are," Jerry Nagel told her. "I'll go up and make the call. I can't fly it but I sure can do that much."

Nagel managed to climb the aft interior stair by sheer willpower and make his way down the corridor towards the shuttle airlock. He was surprised to see that it was closed and all the controls were red. They'd done that with the worm business to seal things, but it wasn't common practice and it sure shouldn't have been that way now.

Something caused him to get a last burst of adrenaline, and he almost ran to the hatch and checked its settings. He put his palm on the code bar, and then could hear the compressors working inside the airlock. There was a slight difference between inside and out for their comfort, so this didn't bother him, but now he began to wonder. The inner hatch rotated, irislike, and he stepped into the airlock itself. Now, just ahead, he could actually see through to the interior of the shuttle through the small window in the far hatch, or, rather, he *should* have been able to see it.

He put his bruised face right up to the lock and looked out.

What he saw was Melchior, just lighting up from planetrise, and the dock and associated hooks that held the shuttle to the larger craft.

The shuttle was gone.

Something made him turn and rush back along the corridor, over the quarters, and to the aft compartments designed for salvaged material. These were removable but sealable airtight containers, and they'd dumped the half ton or so of harvested gems and obsidian mixture into two of them.

Those two, and only those two, were now missing. He didn't have to look; the master board told him so.

It didn't make sense. Even if the captain had double-crossed them or gone nuts herself, she could only have recalled the shuttle and whatever it was hooked to. It was strictly an emergency procedure. And yet, he, Randi, Lucky, Li, and Sark were all accounted for. Who the hell was there left?

He turned and rushed back to tell the others, but he was yelling one single name, the only name that really fit the evidence.

"*Eyegor*, you programmed bastard!"

"Base C&C to *Stanley*, come in, Cap," Nagel called for the hundredth time. He and Cross had taken turns for a full Melchior day and night and had gotten no response.

"I can't figure out how it's possible," Cross told the other two. "I mean, even if Eyegor made it back up there, the captain would *never* leave us without us or proof or death. I just can't believe she'd do this, and I sure don't see how Eyegore could, or did."

Jerry Nagel sighed. "You missed the point, Lucky. Eyegore's nothing more than a glorified camera, or so we were told, right? So how did it fly the shuttle? How did it control it so precisely, with full knowledge of how to detach, and, most importantly, even if we go with the idea that it just triggered the automatic emergency retrieval, how then did it detach, float to the back, pick just those two containers, lift them into the very limited bay of the shuttle, and then take off for the ship? There's only one answer. Because it was designed and programmed to do it right from the start."

"Sanders! That slimy son of a bitch! If I ever get my hands around his throat I'll bite off more than *his* private parts!" Cross snarled.

Nagel nodded. "But the idea is to stick us here. Eyegore even has the exact place recorded where it left us, and it probably has scenes of our madness to explain to anybody back home that we succumbed to something weird and killed each other in some orgy of violence. Nobody will ask questions. He'll probably even make a movie out of it. And he'll sell the stones in little bits and pieces and make more millions, and he alone will still know how to get to the Three Kings."

"But how did he get Cap to go along with this? And what keeps her quiet?"

"I dunno, but he's got this all worked out, you can count on that," Nagel asserted firmly.

Randi Queson looked over at both of them. "Remember that they said they did work on her memory and logic chips? Even she told us that she got the navigational information only when she needed it and that it was wiped as soon as she got back. Remember?"

"Yeah, I—oh *shit!* I see what you mean! She isn't gonna remember *anything*. Probably not even us or this whole job. One command and as far as she's concerned she's been in orbit getting overhauled all this time and we're long gone to other jobs. *Great!* Just *great!*"

Cross chuckled. "If we'd'a been smarter and not suckers and known this was comin', too bad we didn't stay up on Balshazzar. At least that's a kind of no-work tropical paradise."

"Maybe for the rest of you, but not me," Jerry Nagel replied. "I think I'd rather see what's here than be trapped for the rest of my life around telepathic aliens and thousands of Holy Joes."

"Well, we don't have that option, and we can't stay here," Randi Queson pointed out. "Another of those storms could come along at any moment, and I don't think any of us would survive a second one like that, at least mentally. That means moving out of this valley, taking with us whatever we can and leaving this here, probably like *they* did years ago."

Nagel nodded. "Well, I think the scooters will still work, which will help. If we can get off and find a safer, more stable area to camp and near some source of water and maybe even food, and ferry what we can from here to there, it'll be a start."

"What about An Li? How can we move her until she wakes up?" Randi asked him.

"If necessary, we'll strap her on and move her that way," he replied. "I don't see anything else we *can* do."

The two women said nothing. There wasn't much else to say.

Jerry Nagel sighed. "But first I'm going to bury Sark. He deserves that. Then we'll start exploring and see what we can find. One step at a time, but I think we need to get out of here before the next storm no matter what. In fact, I'm prepared to say that if another storm looms, we all get the hell out of this big expanse, away from whatever is inside that cliff. We come back *only* when it's relatively clear and breezy."

"I'm for that," Randi Queson told him.

While Nagel was preparing the grave for Sark's body, he suddenly heard Lucky Cross calling from the underside hatch. "Jerry! An Li's moaning! I think she may be coming to!"

He put down his excavator and ran for the hatch. Sark had waited this long; a little longer wouldn't hurt.

She *was* coming around, twisting and turning and grimacing in her bed, although her eyes remained shut. It took another fifteen or twenty minutes, with a lot of soothing words, hands-on guidance, and wet cloths, but she finally lay still for a moment, then opened her eyes. She had two black eyes—they all had one or two of those—but inside, the pupils looked relatively clear if slightly vacant. She looked up at their faces and smiled, but it wasn't an An Li smile, rather it was an innocent smile, a child's smile. "Hello!" she said with a slight lisp.

"Hello yourself," Randi responded softly. "How do you feel?"

"I hurt. And my arm hurts, too."

"You have a lot of cuts and bruises, and you broke your arm, but we have treated them and your arm's in a splint and cast. It should be okay over time."

"What's a splint?"

"That thing you can probably feel under the cast. It keeps you from moving the arm until it's better."

"What's a cast?"

They all began to sense that something was wrong. "Do you know who you are and where you are?" Randi asked her sweetly.

"My name is Li Li," she responded. "What's *your* name?"

Queson had a feeling that the head injury had done a lot more than it appeared to have, either that or the consequences of the coma. "My name is Randi. This is Jerry, and that's Lucky. How old are you, Li Li?"

"I dunno, Randi. I never learned to count yet."

Queson stood up and whispered to the others, "It may come back. Things like this are really rare. Damn! If we just had the ship, we could find out if there's a physical cause and treat it. Here . . . ?"

Nagel looked down at the one-time tough woman of the bunch and said, "Well, we can't wait for any miracle cures. We're going to have to move, and she comes with

us or for sure she dies. If either of you has any mater-
nal instincts, you may need them in the days and weeks
to come, though, that's for sure."

"I'll look after her for now," Randi Queson told them.
"Lucky will continue with the inventory and packing so
we move what we can. You finish up outside, and then
find us a place to live for now that's far enough away
we won't have nightmares, but close enough we can
actually move stuff."

Nagel nodded. "Then we're all agreed. No matter what,
we survive. We survive until one of us, or somebody
for us, can demonstrate how we were left here and go
back and slowly roast a certain son of a bitch."

"One more trip," Jerry said insistently.

"Okay, one more, but that's *it* for now," Randi told
him. "Every time I've been left here I get the strangest
feeling that an alien voice is going to come out of
somewhere and tell me that negotiations are irrelevant.
We're already down to little things we forgot and some
things we're never going to use that somehow we feel
paranoid about not taking. Face it."

"Yeah, I know, I know," Nagel told her. "Still, one last
look around. It's bright and clear, and that one storm
we went through here didn't do much except wet us
down and keep us awake, so one more trip."

They were in one of the dense forests that abounded
all over Melchior, with varicolored trees and bushes and
a canopy of leaves and fronds that at least helped filter the downpours. There was fresh water in pools, even
a pretty little multiple waterfall dropping three or four
meters, then filling an indentation in the rock, then
spilling over another few meters, and so on.

They had the advantage of some of the portable testing
equipment, too, as long as the power lasted and so long
as nothing malfunctioned. One included a kind of syringe
that, inserted into plant matter, gave its entire composition

and, most importantly, if the plant matter or fruit or whatever was edible by humans without risk and what sort of nutrition it delivered.

There were at least a half dozen fruits and some ground and vine-based vegetables that were surprisingly nutritious, if not always very good tasting to the human palate. It was amazing what you could get used to and no longer even notice once you were forced to, though, or so they discovered.

Randi suspected that the other two were sneaking back and getting heated meals from the food synthesizer in the C&C unit, but it wouldn't matter much longer. Sooner or later they'd have to adapt to eating this gunk just like she and An Li already had. Better to go cold turkey and simply dream of the tastes of yesteryear.

Although technically on the slope of one of the monster volcanoes, they were more than forty kilometers from the internal valley and the obsidian cliff and the abandoned C&C unit.

They'd had a little informal service for Sark, the best they could do, and now, as this was to be the last trip, or at least was intended to be the last trip, they were going to turn on the locator beacon inside the unit just in case.

Normally this would have been standard operating procedure from the start, but they didn't know how many nonhuman receivers might be able to hear it as well, and the last thing they wanted right now was that kind of company. This was hard enough; acclimating to the world and its conditions came first and foremost. Later they could explore and see about communications with whoever or whatever else might live somewhere on this big piece of land.

Randi's suspicions were correct on the food situation, but the place still stank too much for eating. When Lucky and he got what they wanted, they came outside and ate it, calling it their "reunion picnics with Sark," always toasting him with something good and pouring a little symbolically on his grave.

"You got the remote?" he asked Lucky when they were done.

She nodded. "One push and we arm the security perimeter, turn off all but standby power inside, and activate the beacon. God only knows when anybody might hear it and come runnin'."

Suddenly there was a rumbling sound, and the ground began to shake. The scooters toppled over, and so did they.

It stopped for a moment, and Jerry picked up his scooter and hopped on, and Lucky did the same. "What the fuck was *that*?" she yelled to him as they rose into the air.

"Quake!" he shouted. "Push the button and let's get the hell out of here! Something's gonna blow and it's not gonna be pleasant!"

They both accelerated to the maximum but—now in particular—excruciatingly slow speed away from the C&C. As they made it to the rise that would take them out and towards their camp, Cross slowed, turned, and looked back. When Jerry realized that, he did the same.

She pushed the button, and the place they'd just left became a beacon and a fenced-in security area. Human searchers would have little trouble with it, but anyone else might have problems.

"Goodbye, Sark," she said with a sigh.

At that moment the whole interior valley began shaking so badly that she could actually see it with her own eyes, and there were blasts of disturbed air coming from inside.

Slides began to happen, and then, without further warning, tiny cracks began to appear in the valley's rock floor. The cracks expanded more and more, until they were like some kind of massive jigsaw puzzle, and then out of the cracks came yellow and red ooze and acrid smoke.

"Holy shit!" she said. "Another ten minutes . . ."

He understood her perfectly, thinking the same thing.

And now, here and there, things widened even more. The C&C appeared to be floating now, uneasily trying to balance itself on a large block of rock now resting on a sea of magma.

All at once it tipped over, and magma started running up one side and dissolving the rock shelf, causing even more instability. When it was about a third dissolved, the weight of the C&C became too much to support and the rest of the solid rock suddenly and completely flipped over, leaving a pool of bubbling, churning liquid rock where it had been.

"Well, so much for the rescue beam," Cross said, turning and starting slowly away.

Nagel paced her for a bit. "Well, there's one thing. At least we don't have to worry about the security system being inadequate. . . ."

"Now we're citizens of Melchior, I guess," she said to him. "But, God, I hope I live long enough to see Normie show up to film his epic. . . ."

XIV:

THE CURSE

True to its programming, Eyegor had used the special interface Norman Sanders's workers had put in while refitting the *Stanley* that effectively gave it, not the captain, control of the ship.

The captain found herself totally helpless, cut off from any control other than simple automated systems, unable to even see where or what Eyegor was doing. Still, she *could* communicate with the robot, so long as the robot allowed it.

"Eyegor," she pleaded, "you cannot do this. You have left humans who might still be alive in a hostile and probably fatal position, violating every bit of mandatory robotic programming, and now you believe you can pilot this ship safely back. You can't. It was built around and designed for a cyborg unit such as myself. It cannot be handled by someone not designed for it."

"All basic directives of robotics have been suspended in my logic core," Eyegor responded. "I am left entirely with the compulsion to carry out my primary mission at any cost. I have been fed all details on celestial and wormhole navigation and the capabilities of this ship by the auxiliary programming modules placed in this manual override chamber, and to supplement I have access to your entire database libraries. Much of the ship is automatic. I see no reason why I should not be able to pilot it home."

"You don't understand how complex this all is!" the captain pleaded. "All you will do is destroy us both!"

"I have no choice. I must bring this ship and this cargo back. Since any reactivation of your control would also cause you to return to Melchior, I cannot allow this. I am in any event finding this ship remarkably easy to handle."

"You idiot! This is *interplanetary* space. It's complex, but countless thousands have done it over time. Interstellar wormholes, particularly wild holes, are something else. Experience, nuance, becoming totally one with your ship, all those are essential!"

"I do not believe you. I believe it is your programming speaking, or perhaps your human part. I do not have the latter and am unencumbered by the morals of the former. Ah! There is the field up ahead, and we need only one more calculation to determine where and when the next hole will generate!"

"This is our last chance!" the captain pleased. "Otherwise your programming will not be fulfilled because you will not get back! Let me take it! I'll take it through! I swear I will."

"Oaths to a robot are a bizarre and illogical concept," Eyegor noted. "Your crew is dead. You may well be susceptible to the effects of this many stones yourself. I am immune. Ah! There! The last one! My calculations now bear out my contention and the contention of my programmers and the simulations they were based upon. Accelerate, max speed, full shields and ram on, aiming point and destination fixed. Simplicity itself. Now I will demonstrate to you that your major problem is that you still have a human component. Without this component, you would be capable of much more. Now . . . full boost . . . half light speed . . . wild hole opens *thus*. . . . *We're in!*"

"Eyegore, you blockhead! You were almost three degrees off your entry!"

"Impossible! I am incapable of such a simple mathematical error. If that were true, we'd have struck the wall by—"

There was a roar, and the sound of things that could not be compressed being compressed all around.

And then there was silence.

Somehow, back on the Three Kings, there was a sound that almost seemed like laughter. But it did not come from those trapped on Balshazzar, nor those stuck and swearing revenge watching Melchior's fires, but from somewhere else.

Nobody ever looked twice at Kaspar.